YOU SAVE ME

ТЫ СПАС МЕНЯ

SHANNON MYERS

CONTENTS

Cover Design by: The Final Wrap

Photographer: Sheridan Davis Photography

Models: Nikki Logan & Dante Adkins

First Printing: 2016

ISBN- 978-0-9975348-6-3

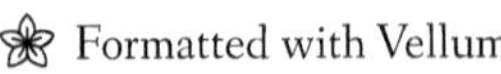
Formatted with Vellum

ALSO BY SHANNON MYERS

From This Day Forward Duet

(David & Elizabeth's Story)

From This Day Forward

Forsaking All Others

Operation Duet

(Dakota & Zane's Story)

Operation Fit-ish

(Kate and Nate's Story)

Operation Annulment

Silent Phoenix MC Series

(Main Storyline)

The Deserter (Book One)

The Protector (Book Two)

The Renegade (Book Three)

The Traitor (Book Four)

The Savior (Book Five)

Standalones within the SPMC universe

The Keeper

The Christmas Trap

Fairest Series (Can be read as standalones).

(Charm & Neve's Story)

Through The Woods

(Killian and Ari's Story)

Wait For It

Fictioned Series

(Hayden & Jake's Story)

Protagonized

To survivors everywhere. When it would've been easier to give up, you fought and persevered.

And

To the brave men and women that put their lives on the line every day, so that we might know freedom—

Thank you.

ACKNOWLEDGMENTS

As always, a lot of research goes into writing these books. This one may very well have been the longest research paper I've ever done. Thank you to all of those who gave up your time to answer my one million questions.

Corporal Sam Schooler- Not many brothers would sit down and let their sisters pick their brains about the Marine Corps in order to write a romance novel. Thank you so much for not only your insight, but the time you took to draw out different scenarios for me to use. I learned so much from you and hope that this story is an accurate reflection of that.

James Ramsey- Thank you for taking the time to visit with me about life with a prosthetic leg. I had so many logistical questions and you were so kind to answer every single one.

DC Renee- Thank you for your help in translating Russian phrases and terms of endearment. It's nice to know that it's never okay to call someone's daughter, *kitten*.

Nikki Logan- You were who I always envisioned for Katya, so naturally I was thrilled when you agreed to the cover-shoot. Thank you so much for embodying everything I wanted Katya to be. I would love to work with you again in the future.

Dante Adkins- I was so happy when you agreed to be on the cover of Operation Fit-ish, and even more so when you agreed to let me use some of the images for this cover. You have a real talent and I hope to work with you again soon.

Sheridan Davis- As always, you nailed it. I can't believe that we're on this little journey together. We've managed to handle the ups and downs of this industry like a Hollywood dream team, and I can't wait to see where we go next.

Rebecca Pau- Your cover designs continue to blow me away. I love how you always manage to capture exactly what I want in each and every one. I can't wait for our coffee/wine date in February.

J.Law- Thank you for your unwavering loyalty. Most days I don't feel like I deserve it, yet you are always waiting in my corner to cheer me on. You are always there when I need a soundboard for my crazy, off-the-wall ideas, and I am forever grateful to have you in my life.

Olivia- Most people would've packed up by now, but not you. You've stuck by my side through both the good...and the really awful times. You + Me = Forever. I love our life together.

Bloggers- You all are amazing. The responses from Operation Fit-ish blew me away and a lot of you became friends in the process. I hope that you all enjoy this book just as much. Thank you for all of the reviewing and promoting you have done on my behalf.

Readers- You should know this by now, but just in case you don't, I do all of this for you. Every review, every email, has pushed me to release a story that tops the last.

Zach- I couldn't do any of this without your love and support. You fell in love with a broken woman, a woman who thought she was incapable of real love. Your unwavering faith transformed me from a timid creature into someone who has the courage to speak her mind and follow her dreams. I don't want to do this life with anyone else, but you.

PROLOGUE

KATYA

THERE IS an old Russian fable about the snow maiden, Snegurochka. An older couple longed for a child of their very own, but were unable to conceive. They decided instead to build a child out of the snow and either due to some intervention by Father Frost or the power of love within the couple, depending on which version you had, the snow maiden was brought to life.

She had skin that was bloodless, yet her lips were a deep crimson. Snegurochka was a good and just daughter to the couple, helping them with their chores and giving them the companionship they had longed for. She never raised her voice in anger, but treated her adoptive parents with the utmost respect.

The little family was perfect, well almost perfect. Snegurochka's mother worried, for her daughter had no friends and never stepped foot outside. The young woman tried to convince her mother that she had no desire to leave, that she was perfectly content to watch the world from her window.

In one version of the story, a carnival arrived in the village and Snegurochka could not resist. She joined the other villagers, enrapturing the men around her, and infuriating a maiden by the name of

Kupava. Kupava accused the snow maiden of stealing her betrothed, Mizgir, and had her brought before the tsar to answer for her crimes. The tsar could not find fault in the young woman and Kupava was ruined. However, Snegurochka no longer felt safe outside of her home and once again insisted upon remaining indoors.

In another version, her mother encouraged her to join a group of girls for a walk in the forest. Snegurochka went along, desiring companionship with people her own age. The girls built a small fire and took turns leaping over it.

In the last version, Snegurochka fell in love with a boy named, Lel. She begged Mother Spring for the gift of love, even though Father Frost warned against it.

All three versions were so vastly different, yet the ending was always the same. In the first, Snegurochka finally decided to venture outside of her home again, only to evaporate in the rays of the spring sun. In the second version, she went to jump over the fire with her new friends, and promptly melted. In the last version, she was given the gift of love and her heart warmed—ultimately destroying her.

Snegurochka was obliterated—dissolved into nothing more than vapor—all because of love. I remember reading the story as a young girl, and feeling nothing but sadness for the snow maiden.

Later on in my life, I felt envy. Snegurochka endured such suffering and pain in her short life. I was jealous of the Snow Maiden and her ability to evaporate into nothingness afterward.

If only it would've been that easy for me.

ONE

TRAVIS

November 4, 2006

"CARLSON!" I cough and try to move my head, my heavy gear preventing full range of motion.

The sound of gunfire echoes all around me. A roadside bomb—we've survived living in this hell for the past year only to be taken out like this? "Carlson!" I groan the name, even as my eyes continue to search the desert for the rest of my men.

"Logan, lie still." Hill's voice breaks through my panic.

I cough again, spitting up blood in the process. "Where is everyone? Where's Carlson?"

He doesn't answer and I struggle to sit up. A minute ago, we were going to recover a stalled vehicle—Carlson was asking everyone in the Humvee what they wanted for Christmas, like some demented version of Santa Claus.

Pain, like I've never felt before, pulses through my body as I move to sit. My efforts leave me lightheaded, but I need to know what we're up against.

Hill speaks to someone near him. "Hold him the fuck down."

I shove his hands away. "Stop—where's Carlson?"

Hill's mouth moves into a grim line and he won't meet my eyes, instead pushing me back toward the desert floor.

"Lay the fuck down, Logan. I need that tourniquet tighter."

The other voice speaks up. "We're gonna have to cut his pants."

"Then fucking do it," Hill turns to someone else. "Hernandez, call it."

I grit my teeth, the copper tang of blood coating every part of my mouth. "Fuck that, Hill. Where the fuck is Carlson?"

"Logan—don't fucking fight me on this. You've been injured."

As if seconding his statement, pain pushes through the blanket of adrenaline, and my head drops onto my chest. I am hurt, but it can't be serious if I'm talking and moving like this. I look at my chest, my arms—everything is intact. Hill tightens something on my leg, and my body roars in pain. My right leg's fine, but my left—my left leg is unrecognizable.

Muscle has been torn away from bone, my knee torqued. Shrapnel is deeply embedded in a leg that no longer even looks like mine. Hill gently pushes me back and this time, I don't fight him.

"Bravo five this is Artic Cobra, request 9-line MEDEVAC."

"Artic Cobra, this is Bravo five, prepared to copy."

"Line one, Delta Charlie three two zero one two one four seven. Line two, two seven zero zero, Artic Cobra. Line three, Alpha one, Bravo two. Line four, Alpha. Line five, Alpha three. Line six, Papa. Line seven, Charlie. Line eight, Alpha three. How copy, over?"

I'm going to be fine. MEDEVAC is going to get us out of here—it's fine.

Maybe use the word 'fine' one more time, asshole. Just to make sure.

I lay my cheek against desert rock and finally find Carlson. He's lying three feet away, unfocused eyes staring in my direction. The lower half of his body is still lying near the Humvee.

No.

Not when we were this close to being back home. I struggle to find the other men, exhaling little bursts of air through my nose. Where the fuck is Moore? Using every last bit of strength I possess, I look over to the right...and there he is.

I hear screaming and black out before realizing that it's coming from me.

TWO

KATYA

August 2014

I TAKE another sip from the cardboard cup of gas station coffee, recoiling slightly at the bitter taste. I could've flown from Denver to Lubbock—it would've taken me an hour and a half. That's it. I could've slept the entire way too.

Unfortunately, I'm deathly afraid of flying. The thought of being in such a small space with nothing more than an armrest between me and the stranger beside me makes me feel claustrophobic. So, here I am—making the nine-hour drive to reach a man I'm not even sure I want to see again.

We've been in an on-again, off-again relationship for the past few years. It's cliché, I know that. Somehow, no matter what life throws our way, we always find our way back to each other.

Well, we *did*. I'd sworn to myself that I wouldn't fall for the lies again, yet here I am. Landon Scott is so persuasive; he could sell a glass of water to a drowning man. Sadly, even with all of our ups and downs, I'm not immune to his tactics.

I shake my head at my own idiocy. He cheated on me.

I'd tried to make the long distance thing work—for nothing. He'd met someone...her. Never mind that she was already married. It didn't matter once he turned the charm on. She was like putty in his hands...for a while. Then she seemed to have second thoughts about leaving her husband for Landon and he came crawling back to me.

I should've slammed the door in his face—forced him back to Texas with his tail between his legs. But I didn't.

I welcomed him back into my life and tried to make him forget her.

What am I doing?

I should turn around and head back to Denver—forget this crazy idea of reconciliation. I just have to convince my heart to give up this vision of the two of us getting married and starting a family.

The song on the radio is soon replaced with static, pulling me from my thoughts. I crack my neck and roll my shoulders to relieve the tension before shutting it off.

Silence.

Four more hours.

LUBBOCK POLICE SEEKING INFORMATION IN MISSING WOMAN'S CASE

Lubbock police are asking for the public's assistance in finding a woman who has been missing for almost two weeks.

The woman, Ekaterina Egoricheva, last spoke with family on August 7. Police confirm that her father reported her missing on August 9.

Since then, police have launched a full investigation into Egoricheva's disappearance. "We've got the entire detective division, along with the state bureau committed to finding her. There are signs that she did not go willingly and some circumstances that lead us to believe that this was an abduction," said Detective Michael Sullivan with LPD.

Sullivan recently spoke at a news conference saying that investigators hope Egoricheva is still alive. "The longer she's gone, the more concerned we become."

Egoricheva is originally from Denver and was in the area visiting a friend when she disappeared. Her car was discovered in the parking lot of the hotel she was staying at, along with many of her personal belongings. Police would not comment on any specific items found on scene.

A former boyfriend was brought in for questioning, but has not been formally charged. According to Detective Sullivan, "He's given us his full cooperation...that's all I can tell you at this point."

Egoricheva, 32, is 5'11 with brown hair and green eyes. If you have any information on this case, you are urged to contact the Lubbock Police Department immediately.

THREE

TRAVIS

June 2009

"I'M DOING A LOT BETTER, *you know? It's been almost three years. I'm lucky to still be here."*

"Travis, you seem to have recovered well. What would you say to other veterans returning home from war?"

"I'd tell them to not take another day for granted. Keep a positive mindset and take it one day at a time."

"That's good advice for every—"

I growl and launch the remote at the television with enough force to crack the screen. The picture goes black immediately, minus a few vertical lines of color at the point of impact.

I shouldn't have done the interview. I'm nothing more than a fraud.

I take a long swig from the bottle of Pendleton in my hand, letting the whiskey burn its way down to my gut.

I'm nothing like the man I just portrayed. I can barely get out of bed most mornings. Every time I close my eyes I'm taken back to that moment—lying helplessly on the ground, seeing their faces. I haven't showered in days...haven't done anything other than sit and drink myself into a stupor.

I clench the neck of the bottle tighter in my fist, my bruised knuckles reminding me of my last altercation.

That's what I do.

I drink. I fight. I fuck—and still I see their faces.

I can put on a mask for a while—be the kind of man my parents are proud of, a man who honorably served his country, all while hiding the monster beneath.

Coming home was like wearing a shirt that didn't quite fit right anymore. You could manage a few hours in it, but after a while you had to strip it off and breathe.

That was the one thing I wasn't prepared to deal with. Being over there, I dreamed of the day I'd come home and get back to normal.

Almost three years later and I'm still waiting.

FOUR

KATYA

I STRUGGLE to open my eyes. My tongue is like cotton in my mouth and every part of my body aches. I try to remember what I'd been doing to end up in such a state.

Landon.

He invited me over to his house for dinner, said he missed me. He promised me that he'd given *her* up. For good this time. I'd wanted to believe him, had driven to the desert that was west Texas, with this hope that we would fix everything.

Now, I'm not so sure.

I force both eyes open. The room is dim, with wooden slats running along the ceiling. I don't recognize this place at all. I shift my shoulder, trying to find a position that doesn't hurt, when I realize that I'm lying on a mound of dirt. A radio is playing somewhere up above, the tinny sound drifting down around me.

"La-Landon?" My voice cracks and I have to force his name out. I just need some water...and answers.

"Hey, sleepyhead." I blink several times until Landon comes into focus. He leans over me, an excited smile on his lips.

My heart beats out a warning. He looks almost maniacal as he watches me.

"Where am I?" I force the words past my quivering lips, suddenly afraid to know the answer.

His smile widens. "I wanted to get away from it all. I knew you would try to leave me again. I can't have that."

My pulse picks up at his words, while my brain scrambles to formulate a response.

"What did you do, Landon?" I try to keep my tone neutral.

"What did I do? I did what you forced me to do. David's trying to get close to you again...I'm not giving you back to him this time."

David?

I force my addled mind to remember someone called David. I have no idea who he's talking about.

"David? Who is—?"

His hand comes down hard across my cheek. The entire left side of my face stings and black spots dance before my eyes.

"Do not ever say his name around me again," he pauses and regains composure. "Now, let's get your hair back to normal."

My hair?

I self-consciously reach for it, pulling several dark strands toward my face. "It's the same as it's always been, Landon."

He brings his hands up, and I immediately flinch. Instead of hitting me again though, he runs them through his own hair in frustration. "Stop lying to me!" He roars the words.

Before I can come up with a response, he yanks me to my feet, even as my entire body protests. *Fight back!* My brain screams for me to do something, but my fear is paralyzing.

"You're hurting me, Landon." My eyes begin to fill with tears and I feel each and every step as he drags me upstairs. The music grows louder the closer we get to the top and he begins singing along as though nothing is amiss.

"Blame it all on my roots. I showed up in boots..."

I focus on the words. I know it's a Garth Brooks song—He

listened to a lot of country music when we were dating. I just can't remember the name of this one though.

Maybe I can distract him.

I bring my hand up and place it lightly on his arm. "I've heard this song before. What's the name of it?"

"Did I give you permission to talk? You broke my heart, Elizabeth. Do you think I'm going to let you outsmart me this time?" The sickly sweet smell of whiskey permeates the air around us as he hisses the words in my face, before shoving me through the upstairs doorway and into hell.

Elizabeth?

He called me by *her* name. I'm going to be sick. Something is very wrong. I just can't wrap my mind around what's taking place right in front of me.

He half pulls, half carries me through the living room and I fight to breathe through my mouth. Whoever lived here before was definitely lax on their housekeeping standards. There are mouse droppings everywhere, along with the strong stench of rotting garbage and urine.

"Landon, baby it's me. Katya." I fail to keep the fear out of my voice. I've never seen him like this before. His dark hair is sticking straight up and his emerald eyes glint with madness.

He stops walking and roughly grabs onto both of my arms. "Don't you lie to me, Elizabeth. Katya would never betray me like this."

I wrench my arms free from his grasp, staggering backward slightly as I do. "I am Katya!"

He laughs as though I've told him a joke and shoves me forward into a bedroom. "You can try and stall, but I'm fixing the hair regardless."

I need an escape. Landon's obviously on something. My eyes land on the window and I run over to it, without a second thought. I yank upward, using what little bit of strength I possess, but it won't budge. It's been painted shut and I'm fighting a losing battle with decades of paint in my attempt to get it open.

His arms come around my body and he easily picks me up before tossing me onto the mattress masquerading as a bed.

No.

"Elizabeth, I've tried to be patient with you. Obviously, a little tough love is in order."

"No. I didn't mean it. I didn't mean it. I'm sorry."

He pins me down, forcing my face into the moldy mattress, and cutting off my air supply.

"Elizabeth, stop fighting me. You need to be punished." His arm slips under my throat and he pulls me up into a chokehold. As he does, I feel a stinging sensation in my right arm.

Did he just inject me with something?

I can't breathe. My hands come up and I work to free myself. He laughs softly in my ear. "Not feeling so good about your decision to brush me off now, are you?"

I scratch at his forearm, my vision blurring with tears. He's going to kill me while he's high on something, thinking I'm Elizabeth.

He loosens his grip just enough for me to suck a little bit of air into my lungs with a gasp. I've only managed to take a couple of shaky breaths when he tightens his hold on my throat again. I claw futilely, my lungs burning and mind scrambling for a solution. This time he doesn't let go though, and my bladder releases before everything goes dark.

FIVE

KATYA

December 14, 2014

THE DESERT SAND beneath me cools rapidly as the last rays of daylight fade away. I shiver and look around the basement for something to cover myself with. I push myself up onto my knees, my head swimming with dizziness and pain from the sudden movement. I'm forced to stop and rest my palms on the dirt floor until it passes.

I need water.

My muscles scream in agony as I force myself onto my feet, using the basement wall as support. I slowly make my way toward the stairs, using the last bit of sunlight coming from underneath the door as a guide. My stomach cramps up and I double over, my hands resting on my thighs.

I need water.

The thought plays on a loop in my head. If I can just make it upstairs, there's a sink. I don't even care what the house looks like at this point, I'm severely dehydrated, and I know it will only be a matter of time before my body starts shutting down on me. I can't wait a moment longer.

I take a deep breath and urge myself to keep moving. I only make it a couple of steps before the pain in my head forces me down to my knees and I silently scream in frustration.

Landon's gone. He's been gone for days, maybe even a week at this point. He's never been gone this long. I'm getting worried that something has happened—maybe the police finally caught up with him. I've been missing for four months and eight days and I know with complete clarity that if I don't move, I'm going to die alone in this hell hole.

Abducted.

One decision that changed everything. I'm no longer Katya Egoricheva, aspiring model. I am nothing more than Landon Scott's prisoner—his toy. A proxy for the woman he truly desires.

He holds all the power; I am nothing but a slave to his desires.

I originally hoped that he would come to his senses and let me go. He'd seemed so convinced that I was Elizabeth when he took me, but I thought the drugs would wear off and he'd get me help. It quickly became apparent though that he hadn't taken anything. He alternated back and forth between the man I'd fallen in love with and someone suffering from a severe mental illness.

He'd drugged me long enough to bleach my hair until it was as white as hers, and I quickly learned that it was better to let him play out his sick fantasies. He's most dangerous when he pretends that I'm her. Fighting him only makes it worse. He claims to love Elizabeth, but the marks on my body tell a much different story. He wants to destroy her, to break her apart until there is nothing left.

He's better when he remembers who I am. It's what has kept me here and I think he knows that. He's left me for days at a time and I've stayed.

No restraints.

Like a well-trained dog.

I see glimpses of the man I loved and I hold onto them, begging him to come back to me. The problem is that he's getting worse, not better. His beatings have grown more vicious, his mind gone for longer periods of time, and I don't know how much more my body can take.

Goose pimples rise up on my skin, reminding me of my original mission—to find a blanket. The wind has picked up outside; I can hear the house groaning from the assault.

I try to stand up again, but my legs give out and I'm left with no other choice but to crawl. With no water and no way of keeping warm, I'm as good as dead right now.

The thought makes me want to cry, but I don't think my body's even capable of producing tears anymore. I bump something plastic in the dark and my hands seek it out. I silently rejoice as I wrap my fingers around what feels like a water bottle before realizing that it's empty.

That was it. My last chance. I give my aching arms a rest and drop onto the dirt floor, inhaling sand with every breath, but too exhausted to move.

Those first few weeks, I'd sworn that I'd fight to escape. I would find a way back to town, jump in my rental car, and speed back to Denver—join the witness protection program if necessary. I was bound and determined that I was going to save myself.

I gave up on that halfway through week three. I remembered the exact moment it happened. Landon pulled out his cell phone and began streaming the press conference he and my father held, pleading for my safe return.

"See those tears? They're real and the press just eats that shit up. Look! Right here at 4:12, Nikolay grips my shoulder. Man, you should've seen your old man. He was so distraught—promising all amounts of money to get you back."

That was the moment I broke.

Seeing my father plead for my kidnapper to bring me home, while standing shoulder to shoulder with him, had been too much for me and I couldn't hold back the sobs. His eyes had shone with excitement and I saw how far gone he really was. I knew then that Landon was never going to let me walk away from this. They'd find my remains down in this basement years from now. I'd be nothing more than a cautionary tale for other women.

It didn't matter how hard I fought. He was never going to let me go, and if by some miraculous chance I did escape? He would find me. He'd find me and the beatings would be even worse than they were now. I close my eyes, fully surrendering myself to the dirt below me.

I've made my peace.

Now, I'm ready to die.

I've just closed my eyes when I hear the familiar slam of a car door from somewhere up above me. I ignore the fogginess in my head and move into a kneeling position near the wall. Using the last bit of energy remaining, I sweep the sand in front of me clear of my handprints.

He's back. Maybe this time he'll end it and put me out of my misery.

SIX

KATYA

"HONEY, I'M HOME!" Landon calls out as he enters the house and I force myself to stop shaking.

I don't have much left in me. Another good hit to the head will probably end things quickly. If I can just get him to hit me there first, I won't feel anything else.

I'm trying to calm myself with thoughts of death?

"Now, I'm only doing this because you're not going to run again. Right?" His deep voice carries throughout, but I'm not sure who he's talking to up there.

The hall lights kick on just as the door opens up, flooding the room with light. It feels as though someone has shoved an icepick into my skull and I squeeze my eyes shut. I've grown accustomed to the dark.

"Don't be a bitch. We have a houseguest who's been dying to meet you."

I can hear him coming down the stairs and my heart beats faster in anticipation of what's to come. My plan is to just keep my eyes closed. That plan goes right out the window when she begins screaming.

I slowly open my eyes and there she is. The woman responsible for all of this. Elizabeth's face is grotesquely swollen on one side, her hair matted with blood. Her eyes scan over my body, starting with my bleached hair and I keep my eyes focused on hers as she looks down, the horror plainly showing on her face. I'm wearing a sleeveless wedding dress that stops just below my knees. I'm sure it would be beautiful were it not caked in blood and dirt. There's a gash down the front from Landon's knife. Elizabeth's eyes drift lower and widen when she sees the dried blood coating the inside of my thighs. I resist the urge to pull the dress back down, to cover myself. I should hate her, but I recognize the fear in her eyes. I've lived it for the past four months.

"K-Katya?"

He's going to kill us both.

I nod, not breaking eye contact with her.

"Now that we're all acquainted, let's get started. Did you see all the hard work I went to for you, Elizabeth? I tried to get her look just right, but no matter how hard I tried, she couldn't compare to you." Landon roughly yanks her to her feet and it's then that I see it.

Damn you, Elizabeth.

I was ready to die...would've let him kill me.

Now? Now, I have her to think about. Well, not just her, but her and the baby she's obviously carrying.

She points somewhere behind me. "Is that my picture? You're the one who broke in and stole it that night!"

Landon calmly grabs onto Elizabeth's hand, bending her finger until it cracks, and she screams out in agony.

I want to pull myself away mentally, as I've done every time before when he's like this, but I need to help her.

"It's rude to point at people, Elizabeth! Davey let you get away with so much, but not me. I'm going to make you into a proper lady."

This is not good.

Think, Katya. Think!

He pulls her over to a chair and pushes her until she's sitting before him. "Are we ready? Good."

He holds something up to her and she begins scrambling out of the chair, fighting to get away from him. If he's surprised by the movement, he doesn't show it. He walks over and grabs her by the hair, before leading her back to the chair.

"Do I need to use the handcuffs again?"

I watch as she shakes her head. I'm trying my best to come up with a plan to help us escape when I see what he's shown her. He runs the blade of the knife down the side of her face and a shudder passes through me.

"Good girl. See—you're learning. Now, I know you're probably as anxious as me to consummate this relationship, but there is one small problem—"

He can't mean—

He moves the blade down to her stomach. "I can't let this go unpunished."

My lips begin trembling in fear. He's going to kill the baby...and most likely her in the process. I force myself to think of something, but my brain is blanketed in fog.

"Landon, what are you doing? You don't want to hurt me." Elizabeth's eyes are fixed on him.

"Of course I don't want to hurt you, sweet girl. I love you. I just can't allow you to have any piece of him though. You belong to me. We're going to cut that reminder out and you'll be mine again. Just like before."

She strokes his arms, much like a mother would a small child. "Landon, I've missed you. And I know that you're mad, but if you try to cut this baby out of me, I'll bleed to death. We're too far away for help to get here. Please don't make me leave you when I just got back." She begins crying and I hold my breath, praying that he'll listen to her.

He drops the knife into the dirt before pulling her into his arms, and I breathe a small sigh of relief.

It worked.

"I've waited six months to hear those words from you. Six long months." He leans his head down and kisses her hair before stepping back. "You're right. I can't take a risk like that with your life."

I watch as Elizabeth closes her eyes, thinking she's won. I scream out a warning, but his fist moves back so quickly that she doesn't have enough time to register what's happening. Landon hits her right in the abdomen and she drops to her knees, gasping for breath.

He stands over her prone body. "You are mine, Elizabeth, and you will not walk out of here pregnant with that bastard's kid."

He begins kicking and punching her, while she struggles to move away from him. I need to help her, but I'm frozen in place. It's then that I realize I'm still screaming. Elizabeth grabs the knife out of the dirt just as Landon pulls her up by her hair. She begins stabbing back toward him, managing to get the blade in despite his erratic movements.

"You fucking bitch! You stabbed me!" He drops her back into the dirt.

We are going to get out of here and get help.

He leans down and roughly yanks her into a chokehold, pulling her up until her feet are dangling off the ground. "I tried to make this easy for you, but now I'm afraid to say that it's going to hurt you...a lot."

She begins kicking wildly.

He's choking her. Do something, Katya.

I search around the dim room for the weapon I'd found a few weeks ago. I hid it against the cinderblock wall, all the while praying I'd never have to use it. A truck door slams from outside and I can hear men's voices.

"Help us!" I scream the words just as my hand makes contact with the flat head screwdriver I had hidden.

"Beth?" The voice shouts from up above.

I open my mouth to scream again, but no sound comes out.

Down here, please come down here.

Elizabeth is silent and her attempts to fight Landon off are becoming weaker. A dark-haired man appears at the bottom of the stairs, his gun drawn. Another follows closely behind.

I wait for a fraction of a second, but they make no move to stop him. Using everything I have left, I launch my body at Landon's, forcing the screwdriver right between his shoulder blades. It's enough to cause him to drop her body before immediately turning on me.

He grabs me by the throat, backing me into the wall as I defiantly stare into his eyes.

Kill me.

I've expected it for months—forced myself to hang on. I won't fight this time. I'll take it if it means that she's safe. I won't close my eyes either. The bastard's going to have to look me in the eyes as he does it.

There's a loud pop and then Landon's eyes widen in shock. He loosens his grip and falls to the dirt floor with a loud exhale. My weak legs give out almost immediately and I fall down next to him.

"I'm sorry, Katya. I'm sorry, baby." His voice is barely above a whisper. He tries to reach for my hand, but the man who shot him pulls me into his arms and moves me across the basement.

Away from him.

"I'm Detective Michael Sullivan. Can you tell me your name, ma'am?" He kneels down, intensely studying my face.

"Ka-Katya." I want to say more, but my throat is so dry and it hurts to talk.

His eyes widen. "Egoricheva?"

I nod and he gently brushes the hair back off of my forehead, inspecting the various cuts and bruises marring my skin. His touch stings and I try to turn away.

Elizabeth moans in pain just a few feet away, bringing my focus back to her. The detective pats my arm gently and moves over to them.

"Mike—we're going to need to call an ambulance. She's in bad shape."

Elizabeth screams again and the detective—Mike, grimly responds, "We're going to need an ambulance for both of them. We just found Katya Egoricheva."

Both men are crouched down near Elizabeth as she continually cries out in pain. The dark-haired man, I assume is David, has a death grip on her.

"Beth, stay with me baby. Hold onto my voice. We're going to get you help."

She might not make it. The baby could die.

It's enough to snap me out of my numbing shock and a tremor passes through my body, wracking my body with silent sobs. "I tried to save her...I'm so sorry—I tried."

Maybe if I hadn't hesitated, she'd be okay right now. There's a deep groan from the other side of the basement as the detective wraps his jacket around my shoulders. A part of me wants to grab his gun and empty it into Landon's chest. The other part of me feels obligated to go check his wounds and help him.

It would be an easy decision had he been a monster the entire time. There were moments though, where I expected him to hit me, only for him to stroke the side of my face lovingly. Those intimate gestures conjured up all sorts of feelings that were confusing to me. He didn't just bring me food, he sat next to me and fed me by hand. If his beatings had been particularly vicious, and I couldn't do it myself, he'd hold the water bottle to my lips for me.

I was grateful for his kindness. I'd pretended that we were a normal couple again. I thought I could reciprocate the kindness he'd shown me and break through to him. Make him see what he was doing to me.

The detective's shouting interrupts my thoughts. "How long will it take an ambulance to get to us?" He pauses as the person on the other end of the line responds. "No, dammit, I don't have that kind of time. One of the female victims is twenty-eight weeks pregnant and in active labor due to trauma. How fast could you get a chopper in the air?"

I look over at Elizabeth, struggling to sit up in the dirt, panting from the exertion on her body. Blood is pouring steadily from between her legs.

I blame myself.

I did this. If only I'd tried a little bit harder, he never would've gone after her.

The detective raises his voice again. "Fuck! I'm aware that we're under a blizzard warning—I've got two women who need immediate medical attention!"

We're in the middle of nowhere. I'd ventured outside once when Landon was gone, but there was nothing around, as far as I could tell.

David cradles Elizabeth in his arms and carries her up the stairs. "I got you, baby. We're going to get you help." He looks back to the detective. "Mike, tell them I'll meet them, but I can't sit here and wait. She doesn't have that kind of time!"

Mike relays the message and gives the person instructions on where to meet us. Without missing a single beat, he gently lifts me up off of the ground and into his arms. I want to argue and tell him that I'm fine, but the small movement sends a wave of pain through my skull, leaving me disoriented.

Instead, I cling to him as he mounts the stairs. He places me in the backseat of a truck, straightening the jacket around my shoulders as he buckles me in. I keep a death grip on his shirt as he moves to back away.

Don't leave me, please.

He hands his phone over to David in the front seat. "Go, I'll catch up with you! They'll get you to the chopper. Hurry—this storm won't hold back much longer."

He gently removes my hands from his shirt and points back to the house. "I'm going to take care of him. I will come to you, I promise."

I nod and reluctantly bring my hands down to my lap.

David navigates the dark dirt roads as best he can, each bump sending jolts of pain throughout my body. From the sounds of it, Elizabeth isn't faring much better in the front seat either. I stare out the front windshield into the sea of darkness and silently urge him to drive faster. We need to be moving faster. I will my body to stop shaking, but it's flooded with adrenaline and I'm too weak to stop it.

He continues getting directions from the person on the phone, leading us closer to salvation. By the time we pull off the dirt road, the highway is lit up like the fourth of July. Red and blue flashing lights illuminate the desolate landscape, like a beacon in the night. There's a barricade being set up as we approach, with various officers laying flares down on the asphalt.

People begin running toward the truck immediately as the helicopter touches down on the blacktop. They waste no time in pulling Elizabeth from the front seat and getting her onto a stretcher, the flight team shouting to one another as they load her. David fights his way through the police officers to get to her.

My head bobs slightly and I close my eyes, fighting the blanket of fatigue that has settled over me, when the back door opens suddenly. The dome light hurts my eyes and I have to blink several times in order to make out that it's David and a uniformed officer.

The officer directs David into the truck. "Can you ride back here with her? I'm going to get you to your wife as fast as possible."

He nods, looking shell-shocked. I don't know what it means that they won't let him go with her. I don't know if that's normal or not. His face is devoid of emotion as he stares listlessly ahead. He looks so incredibly lost that I don't think twice. I just reach over and grab his hand in mine. I squeeze tight, my thumb making small circles along the back of it.

And I pray.

I pray that his family is safe.

I pray that Landon will be arrested and imprisoned for what he's done.

I don't know it yet, but this will be the last time I touch a man for a very long time. I don't realize that being rescued was the easy part.

Therapists will later say that I'm in shock right now, and my actions are nothing but a reflex, but I know that's not the reason. I want him to know that I see his pain. I want him to know that he isn't alone.

So, I join him in the darkness.

It's the only place that feels like home.

MISSING MODEL FOUND ALIVE

Lubbock, TX - The Lubbock Police Department confirmed tonight that Ekaterina 'Katya' Egoricheva, the Selvaggia model last seen August 7, has been found alive and safe.

The disappearance of Egoricheva sparked a massive search and several vigils, pleading for her return. Those same family members are rejoicing tonight as Egoricheva has been returned to them.

The aspiring model had just done a photoshoot with well-known lingerie company, Selvaggia, when she went missing. The company became integral to the investigation, when they obtained permission from family members to release the photos with Egoricheva on the cover of their winter catalog. The catalogs became impromptu flyers, aiding police in their search for the missing woman.

Police are still investigating what happened during the four months Egoricheva was held captive. Egoricheva's former boyfriend, Landon Scott–initially a person of interest in the investigation, is now being sought by police as the primary suspect. It's unclear whether formal charges were ever brought against him in her disappearance.

"We don't usually get a happy ending when a person has been

missing as long as she was." Detective Michael Sullivan, who is credited with rescuing Egoricheva, said.

Police also discovered a second woman when rescuing the model. This woman had only been missing a few hours and few details have been released regarding her or the condition she's in tonight.

This investigation is ongoing and this story will be updated as soon as we receive more details.

SEVEN
TRAVIS

August 2012

"SO, she's mine? I can take her home?" I look down at the gorgeous yellow Labrador to find her staring up at me, tongue lolling out of the side of her mouth as if she's smiling.

I smile back at her in spite of myself.

I'm getting my shit together. I've been sober for two hundred and eighty-two days. I'd spent the last anniversary of my nightmare, alone, getting wasted.

The next morning had been a low point for me. Not only did I have the hangover from hell, but I'd trashed my apartment. The picture frame of Carlson, his arm slung lazily around my shoulder, was shattered.

Seeing that ripped through the numbness.

I sat in the floor, holding that photograph like a lifeline, and feeling like a complete failure. I was pissed at myself. Carlson and Moore died that day and what was I doing? Just fucking my life away in the bottle.

Some way to honor their memory.

So, I made the decision then and there—no more drinking. I'd sober up and do something with my life. I'd find a way to honor them and everyone who'd put their asses on the line that day to save mine.

I found a psychiatrist who recommended a service dog, and almost a year later, here I am. They were able to match me with a dog sooner than I expected. I'd been told it could take a year or more. Once they paired us, Charlie and I spent almost a month working through various trainings, until she knew me better than anyone else.

That part was almost as challenging as boot camp. Now, she's seen every emotion from me and has proven her worth ten times over.

"Charlie's all yours, Travis."

I fight back the wave of emotion trying to creep up on me and briskly shake Sam's hand instead. He's a fellow marine, one who found it hard to integrate back into society after the Gulf War. So, he wanted to ensure that other veterans didn't struggle for years like he did. He'd always been interested in animals and he used that to find a solution.

He'd taken a lemon and made fucking lemonade. Thank God he hadn't sat around drinking his problems away like I'd done. Sam picked himself up by his bootstraps and helped himself by helping those around him.

I'd like to be able to give back like that.

Baby steps, Trav.

Baby steps.

EIGHT

KATYA

January 3, 2015

"HERE YOU ARE, my Katya. Home sweet home." My father carries my bags inside before turning to face me.

After ensuring that every light is on, I wrap my arms around myself and look around. "Has someone been in here?"

Papa gives me a puzzled look. "There were a couple of police officers that looked around after you were ab—when you were not here, but I swear they touched nothing."

I inhale and there it is again. It doesn't smell like my apartment anymore. Maybe I'm imagining things—maybe I've been gone too long to even remember what it's supposed to smell like.

I sit down on the couch, feeling like a stranger. "Thank you for bringing me home, Papa. Would you mind if I laid down for a bit? My head's hurting."

"I could unpack this for you—make you some dinner..." My father trails off as I shake my head. "*Lyubov moya*, let me take care of you."

"I really just need some sleep. Maybe tomorrow we can spend

the day together." I have no intention of ever leaving my apartment again, but I'll humor him for the time being.

He sits down next to me and kisses the top of my head. "I could sleep in the guest room. It's your first night back—you shouldn't be alone."

I lean into him and squeeze his hand. "Papa, I've been poked and prodded constantly for the past few weeks. There hasn't been a moment of peace. I'd really just like to be alone tonight...please."

He frowns. "Are you sure? I will be back early tomorrow morning —I'll bring you breakfast. The nurses said you need to keep your strength up."

"I'll be fine. Just let me rest, please."

Once he leaves, I lock the bottom two locks and put the chain on, before going into the kitchen. I open the fridge to find a molded sphere that might've been an orange at one point and a bottle of vodka. I grab the vodka and uncork it. I debate getting a glass for a brief moment, before downing it straight from the bottle.

The warmth spreads to my limbs, instantly relieving the tension in my body. Tucking it under my arm, I walk down the hall to my bedroom, passing the wall of windows overlooking downtown Denver. I'd bought the condo for the view—no matter where I was at inside, at least one wall was solid windows.

Now, it's as if I'm viewing a foreign planet from inside my glass prison. I catch movement in the building across from mine and I startle, nearly dropping the vodka. I could've sworn the person had been holding a gun. I crouch down in the hall as he moves near the windows again, looking out over the city. He brings his hand back up and I bite back a scream, trembling in fear.

It's a flask. Not a gun.

He carelessly takes a long drink, looking down over the busy streets—unaware that I'm ten feet away, dying from heart failure.

My hands shake helplessly as I force another swig down. I have to get ahold of myself. I push myself up onto my feet, feeling as though my heart is going to burst through my chest.

I'll just get into bed and try to sleep. The nurses were giving me Ambien in the hospital, but I haven't filled any of my prescriptions yet. Maybe I'll sleep so well that I won't have to fill it. I just need my own bed and I'll be fine. I place the bottle down on the nightstand and pull the comforter back.

There's a Selvaggia catalog resting underneath, with me on the cover. I stare at it for a long time, trying to come up with an explanation that doesn't fill me with a sense of dread. The catalog was released after I was taken. My father had said no one touched anything in my house. Swore to it.

Yet, here it is.

Lying there.

Mocking me.

The sick feeling of dread intensifies when I see that someone has written across my body in permanent marker.

"What do you know about the disappearance of Katya Egoricheva?"

"KATYA—*MYSHKA,* open your eyes! You are safe." My eyes shoot open in fear. Papa leans down and brushes damp hair off of my forehead. "It was just a nightmare. See? You are home."

I look around the room. "You left and someone was in here, Papa. There was the catalog—my face. Someone wrote on it. Someone was in here—I told you."

My father's lip quivers slightly as he shakes his head. "No, my Katya. I went to get dinner for us. I told you that. I came back and you were crying out—I was only gone for a few minutes."

Tears begin to leak from my eyes. "There was a man in the other building—I thought he had a gun. Maybe I imagined it." I lift the comforter to see if the catalog is still there, but the only thing next to me is an empty vodka bottle. I try to cover it back up before he sees it.

"You told me you were not drinking anymore."

I hadn't agreed to that…had I?

"Papa, I just got home from the hospital. I just need something to take the edge off for a few days. Then I'll get back to myself."

He pinches the bridge of his nose and looks down; his shoulders shaking with silent sobs. "*Milaya moya*…you have been home for a month now. I am worried sick right now, Katya. You are not well."

I shake my head vehemently. "No, we just got home tonight. You were going to come back tomorrow. You left and I saw the man with a gun—but maybe it wasn't a gun. Then, I found the catalog and I wanted to call the police."

He stands up, hastily swiping at his eyes. "You have called the police almost daily since coming home. They have searched, but there's never been any sign that anyone's been here but you. It's February, Katya. It's time to get out of the condo. You need some help."

A whole month of my life—gone. I've slipped away from reality and taken up residence with paranoia and delusions. I do need help.

I climb out from the nest of blankets and walk over to him. He gestures to the mirror in the bathroom and leads me toward it. My hand comes up to my mouth in horror. I look worse than I did when they rescued me.

My hair is still bleached out, but it's grown out about an inch, leaving me with a crown of jet black roots. It hangs in clumps and I wonder if I've even washed it since coming home. I look almost skeletal, my ribs poking through my t-shirt. Judging by the fact that I'm incredibly lightheaded right now, I haven't been consuming enough calories either. Tears pool in my eyes, threatening to spill over onto the dark blue shadows underneath.

He may not have killed me physically, but I am nothing more than a walking corpse. I rely on vodka to numb me enough to sleep and even then, the nightmares pierce the fog, traumatizing me all over again.

My father grips my shoulders tightly, our eyes meeting in the reflection from the mirror. "I cannot always be here with you—maybe it would be better if you kept yourself busy."

I nod. "Maybe I go back to work. I just don't know if they'll take me looking like this."

He studies my reflection. "I will handle that. I can take care of everything. You will be good as new. You'll see."

He kisses the top of my greasy head and I close my eyes. I'll go back to work and everything will get better.

It has to.

I'm disappearing before my own eyes.

NINE
KATYA

April 7, 2015

"IT'S BEEN one hundred and fourteen days. I'm fine."

"You feel that's enough time to recover from being abducted and abused?" The woman gazes intently up at me as I pace her office.

I walk over to the floor to ceiling windows and rest my head against the cool glass, looking down over the busy Denver streets. People in a hurry to be somewhere—that's all anyone did here—rush to be somewhere else.

I didn't want therapy. I didn't want to talk about the four months I'd spent with Landon. I wanted to pretend it never fucking happened. I craved normalcy for all the good it did me.

Before, I was a nobody model, trying to make a name for herself. After, when I wanted nothing more than anonymity, I was a household name. In addition to my agent, I suddenly have a nutritionist, a publicist—hell, I even have an assistant. My father went a bit overboard in his desire to help me.

"You've also kept track of how many days it's been since you were rescued? Why is that?"

One of my psychologists had pushed me to take pride in the fact that I survived—to wear it like a badge. I never went back after that. I couldn't fathom meeting someone and sharing my "survivor story," as though it was something to boast about. Another tried to convince me that the nightmares were a free version of exposure therapy and couldn't understand why I didn't want to sleep.

This one probably won't work out either, but I can humor her for the hour I'm here.

"I keep track of the days because I don't ever want to take my freedom for granted again. I'm truly blessed to be alive." I try not to gag on the sugary sweet words as they leave my mouth.

The psychologist, I didn't take the time to remember her name, cocks her head to the side. "Really? That's it? You return to working full-time as a lingerie model a month after being rescued, and you're fine? You've worked through the abuse—"

"And emerged a stronger person." I cut her off to add helpfully.

She sighs and flips through my medical file. I can see that she thinks that she's about to 'bring out the big guns,' but she has no idea that this has all been done before.

"What about the rape? It says here in your file that you presented with abrasions and tears, along with bruising of your cervix. Those are some pretty severe physical injuries. Have you recovered from all of that?"

I cringe. She doesn't beat around the bush like some of the others did. In spite of my personal thoughts on the matter, I nod at her.

She doesn't need to know that some mornings I wake up with severe pelvic pain—as if the wounds have been reopened. As if he's breaking me apart all over again.

"I have. Physically and emotionally, I've healed. I've also found a way to turn what happened to me into an entire campaign against domestic abuse and—"

"This wasn't a case of domestic abuse though, Ms. Egoricheva. You weren't even in a relationship with Landon Scott when he abducted you. I cannot fathom how you've recovered so quickly. Have you been sexually intimate with anyone since it occurred?"

Her rapid-fire questions leave me feeling slightly off-kilter, and it takes me a second to recover my composure. "There have been a few special men, but you know with my work schedule it's hard to find time for a relationship." I smile brightly at her, resisting the urge to wink, but she doesn't return it.

"What about Landon? This man holds you against your will for months on end and police still have no leads on where he might be. You're not worried he'll come after you again?"

I shrug. "I can't live my life always looking over my shoulder."

She closes her notebook and stands up, walking toward her office door. "Everything you've said in here today is nothing more than media stock answers. When you're actually ready to confront what happened to you, I'll be here."

She looks like she wants to say more, but purses her lips instead as she holds the door for me.

Twenty-seven minutes in and she's thrown me out. That has to be a new record for me.

"KATYA, get lower. These are pistol squats. Take it to the ground." My trainer pushes me harder, leaving no time to dwell on my botched therapy session.

I sink down until I'm hovering over the ground, my right leg extended out in front of me, sweat coating my body in a fine sheen.

My body wants to quit, I'm still not where I was before—well, before *it* happened. Adriana's been tasked with getting me back to my runway physique, something she hasn't taken lightly.

I'm not even sure I wanted to know what all of it costs. My father wants me to have whatever I need to get back to the old Katya—hence, the five million psychologists I've seen over the past four months. Every time I tell him one isn't going to work out, he has another already lined up.

I'd jokingly told him he'd have to wipe my memory to get the old Katya back and he'd teared up. Now, I just agree to whatever he offers. It's easier this way.

"Ms. Egoricheva, I'm sorry to interrupt, but I've got you down for a one-fifteen with your nutritionist and then we have an interview at five with *9NEWS* regarding your NFL campaign spot."

I nod, only half-listening to my assistant, Amy, as I clench my core muscles in an attempt to keep myself upright. "Got it," I huff out the words.

It took a while to get used to someone else running my schedule, someone else knowing every aspect of my life. With her platinum blonde hair and no-nonsense attitude, she looks ready to strut a catwalk at any given moment.

Adriana speaks up. "Speaking of nutrition, what's she weighing in at? If we can't get some meat back on her bones with what we're doing here, it might not hurt to have Therese revamp her meal plan."

Amy consults her notebook, "She weighed 105 yesterday morning. So, she's put back on a total of ten pounds since December."

Adriana shakes her head. "It's not enough. She needs to be 120-125 ideally. Other fashion designers would gladly take her now, but VS? They won't even consider her when she's that underweight."

Amy nods and begins scribbling notes down, neither of them aware that they're having a conversation about me without actually taking the time to involve me.

Adriana breaks eye contact with Amy and glares at me. "Why'd you stop? You have three more sets of five. Then we're going to figure out your meals."

I nod slowly as I lower myself into a squat. "You got it, boss."

This is hell.

I haven't made one decision for myself since December.

I've simply traded one prison for another.

NFL "IT ENDS WITH US" DOMESTIC VIOLENCE CAMPAIGN SCRIPT

[IMAGE OF SEVERELY BEATEN WOMAN IN A HOSPITAL BED APPEARS ON SCREEN]

Female Voiceover: "It's hard to believe this picture was taken four months ago. When I was planning my future, I envisioned something else entirely."

[*Image replaced with the winter 2014 Selvaggia photo shoot*]

Female Voiceover: "I'm Katya Egorichev, Selvaggia model, and these photographs were taken right before I was abducted. Twenty-four people are physically abused by an intimate partner every minute in the United States and one out of every five women will be the victim of severe physical violence by an intimate partner."

Male Voiceover: "I'm Brody Rodgers, wide receiver for the Dallas Cowboys. One out of every five women will be raped in their lifetime, half of them by someone they know and trust. When 12.7 million people are being physically abused, raped, or stalked within a one-year period, we cannot allow it to become a blind spot."

[*Screen flashes various domestic violence statistics, each covering the last until the screen is a jumble of statistics*]

[*Katya and Brody enter room, arm in arm*]

Katya: "I am one out of five."

Brody: "And that's one too many in my playbook."

Katya: "No more turning a blind eye. No more, 'she seems fine.'"

Brody: "No more, 'she shouldn't wear that,' or 'boys will be boys.' If you see something, say something. Join the NFL and Selvaggia in our campaign to end domestic violence."

[*Website displays along the bottom of the screen*]

Katya: "Please visit the website to learn more about how you can help out."

[*Brody looks affectionately at Katya*]

Brody: "No more statistics. No more excuses. It ends with us."

[*Fade to black*]

TEN
KATYA

"WOW. To come from that level of abuse and turn it into something positive? Katya, I am blown away. How was it, shooting this PSA?"

I catch Amy out of the corner of my eye, off-set, nodding and smiling. I mimic her actions and answer, "It was a very empowering experience, Candice. I was powerless for four months and for me to be able to regain that power and help other victims at the same time? There's no better feeling in the world."

Candice leans in, conspiratorially. "Woman to woman, what about the rumors that you and Brody have been spotted out and about since the campaign? Is there an off-field romance blossoming between the two of you?"

Amy gives me a stern look. We knew this question was coming, having reviewed everything beforehand, so I stick to the agreed-upon script. "While Brody is quite the heart-throb, I'm sorry to say that we are nothing more than friends."

She laughs easily, "Well, there you have it. Women of America, you can rest easy with that knowledge. So, what's next for you?"

As instructed, I glance down at my lap and answer shyly. "I don't quite know. I love my relationship with Selvaggia and I'm just looking forward to working more closely with them in the near future."

Candice affectionately pats the arm of my chair, not a single blonde hair on her head moving in the process. "Katya, thank you for stopping by. We look forward to visiting with you again soon. Next up, could your home be making you sick? We've got the dirt on how clean your house really is."

Once they go to commercial break, I unclip my microphone and leave it with someone on set before making my way over to Amy. She passes me a cell phone without so much as a greeting.

"That was perfect. You balanced that fine line between victim and victor," I pull the phone away from my ear, my publicist's voice grating on my nerves.

"Yep. Everything went according to plan. Listen, I hate to cut you short, but I have dinner plans tonight."

Cindy laughs heartily. "Katya, you have group counseling tonight. Remember?"

"I never agreed to that. We looked it over and it seemed geared more toward sexual assault survivors—which doesn't apply to me." I've done enough therapy today.

"Katya, it's good publicity. We're going to have a camera crew waiting for you a block away—we don't want to give the location away out of respect for others who might be attending. They're going to ask you some questions and you're going to tell them how therapy has done so much to help you recover. We'll "leak" the story to the major news outlets and wait for that Selvaggia contract to come through. They want women who empower others—that's you. You have one hour."

"And if I refuse?" My phone beeps, signaling that the call has been disconnected.

I glare at Amy. "You failed to mention therapy when we went over everything earlier."

She looks away. "It was a bit last minute..."

It doesn't matter. I don't know how to say no anyway.

"OKAY, let's get started. Remember, this is a safe space. These are our stories, we own them. These are not the stories of our abusers because they hold no power over us anymore."

A small giggle works its way out and I cup my hand over my mouth in horror.

The woman at the front of the room looks around for the culprit and I sink lower into the cold metal folding chair. She shields her eyes against the bright fluorescent lights, squinting into the small group. Her long brown hair is in dreadlocks and her clothes look as if she made them herself, but she seems nice enough so I remain seated. That, and I'm fairly certain that if I get up, she'll immediately know that I was the one laughing.

"I don't believe we've met you. Would you mind introducing yourself to the group?"

I look left and right, hoping someone else has joined me in the last few seconds. Realizing I'm not that lucky, I slowly stand, wiping my damp palms on my jeans.

"Hello, I'm Kat. I'm- I'm here for a friend of mine—not me." I manage to clear my throat awkwardly before sitting back down.

"Well, hello Kat. I'm Josephine, but everyone calls me Jo. I hope that you find this session beneficial for your friend."

I nod, my eyes zeroed in on the chair in front of me. Jo sits down and a young woman stands up. She's barely five foot, just this tiny little thing with fiery red hair and blue eyes.

"Hi, my name is Marissa. Um, I'm a little nervous, so I want to apologize up front in case I screw this whole thing up. I haven't talked about that night in a really long time," she swallows nervously.

"I dated Tony for a while—almost a year. We broke up, but you know, we stayed in touch. We'd gotten a lot closer and I wanted us to get back together...I missed him. We'd see each other out from time to time and there was still this pull between us. He called me one night because he'd been drinking and I went downtown to find him—didn't want him trying to drive home intoxicated.

"Um, so I found him and drove to his place. I had a roommate and didn't want to wake her. So, we're at his house, kissing. We were standing in his living room and he kind of shoved me back onto the couch, falling on top of me in the process. He's six feet tall and probably weighs over two hundred pounds. I struggled because I couldn't catch my breath. I thought that he'd realize that he was hurting me and ease up, but he didn't. He had me pinned beneath him and all I could manage to do was breathe shallowly. He um- he put himself inside me. I wasn't ready, so it hurt, a lot."

The woman pauses and wipes away tears. I lean forward in my chair, knowing exactly how this story is going to end, but needing to hear her tell it anyway.

"Sorry—this part is hard for me. I didn't say anything. He hadn't done anything when I told him I couldn't breathe, so I didn't think he'd listen. I just let him move in and out of me.

"I remember staring at the canned lights in the ceiling. They'd been dimmed, and it reminded me of Christmas, like when you leave the Christmas tree plugged in. There was this disconnect happening within me. I just wanted it to be over, so I focused on the fact that it looked like Christmas. I pulled myself away from each thrust and focused on those lights, and I prayed that it would be over soon.

"He finished and I got the hell out of there. My shirt was torn and I had bruises on one of my shoulders. I spent the night in the bathroom floor, bleeding and crying. I was so disgusted with myself, felt like I was to blame for it even happening.

"Tony showed up at my work the next day with flowers. He wanted to know if I'd told anyone about what happened and I told him no. Then he apologized for what had happened the night before —said he'd never been so drunk. The thing is, up until he asked me if I'd told anyone, I'd blamed myself for letting it go that far. I could've stopped him. I should've kicked and fought. After...after he asked, I realized that he knew it was rape." She finishes weakly and Jo has to help her back to her chair. Other than the sound of her sobs, the room is deathly quiet.

"Marissa's shown incredible bravery here tonight. It's not easy to acknowledge our trauma—to give it a voice. Our abusers want our silence—silence is consent. The thing is, we may be quieted while it's taking place, but we refuse to remain there."

I work feverishly to brush the wetness off of my cheeks and compose myself. I've found the first chink in my armor. When she described the disconnect—I knew exactly what she meant. I had stared at that moldy mattress so many times, envisioning myself a million miles away. Suffering through the pain, and praying with every breath that it would be over soon. I thought of my father and my friends and I created a fantasy inside my head; one where I wasn't being abused.

Jo gives us a five-minute break and I make a beeline for the coffee pot in the corner.

"That stuff will put hair on your chest."

I turn to face the man behind me. "Excuse me?"

He laughs easily. "I just meant it's like drinking sludge. God knows when they last cleaned the damn thing."

He thrusts his hand out to me. "I'm Lee. It's Kat, right?"

I give a small smile and take his hand. "Nice to meet you, Lee. Do you come here often?" I realize what I've implied just as his eyebrows arch up in surprise. "God, don't answer that. It sounds like a bad pick-up line."

He smiles and everything feels normal again. We're just two people, chatting about therapy attendance. "I do come here often—my wife was assaulted and I find that coming here has helped me better understand what she went through."

My smile fades and I focus on the empty Styrofoam cup in my hand. "I'm sorry to hear that. Well, nice to meet you—again."

Without waiting for a response, I turn and quickly walk back to my seat. I place the empty cup on the floor and work on distracting myself. I count cracks in the concrete floor and try to clear my mind.

This was a mistake.

"Is this seat taken?" Lee gestures toward the empty chair next to mine with the bottle of water in his hand. I stop twirling the strand of hair around my finger. I'd been so focused on wrapping and unwrapping it as my finger turned purple, that I didn't see him walk up.

I give a small sigh, but shake my head. "No. Help yourself."

I stand up to let him around me, his body mere inches from mine. It's then that I fully take him in. He stands only a few inches taller than me—I'd guess he's maybe 6'2 or 6'3. His dark hair is tousled in a way that looks like he just rolled out of bed, but you know it probably takes him hours to perfect it. He has just the right amount of cologne on, but it's his eyes—that same shade of green, that causes me to take a step back.

I don't know how I missed it before. He resembles Landon in a way that is almost uncanny. I'm not sure whether to run for my life or throw myself into his arms and apologize for ever leaving. I swallow nervously and sit back down, my thoughts spiraling out of control.

Jo steps up to the small podium. "Alright, is everyone back? Good. Lee, you wanna start?"

He nods and stands up slowly. "I'm Lee and I love a victim. My wife was abducted and assaulted. The things that she endured at the hands of her attacker—they changed her. It took me a long time to see past my own anger and realize it. She startled at every little sound... wanted to sleep with the lights on. She tried to pretend that everything was okay...like it never happened.

"I think I took a lot of my anger out on her, even though she was the last person in the world I would ever want to hurt. She saw counselors and begged me to go with her, but I just didn't see the point. What good could come from reliving that nightmare over and over?"

I lean forward in my chair. "What happened? Did it work?" I don't even realize I've spoken the words aloud until Lee looks down at me.

"She killed herself, Kat," he rubs his hand roughly across his face. "I could've prevented it had I done more to help her recover. That's part of why I'm here—to atone for my past mistakes...make sure no one else has to endure what I endure every day now."

I exhale slowly. *This was a huge mistake.*

Feeling panicked, I quickly stand up and grab my purse. "I'm sorry, I just remembered I have to be somewhere." I glance wildly around the room; certain someone is watching me.

"Kat—wait." Lee takes a step toward me just as Jo does the same. She gets to me first and presses her card into my hand as she walks me to the door.

"When you're ready to talk, I'm ready to listen. Call me anytime. Okay?"

I nod reluctantly and get the hell out of there, my hands trembling the entire time. *What if he'd been in there with me?* What if he followed me out? I turn around several times, but the sidewalk remains empty behind me.

I need to get back to my condo.

I've only made it a few steps before the cameras stop me in my tracks. Several reporters call my name and I know I'm supposed to give a vague statement about therapy.

I don't.

Instead, I stand there, blinking amid the flashbulbs, looking like a deer caught in the headlights.

ELEVEN
KATYA

May 2015

"YOU PROMISED you'd go out with me, Kat. After the five billionth time you blew me off...remember?" My best friend, Aja, gets right up in my face as she says it, her jet black hair dropping over one eye in the process.

I have blown her off...a lot. I've avoided so much in the last month. I haven't told anyone, but I've gone back to the victim support group meetings. Repeatedly.

It's silly.

I'm not a victim anymore—I shouldn't want to go to something like that. And it's not like I need to be there...I just feel bad for those people. Part of the *It Ends with Us* campaign is supporting the victims of assault.

That's all I'm doing...supporting the victims. Maybe we'll use them in an ad spot in the future. Lee's story would have such an impact, with losing his wife like that. I'll have to get with the execs and see if they'll consider my ideas. It's research—nothing more.

"Hello, earth to Katya. You in or not?" Aja cocks her head to the side, hands firmly on her hips.

I am not a victim.

"In." I say firmly, clasping her bronzed hand in mine. "Let's do this."

THE MUSIC PULSES LOUDLY, my thoughts getting jumbled with each pounding beat. "Aja!"

The blue lights overhead give everything an ethereal appearance while the city skyline, clearly visible from the wall of windows, lights up the night sky beyond us.

"Katya!"

I jump at her touch on my arm. "Aja—it's so loud. Did you find a table?"

She shakes her head and gestures wildly with the two martini glasses in her hand, pink liquid spilling over the sides. "Let's try over in the corner."

I take a small sip and shudder. It's sweet and fruity, not at all the way alcohol is supposed to taste.

Aja leans into me as we stand in a small corner of the bar, shouting to be heard. "So, Chris tells me that you're getting serious with the VS stuff. Are you considering going exclusive with them?"

I feel as though I'm underwater. Aja's voice sounds so far away. Just like clockwork, there's a high-pitched ringing in my ears, quickly followed by a stabbing pain in my head. I've seen several doctors in the past few months and all agree that there is no brain damage. I was just given prescription strength migraine medication and told to wait it out.

I shake my head slightly, trying to clear my thoughts and stop the buzzing. "Do you want to step outside?"

Aja cups a hand to her ear. "What?"

I point out to the balcony, where several people are standing around smoking, and she nods. My hands begin to tremble so I down the fruity cocktail like a shot.

Aja turns back to me as she reaches the railing. "Wow, sister, you did need a night out. Want another?"

I do want another, but not with this many people around. I make sure no one is staring for too long in our direction. "No, I'm fine. What were you asking me in there?"

She sways back and forth to the music from the outdoor speakers —clearly she started drinking before I arrived. "Hmm? Oh, right. I was asking if you think you're going to go exclusive with Selvaggia. I've heard some rumors..."

I smile without showing any teeth, a move I've perfected in the last few months. "I'm a little too old for that, don't you think? I don't think they consider anyone over the age of thirty for a long-term contract."

She shakes her head earnestly while taking a sip, little droplets of liquor splashing onto her cheeks. "No ma'am, you do not get to pull that card. You've been modeling with them for years. They put you on the damn cover of their winter catalog—surely it's not a stretch to think that next you'll be wearing the multi-million-dollar fantasy bra."

The throbbing in my head worsens, as though someone is taking an ice pick and jabbing it in at random. I give a small groan and massage my temple. Aja lays a hand on my arm. "You okay, Kat?"

I close my eyes against a wave of dizziness. "Yeah, I'm fine. It's just a headache."

She downs the rest of her drink. "You're not fine. I knew this was a little too much for your first night out. Let's get you home." She doesn't allow any room for arguing as she wraps her arm around my shoulders and guides me back inside.

I watch the faces around us, making sure no one is looking in our direction. I also glance back to make sure we're not being followed. It isn't a big deal—every single woman that lives in a big city does it.

Aja confidently pushes us through the throngs of sweaty bodies drinking and dancing, with me glued to her side. Once we reach the sidewalk out front, she hails me a cab.

"Text me when you get home, okay? We'll do brunch this weekend."

I nod and lean back into the cloth-covered seat. The entire cab reeks of cigarette smoke even though there are "No Smoking" signs posted everywhere.

The cab driver gets me dropped off at my building and I quickly pay him before unlocking the main door and taking the elevator up to my condo.

I breathe a sigh of relief as the doors click open. *I'm safe.* I've only taken a couple of steps when I see it, and I freeze in my tracks.

There's a picture of me taped to my front door. I stare at it dumbly for a few seconds before realizing that it was taken when I left a few hours ago.

Underneath it is a hastily scrawled note.

"My darling, you looked wonderful tonight."

No.

Not again.

I rip the note and picture off the door and crumple them up in my pocket as I quickly let myself in. I relock the door behind me and put the chain on, before pulling my laptop from the couch and into my lap. Shakily, I grab the bottle of vodka and a room temperature energy drink from the coffee table, alternating between the two, as the computer hums to life. My body's ready to slip into fight or flight mode.

I log into Facebook and immediately go to Landon's account. It's what I did when I got the previous message. The last thing posted is a photo of me along with a phone number to contact if I'd been seen. Never mind the fact that he knew damn good and well where I was the entire time.

I take a drink of vodka and chase it with the *Redbull* before looking over at the column of friends currently online. I could've sworn his name just popped up on that list. I blink again and scroll through, but I must've been mistaken. I can't find his name anywhere.

Without looking at the time, I call the one person who can answer my questions and calm my fears.

"Hello?" The sleepy male voice answers.

"Detective Sullivan? Did I wake you?"

There's a small yawn. "Katya, are you okay?"

I inhale deeply. "It happened again. I got home tonight and there was another note on the door. I checked his Facebook profile and I could've sworn he was just online too. Detective Sullivan, you told me—"

"Katya, please call me Mike. As I've said multiple times, I think we're past formalities by now. And I know what you're thinking, but it's got to be a copycat. What was on your door tonight?"

I pull the wrinkled note and photo from the pocket of my jacket, smoothing the papers as best I can, before laying them on the coffee table. "It's a picture of me that was taken when I left my condo tonight and a note that just says, *'My darling, you looked wonderful tonight.'* I followed your advice, I swear. I checked the hallway before I stepped out, but I didn't see anyone when I left."

I can hear the clicking of a pen through the phone and I know he's thinking. He does it almost every time we talk, like a nervous habit. "Well, this person is consistent. The last note was a song lyric too, wasn't it?"

I get up and walk to my closet, finding the note buried in a shoe box in the back. "Yeah, that one said, *"These days when I see you, you make it look like I'm see-through."* Isn't that an Adele song? So, we've got Clapton and Adele—but what does it mean?"

"Was Landon into any of that music? Anyone he might've told about that music?" The clicking becomes frantic and my anxiety ratchets up another notch.

"No, he listened to country music. That's it." I walk out of the closet and catch the time on the digital clock on my nightstand. "It's four in the morning there. I'm sorry, Det—Mike. I just didn't want to wait to call."

"Hey, I made you a promise a few months ago. One I intend to keep. If I wanted sleep, I wouldn't have gone into law enforcement. I've got some vacation time coming up next week. I think it's time I came up there. In the meantime, I want you to keep a low profile—don't go out at night. If you do, make sure you've got someone with you."

I brush a tear from my cheek and clear my throat. "Got it."

Mike continues, "We're going to find Landon. We've been monitoring his house here, watching for activity on any of his bank accounts—the minute he makes a move, we're going to be on it. I'll look into the Facebook thing. Okay?"

It's code for *"we're not discussing this on a phone call,"* something I know all too well.

Landon Scott is dead, has been for months now. I know it. Mike knows it. We just don't necessarily need the rest of the world to know it.

TWELVE

KATYA

December 18, 2014

"WE'RE BACK *tonight with the latest on the search for Landon Scott, the man behind the disappearance of Katya Egoricheva. Egoricheva was found severely dehydrated and suffering from malnutrition. Her injuries are considered non-life threatening and she is recovering in a local hospital tonight.*

"We've just learned that Elizabeth Greene was the unidentified female rescued along with Egoricheva. Greene, twenty-eight weeks pregnant at the time of abduction, was severely beaten. She was taken by medical helicopter to an undisclosed local hospital where she underwent emergency surgery. Both mom and baby are recovering in the hospital and are expected to make a full recovery.

"Landon Scott was injured in an altercation with a police officer, but managed to flee the scene. His vehicle was found yesterday morning buried in a snow drift. Blood inside the vehicle matched that found on scene. If you have any information on his whereabouts, you are urged to call..."

I tune out the rest as hot tears roll down my cheeks. He's still alive. He'll be coming back for us. I need to figure out which hospital room Elizabeth is in—warn her before it's too late.

There's a knock on my hospital door and I reluctantly turn away from the window. "Come in."

I'm expecting a nurse, but it's the detective who saved me. Maybe he's come to get me out of here. I can do some sort of witness protection program. He has a bouquet of grocery store flowers in his hand.

"I told you I'd come back. Is now a good time for you?" He uses his free hand to brush his blond hair off of his forehead, a gesture that women everywhere must go crazy over.

I swipe a hand over my face, trying to rid it of any emotion. "It's fine."

He gently closes the door behind him and sets the flowers on the hospital bed table before coming over to sit on the edge of the bed. "You've been crying, you're not fine."

I take a deep breath just as another sob works its way out. "I-I saw the news story. He's s-still out there. I have to get out of here. Detective, please don't leave me alone." I clutch the bed sheets tightly in my fists, working to regain control of my emotions.

"Katya, listen to me. He's not going to be coming back, I swear to you. I made a promise to keep you safe and I'm going to honor that."

I shake my head, disagreeing with him. "No, you don't understand. They just showed his picture and said he was still at large. I can't stay, detective. He'll come after me. Have you gotten Elizabeth out of here? He might come after her or the baby." My words are laced with panic and paranoia.

When he moves to touch my hand, I scramble back in the bed away from him. He puts his hand back down, a look of regret on his face. "It's okay, I won't touch you. I'm sorry, I wasn't thinking."

I nod shakily and relax. If I react like this anytime a man tries to touch me, I'm never going to recover. The hospital door opens again and my father walks in, carrying bags of food. "Katya, *ya nashol khoroshuyu yedu.*"

He stops when he sees the detective. "Detective, we were not expecting a visit from you tonight."

Detective Sullivan looks over at me in confusion. "Do you understand what he just said? I didn't think you spoke Russian."

My father scoffs, "Of course she speaks Russian. Why wouldn't she?"

In spite of our conversation, I smile. "*Koneshno, detektiv.* My Papa just informed me that he's brought us food that's actually edible. He's not a big fan of the hospital food. How would you know whether or not I speak the language though?"

He looks down at his feet. "I've been trying to find you for four months. I feel like I know everything about you. It was never mentioned. I mean, you were born right outside of Denver, so I just assumed. Sorry."

"Why are you here, Detective Sullivan?" All traces of adoration are gone, my father's mouth set in a hard line.

It's hard to believe that Nikolay Egorichev was thirty-seven when I was born. People never seem to think that I'm his daughter, he still looks so young. His close-cropped dark hair has long since been replaced by silver, but my Papa is still an incredibly handsome man. And right now, he looks like he's going to murder the man who saved my life.

"Papa, Detective Sullivan saved my life. I think he has every right to be here."

"Please, call me Mike."

"Detective, is it done or not? Do not waste my time." I've never heard my father sound so angry.

Mike stands up and walks over to the hospital door, checking to make sure no one is about to come in. "Nikolay, it's done."

I look between the two men. "Wait, what's going on? Papa?"

My father ignores my question and pulls a wad of cash from his pocket, handing it over to Mike. "I have associates that can help with the disposal. I'll reach out to them."

Mike shakes his head. "That won't be necessary."

Fighting incredulity, I hold both hands up. "Will someone please tell me what the hell is going on? Papa?"

My father comes over and sits on the edge of the bed. "*Moya milaya,* I did what needed to be done. Your nightmare is over now."

He roughly grabs me into a hug as I stare wide-eyed over his shoulder at Mike. His eyes plead for me to accept what he's done, but there's something else there as well.

Guilt?

Worry?

"Papa, would you mind giving me and the detective a moment alone please?"

My father releases my shoulders and stands again, gesturing over to the white paper bag on the table. "Of course. I found a food truck that made pirozhki. I thought you could use some comfort food. I'll-uh- I'll just be down the hall if you need me." He's rambling in his attempts to smooth over the situation.

Once the door clicks shut, I fix my eyes on Mike. "Tell me everything."

He comes back and sits on my hospital bed. "David, he-uh- he didn't like the idea that Landon could be sitting in some prison, just waiting on parole. He didn't want Elizabeth looking over her shoulder the rest of her life. To be honest, I didn't like the idea of you dealing with any more shit either.

"Your father was already planning his own form of justice, was ready to recruit his own army to find Landon. I just brought him into our plan and assured him we'd take care of it."

It's all true then.

Landon is dead. I don't know whether to laugh or cry. Just a few minutes ago I'd been ready to sneak out of the hospital to escape the man, but he's never coming back.

I'm safe.

So, why do I feel sad?

"You said you took care of him—how do you know you won't be caught?" I whisper the words, suddenly afraid that someone might have their ear pressed to the door. If anyone were to find out, my father would go to prison for his role in it.

Mike's mouth is set in a grim line when he answers. "You're not the only one with a powerful father. Let's just say that this kind of stuff is my old man's specialty. They'll never find any part of him."

"So what my father gave you tonight...it's blood money. You do realize that, don't you?"

He shakes his head angrily. "No, we all did what we had to do to protect you and Elizabeth from that sociopath. Don't try to guilt me, Katya. I won't apologize for my role in this."

I slide my hand closer to him before reconsidering and bringing it back. "I know; I'm not asking for that. I'm just trying to make sense of it all."

"You can't speak a word of this to anyone. I only told you because you deserve to recover from this. You deserve a chance to live without him tainting everything around you."

My throat tightens and I nod, willing myself not to cry.

A nurse knocks on the door and wheels in a small cart with a blood pressure cuff on it. "Hey love, I just need to get some vitals on you and then I'll be out of your hair."

My hair.

I shudder. My hair is still a bleached out mess. The first time I saw myself in a mirror, I'd jumped back in fright. I don't look like me —I look like a battered skeleton wearing a blonde wig.

She swipes her badge at the computer and begins typing. Mike takes the opportunity to move closer to me, wrapping me up in his arms, his lips pressed to my ear. My body screams at the contact, but he doesn't release his hold on me. "Remember, not a word." He whispers and presses something into my hand as he stands up. The nurse gives a knowing smile as she glances over at us—not realizing that it isn't a show of intimacy. It's a warning.

"I'm going to let you get some rest, Katya. I'll check in on you again before you leave."

He's just reached for the door handle when I find my voice. "Mike? Thank you...for coming by."

He looks back at me and swallows. "You're welcome."

I wait until both he and the nurse are gone before opening my hand.

It's Landon's college ring. Something he never took off. Mike must've known, or maybe my father told him, that I'd want proof. I lean back into the pillow, clutching the ring, and trying to come to terms with the fact that Landon would never be coming back.

I'm safe, yet every time I close my eyes, I see my father in handcuffs.

THIRTEEN

KATYA

"KATYA, welcome. We have not seen you in a while. I set aside a couple of bottles of Beluga for you last week."

"Viktor, thank you. You know I'd be in here once a week if you carried Yamskaya."

He laughs heartily. "As would your father."

I try to pay him, but he refuses, as he'd done every other time in the past few months. "Viktor, this vodka is not cheap. Let me pay you, please."

He grumbles. "No, Katya. You have been through so much. Your money is no good here."

"I'm fine, truly." I can hear the lie as I say it, but luckily Viktor doesn't catch on.

As far as he knows, my busy modeling schedule is the reason I haven't been in. I think the truth would crush him—at the very least, he would alert my father to my drinking.

I don't want to burden anyone so I try to keep my visits to once a month. There are six other liquor stores that carry my brand of vodka and I rotate through them to get me through the other days.

I leave and get into my Jeep after promising Viktor to come by more often. Seeing that he's still watching me from the store windows, I drive a few blocks away before pulling over and tearing into the box. I manage to pull the bottle and hammer out, and with shaking hands, use it to break the wax seal—wax bits falling into my lap and onto the floorboard. I quickly brush away the remnants on the bottle and pop the cork.

Grabbing my empty water bottle, I unscrew the lid and empty the first bottle of vodka into it. It takes me several attempts to get the lid screwed back on, but once it's done, I let out an audible sigh of relief.

I always feel a little rush at this point, I don't quite know how to describe it. It's an intense feeling of pleasure similar to what you might get when you take a lover to bed for the first time. At least from what I remember.

I take a long sip and my body immediately relaxes. All the blood rushes to my stomach, leaving me feeling warm inside. The delicious burn spreads down to my toes, and I let myself savor the feeling for a minute. My hands stop shaking, and I feel like I can finally think clearly again.

Before, I'd probably meditate or do yoga to clear my head. Now, I just have a few drinks. I didn't tell the doctors this, but when I couple it with my migraine medicine, I finally get some relief. I've told my Papa that I only drink a little. If he ever checks with Viktor, he'll verify that. I'm good.

I close my eyes and take another sip. I just need to take the edge off of finding that note on my door last night, that's all. It isn't like I have a problem. I know that sounds like something that all addicts say, but I don't need to drink all day. Just a little bit at night.

Nights are hard for me. Otherwise, I'm fine.

I am fine.

FOURTEEN

TRAVIS

June 22, 2013

THE SOUND of gunfire wakes me.

I quickly look around, realizing I'm back in the desert. Silently, I roll out of bed and onto the floor.

Who the fuck is on fire watch?

I hear a low moan and move toward the sound. It's Carlson. I roughly pull him onto the floor with me.

There's another loud pop and his eyes widen in fear. "Stay quiet."

He nods shakily and then whines loudly in my ear.

"Carlson, shut the fuck up!" I whisper.

He begins crying and shaking his head, the whining growing louder.

The pops continue just outside and I know that he's going to get us both killed if he doesn't quiet down.

"Stop!" I growl the words into his face. "I'm trying to save our asses."

He suddenly sits up, tackling me and knocking me onto my back.

I blink and look up. I'm back in my bedroom. Charlie stands on my chest, licking my face and whining.

I rub her head before shakily saying, "Good girl. I'm okay."

She backs off and then I hear the crying. I crawl over to the other side of the bed. Anne sits, her back to the nightstand, rocking slowly.

"Annie, baby, it's okay. I'm fine."

She continues sobbing and when her head drops onto her knees, I see the blood in her blonde hair.

"Jesus Christ, what happened?"

I move closer to her and she tries to wedge herself in between the bed and nightstand. "Don't touch me! Don't touch me!"

I sit back on my ass, hands up. "I won't. I won't. Baby, what happened?"

She gulps in a breath. "Y-y-y-you! You did this!"

There's another loud pop from outside and my head jerks toward the sound.

"It's fireworks, Travis! It's fucking fireworks!" She cradles her head. "You yanked me out of bed and I hit the nightstand. You wouldn't let me up. If Charlie wouldn't have been here..." She trails off and shudders.

Hearing her name, Charlie comes and sits down next to me. "Baby, I'm sorry. I can take you to a hospital."

She shakes her head violently. "I want to leave. I can't do this, Trav. This isn't new with you. You're always angry and tonight—tonight was the final straw for me." She quickly stands and begins gathering her clothes.

"I'm sorry, Annie." I don't know what else to say.

She gives me a look and it shreds my heart into fucking ribbons. "You need to get help." Then, without another look, she walks out.

Five months. We were together five months and she left the minute she saw me for the monster I am. Charlie licks my face again and I pull her into me, my tears wetting her fur.

"You save me, Char. Every fucking time. You save me."

If it weren't for her, the nightmares would've taken what little humanity remains in me.

DEVIL IN DISGUISE?

Selvaggia model, Katya Egoricheva, is reportedly being considered for a Siren contract with the lingerie giant. But, is she really siren material?

You may recall Katya was rescued back in December after allegedly being held against her will for months by her ex-boyfriend, Landon Scott. Scott has not been seen since and is still considered the primary suspect in her disappearance.

Katya, who was relatively unknown in the fashion world before her abduction, rose to prominence during the months she was missing. Selvaggia went as far as placing her on the cover of their winter catalog in an attempt to help locate her.

An anonymous source close to the model had this to say, “It must be nice to have everything handed to you just because you dropped off the face of the earth for four months. I'm not saying she staged the entire thing, but it has worked out rather well for her.”

“My son is a good man. Ms. Egoricheva ruined him when she broke things off. For her to come out and say that he abducted her...abused her? It's unbelievable. What I want to know is what Ms. Egoricheva is hiding regarding the whereabouts of my son. He should be considered innocent until proven guilty, especially with no concrete evidence pointing to his guilt," said Nancy Scott, Landon's mother.

Police still have no leads on the location of Landon Scott, but assured our local reporter that they are working feverishly to locate him. According to Detective Michael Sullivan, "This is still an open investigation. Ms. Egoricheva has been cooperating with our office and is not considered a suspect in this investigation."

FIFTEEN

KATYA

"SO, it looks like they're going to offer you a contract. Rumor has it that you won them over with your *Academy Award* performance outside of therapy last month. Just keep riding that line between victim and victor. Remember that; victim and victor." My publicist ends the call before I can even respond.

I stare up at the high-rise building in front of me, dread filling me inside. I don't want to go in. The last time I went to the support group meeting, Jo pulled me aside and gave me the names of several psychologists and urged me to sit down with one of them. She said it was perfectly normal to not necessarily want to share my story in a group setting.

As usual, I tried to assure her that I'm fine and only coming for a friend. As usual, she didn't believe me. I blew her off, but pocketed the names. Just in case. This past week has been a ticking time bomb of sorts. There's only been one other note left.

It simply said, *"You live in lies."*

After that, nothing. I've been in this sick waiting game ever since, but the culprit has gone silent. Mike suspects it's someone Landon knew. The police ruled out his mother, as she hasn't left town. I suggested that she hired someone to do it and Mike said he'd considered the same thing. In all honesty though, neither of us knows exactly what we're dealing with.

My phone rings again and I reluctantly pull it from my purse. It's my trainer. "Hi Adriana."

"Katya, I just heard the news. Congrats! Now, get Amy to look at your schedule. We're going to need to go up to two workouts per day. I just don't think once a day is cutting it anymore. 'Kay?"

"Okay, I just—" The phone flashes back to the home screen.

Almost immediately, it rings again.

Amy.

"Hi Amy."

"Kat, just heard the news. I'm trying to schedule an interview with E! News. How long are you going to be meeting with your realtor?"

I might have told a little white lie to my assistant. As far as she knows, I meet with a lot of different people. Massage therapists, reflexologists, my gynecologist, nail tech, realtors...she doesn't need to know that I've been trying out psychologists the entire time.

"I'm hoping no more than an hour. Did Adriana call you?"

There's silence as Amy jots everything down in the notebook that is permanently glued to her hand. I don't have to see her to know that's exactly what she's doing. "Okay, you and Brody are supposed to speak at the NCADV dinner tonight. Lucky for us, it's here in town. Brody is flying in this afternoon.

"Let's see, to recap...if you could wrap it up with your realtor, then we'll get the phone interview with E! done. Adriana did call me and we'll pencil in a workout for one. You've got hair and makeup at three—that'll take approximately two hours. That leaves the dinner and then we can squeeze in another session with Adriana around ten tonight. Am I missing anything?"

I cringe. I'd completely forgotten about the National Coalition Against Domestic Violence dinner. I agreed to speak right after getting back to Colorado.

"Um Amy, is there any way we could clear my schedule tomorrow?" She's my assistant, I should just be able to just tell her what we're doing.

She sighs. "I'm afraid not. We've got you on a flight to San Francisco after your morning workout. You'll be presented a formal contract. From there, we've got you interviewing with various outlets and then speaking at another benefit dinner tomorrow night."

I quickly walk into the building, my heels clicking along the marble floor as I do. The elevator doors are just beginning to close as I reach them. An arm shoots out, keeping them open for me.

I focus on the floor. "Thanks. Listen, Amy, I'm stepping into an elevator with my realtor. I'll call you later."

I end the call just as I catch a tail wagging from the corner of my eye. I stare dumbly at the dog before looking up at its owner. He stands a few inches above me, with close-cropped dark hair. The stubble on his face is trying really hard to become a beard. It just looks like it needs a little pep talk. I snap out of my thoughts and see that he's watching me with a smirk.

"Is your realtor invisible?" His greenish-blue eyes sparkle with amusement, at my expense of course.

I shake my head. "No, I just needed an excuse to get off the phone." I look down at the yellow lab, its tongue hanging out. "No one cares that you bring an animal into the building?"

"She's a service dog."

"You don't look like you need a service dog." His smile fades and I realize too late what I've implied. "I'm sorry—I didn't mean that."

He glances over to the elevator. "You need me to push a floor for you?"

I shake my head. "No, thank you." I'm such an asshole. *Who tells someone they don't look like they need a service dog?*

"Guess looks aren't everything, are they? I wouldn't have pegged you for someone needing therapy." The light that was in his eyes is now gone, replaced by coldness.

I laugh in an attempt to lighten the mood. "Oh, I don't. I'm meeting with my realtor."

He holds my gaze. "That's funny, because the seventh floor is nothing but psych offices."

I look down at my shoes, willing the elevator to move faster. An eternity later, the doors slide open. Still keeping my head down, I all but run out.

"Good luck with your 'realtor.' Hope you find a great place." He laughs to himself and my face burns in embarrassment.

Thankfully, the universe decides to smile on me for once. He goes left and I go right.

"KATYA, why don't we start by you telling me a little bit about what you're looking for with therapy. I just want to ensure that I'm able to fulfill my obligations and help you meet your goals in the process."

I stare at her; my mouth quite possibly hanging open. "You want to know what I want to accomplish here?"

She nods and my mind races. I've seen so many psychologists and psychiatrists over the past few months, but I don't remember any of them asking me what I wanted to get out of therapy.

I don't know...maybe they did.

I had only been going out of obligation. Would I have even been able to answer truthfully?

Am I able to now?

"I don't know what I want to get from this. I've been doing campaigns and raising awareness, so maybe I just need more tools to help other victims I encounter."

It's bullshit. All of it. It's also the only thing I can come up with off the top of my head. A prepackaged answer ready to be heated up and served at a moment's notice.

She jots down a note and nods. *Here it comes.* This is the part where she chastises me for wasting her time while waving my medical record in my face.

"Okay, that seems easy enough. I think I can definitely help you."

I pick my jaw up off the floor. "So, you can help me with my speeches and how to best help those that have been victimized?"

She nods again. "Absolutely. What you're doing is such a good thing, Katya. I'd love to support you in that."

I stand up, smoothing my dress in the process. I take a couple of steps toward the door and then back over to the windows. With my back to her, I ask, "What if it's all shit? What if every bit of it is some elaborate act?"

My forehead connects with a soft thud against the glass. My heart is racing right now. I don't know that I've ever said these words aloud to anyone.

"Then, I can help with that too. I want you to share what you're comfortable sharing."

I catch my reflection in the window, dark shadows still visible-even with all the makeup, and take a deep breath. "It's all a lie. I'm not okay. I've tried to be. I've tried so hard, but I don't know if there's a way to fix this. You've seen the medical report, but that's just scratching the surface of the entire thing.

"The report has photographic evidence of everything I endured at the hands of someone who once swore to love me. What it doesn't capture is the way he would look at me sometimes—like I was something he cherished. It doesn't get into the gray area that was our relationship. I could've fought. He left me alone for days at a time. Why didn't I run? That's what the police wanted to know when they questioned me. They didn't see him in those small moments. He was vicious when he tortured me, but I endured it, knowing he would be the one to nurse me back to health once it was over."

I slowly turn back around, but Dr. Farrell hasn't moved. She smiles warmly at me and somehow, that's all it takes. The walls start dropping. The armor that has protected me for the last few months is stripped away and I stand before her completely vulnerable.

"Everyone acts like they know what happened to me, but they don't. No one does. Do you know what it's like–spending your days trapped?"

"What is it like, Katya? Walk me through a day in your shoes."

These walls don't make a sound as they fall down around me, even if I envision it as an earthquake taking place. I close my eyes and take another deep breath.

One.

Two.

Three.

Five hours ago...

HIS GRUNTS FILLED *the room as his belt connected over and over with my back. I curled into the fetal position, refusing to make a sound.*

He wanted that, fed off of it.

"Scream, bitch. Scream and I'll stop." He snarled the words, but I knew he wouldn't stop. He wouldn't stop until he was physically exhausted and right now, he was far from it.

I wondered if he'd stop if I died...or if he'd continue until his body quit on him.

The lashes stopped suddenly and he stood over me, kicking at me with the toe of his boot. I kept my eyes tightly shut, even while knowing what was coming next. He knelt down, easily flipping me onto my back, before sitting down on my chest. His hands stroked my face gently before settling around my throat.

My eyes popped open and I shook my head frantically. This caused him to smile.

"You afraid to die, Elizabeth?"

Before I could open my mouth to respond, his hands tightened around my throat and everything went dark.

"No!" I suck air into my lungs as I scream. I fight to sit up in bed, expecting to see Landon, but I'm in my condo. Alone.

Safe.

I fall back against the damp pillow, letting my pulse slow to normal, while watching the snow fall outside of my bedroom window. It's May, but obviously Mother Nature isn't ready for spring just yet.

It was just another nightmare. I can't recall one night where I've been able to sleep peacefully. Every single night is the same. I close my eyes and relive what he did. The problem is that my body doesn't know it's just a dream. My body reacts as though the events are still taking place. I've woken up to sheets covered in sweat, vomit, and urine more times than I'm comfortable admitting.

It's hard to feel like a grown woman when you're wetting the bed because of nightmares. I swipe a finger under each eye, brushing away tears. My throat feels tight, either from crying or reliving the choking, I don't want to take the time to dwell on which. I tried to stay awake again, staring at the clock on my nightstand until my eyes crossed from exhaustion, every light burning bright in my entire condo.

I center myself and focus on my breathing.

Inhale.

Exhale.

I study the snowflakes as they fall from the sky. Snow is so calming for me. I was rescued right before that blizzard hit and to this day, there's just something about seeing the world blanketed in white that soothes me—it's like a fresh start. It won't last of course...the snow will be gone by lunch, but I'll enjoy it for now.

My heart rate slows as I continue my breathing exercises. I'm supposed to vocalize that I am in a safe place and acknowledge that Landon can no longer hurt me, but I can't. Not yet.

I'm not ready to let my guard down. He'll be counting on that.

I grab my water bottle of vodka from the nightstand, taking the time to unscrew the lid before downing it. Like some fucked up version of *Groundhog Day*, I know exactly what will happen next.

My trainer will show up.

My publicist and agent will call.

Amy will tell me to be somewhere.

I will smile for the cameras.

I will pretend that I'm okay.

I will do this until eventually, I cease to exist.

SIXTEEN
KATYA

"...AND I couldn't think of any other person more perfect for this than Katya. Someone who experienced this first hand. If you'll look up at the screen behind me, you'll see a woman who went to Hell and fought her way back. She survived that and devoted her life to helping other women in similar situations."

The lights are blinding me—the heat radiating off of them as if the sun itself has entered the hotel ballroom. Someone in the back of the room clears their throat and Brody gently nudges me with his arm.

I squint at the teleprompter in front of us and then back at the screen behind. It's the media's favorite image—me in a hospital bed. My lips swollen and split, face bruised.

Brody breaks through the silence, improvising. "It's tough to look at that picture, isn't it Katya?"

I turn back to the teleprompter slowly, trying to focus on the words; each one slipping and sliding as it moves across the screen. Like snakes.

"Sooooooo true, Brody." A giggle escapes and he turns to me in shock.

I try to cover it with a cough and quickly look back down at the screen. "Stick to the script, Katya." I whisper the words and they're instantly amplified with the microphone in my face.

I giggle again, this time making no attempt to cover it up.

"Where are we at Brody? The part where everyone gasps after seeing my face or the part where we basically say if you've got a vagina, you're going to be raped and beaten?"

Brody's hand shoots out to cover the microphone, seconds too late. He glances around for help and then gently moves the microphone away from me. "Folks, this is hard stuff. I think you'll agree with me that the woman beside me has endured more than any person ever should. I'm going to ask that you excuse us for a few minutes."

People begin standing up and clapping in support, and I try to wave like Miss America would, but Brody's already pulling me through a side door and into another conference room that has been turned into a dressing room just for the event.

"Are you drunk?" He leans down to peer into my eyes and I bring a hand up to his face. I wonder what it would be like to touch him. Could I just lay my hand on his cheek? What would happen if I did?

I nod stupidly at his question, a grin tugging at my lips. "I may have overhydrated a bit today."

"Is she okay? What can I get?" Amy stands nervously in the doorway, clutching her precious planner.

"The precious..." I mutter to myself.

Brody holds a hand up to her. "Just give us a minute, okay? I think she just got a little lightheaded up there."

Amy nods and steps back out, closing the door softly behind her.

I've never tried to touch a man while drunk. Maybe it's easier than trying to do it while sober. I bring my hand down until it rests against his scruffy cheek.

"You're furry." I stroke gently and he sucks in a breath.

"Don't. You are completely shit-faced right now—you're not thinking straight. I thought you were done with that. You promised."

"I put the vodka in the water bottle and the people never know. Never. It's our little secret." I continue petting his face all while moving closer, breathing him in. I could kiss him...just lean in and take what I want.

Do I even want Brody?

I fight through the drunken haze to ponder it. He's been like a big brother type to me since we started this campaign, but could he be more? Is Brody a safe bet? He's seen the images of me—he knows that I'm beyond saving.

"Kat, seriously. Cut the shit so we can get back out there. We'll get through it and then I'll take you home. No one has to know you've been drinking."

I bring my hands around to the back of his head, pulling his mouth closer to mine.

So close.

I can see exactly how it would go. He'd growl with pleasure, as his hands slipped around my waist, pulling me into him. A jolt of pleasure would ripple through my body and I would do a small victory dance inside; knowing that I was doing it.

Brody would capture my lower lip between his teeth, holding me hostage, while his hands would stroke my body through layers of satin. I'd probably orgasm just from his hands on my waist. We'd pull apart long enough to look at each other before moving together again. Our teeth would clink together as he lifted me up onto a long table, taking me roughly.

"Fuck, what are you doing to me?" He'd groan in my ear

I open my eyes and the smile on my face instantly fades. I imagined Brody's voice, but I'm staring at Landon's face. I scramble back, kicking him away from me in the process.

I slide off the other side of the table, keeping it between us as a barrier, while my heart hammers loudly in my chest. It isn't real. He's not real. Landon is gone.

I blink several times and suddenly it's Brody in front of me again. His arms rest on the table, as if he's trying to hold himself up.

"I'm sorry, Brody."

His eyes meet mine and he sighs. "You can't keep doing this to yourself, Kat. You said you were going to get help. Now we've got an entire ballroom full of people that came here to see you tonight. They paid a lot of money for that. You committed to this, so we're gonna finish it together. Then, we're going to sober you up. Deal?"

I nod. "Deal."

He pushes off from the table, adjusting his suit, as I reapply lip gloss. I glance at his reflection in the mirror. "You're really good at thinking on your feet. Thanks for covering for me back there."

He smiles. "Darlin', I play in the NFL. Thinking on my feet has kept me off the injured list and my team in the top of our league."

MY CELL PHONE buzzes and it takes me a minute to locate it. It's wedged between the headboard and the mattress, I must've fallen asleep with it again. My head aches something awful as I scramble to find it.

"Hello?" My voice is raspy, probably from screaming in my sleep again.

I look over at the clock to see that it's almost three in the afternoon.

Oh no.

No. No. No.

"Katya, we've been calling you for hours. Where are you? Your flight landed three hours ago. We called the hotel, but they said you hadn't checked in yet."

"Alexa, I'm so sorry. I wasn't feeling well last night and I overslept. I'm still in Denver." It's a pitiful excuse and one that will not win me any brownie points with my agent.

She sighs heavily. "Does this have anything to do with what's in the tabloids this morning?"

I frown. "The tabloids?"

"Katya, pictures of you and Brody are everywhere. I've tried to be understanding, with everything you've gone through, but you're telling me that you couldn't have waited just twenty-four more hours? Selvaggia is bringing you on because of what you represent, but these pictures are not helping your image."

I try to find a comfortable spot, or at the very least, one that doesn't make my head want to explode. "Wait, —"

She cuts me off. "No, you wait. You wanna fuck '*The Bad Boy from Dallas*,' be my guest. But do it discreetly—and not on the day you're supposed to sign a contract!"

I hold the phone away from my ear, cringing. "Alexa, I can do better. I really need—" My phone's completely silent and I realize she's already disconnected the call.

I drag myself from the bed and stand slowly, trying to gather my bearings.

What happened last night that the tabloids have already picked up?

KATYA: RED HANDED

Denver, CO- Looks like this soon-to-be Siren couldn't resist a visit to the dark side. Media darling Katya Egoricheva was spotted last night with NFL's bad boy, Brody Rodgers, 33. The pair were photographed outside of the model's Denver condo last night, sharing an intimate moment.

A source close to the Cowboys' wide receiver shared that the athlete met the lingerie bombshell when they teamed up for the "It Ends with Us" domestic violence campaign. "It was only a matter of time before they got together. The chemistry between the two of them is off the charts. Brody's been very protective over Katya. And with everything she's gone through, she just might be the one to settle him down."

An attendee at the NCADV dinner noted that the couple "couldn't keep their hands off of each other. He was constantly putting his arm around her, pulling her into his body. It was very romantic."

The thirty-two-year-old model has kept a low profile since being abducted last year. The majority of her appearances recently have all been related to the campaign.

Neither of their reps would confirm anything, but we're rooting for the couple.

Is it too soon to hope for a "Bratya" baby?

SEVENTEEN

KATYA

BRATYA?

Jesus, we sound like the Russian Mafia.

Couldn't keep our hands off each other?

He had his arms around me at the dinner to keep me from falling onto my face.

I rest my phone on the island in the kitchen and scroll up to see the photographs again. We're hugging, but from the paparazzi's angle, it looks like we were doing quite a bit more.

Thankfully, there were no cameras in the hotel conference room last night to capture me throwing myself at Brody.

The phone rings again and Brody's name pops up.

"Hey, I just saw it."

He laughs easily. "I was just calling to see if you wanted to go ahead and hit up Vegas while we're at it. I mean, if we're supposed to have a baby I'd like to make an honest woman out of you first."

I lay my face against the cool granite countertop while holding the phone to my ear. My hands have already begun to tremble, but I can't think about that right now. "Brody, I'm so sorry."

"Why? Nothing happened—well, after we left the dinner. I

hugged you when I left, some paps caught it. Trust me, this is better than the last time I ended up in the tabloids."

I crack a smile. "Well, what do you expect when you use hook-up apps to meet women?"

"I expect to be able to pass out without her taking selfies and broadcasting it to the world."

"Has your publicist released a statement yet? My agent's already called, so I know Cindy's call can't be far behind. What are we saying?"

I don't want my poor judgment affecting anyone else.

He deadpans, "I say we go with the Bratya baby angle."

I laugh in spite of the situation. "Or..."

"Or we remind the public what you've been through. I was comforting you after an emotional evening. Have your publicist release the statement and I'll have mine back it up."

My life has been spinning aimlessly out of control since December. I've tried pushing everything under the rug and pretending to be happy, but skeletons are never content to remain locked away in a closet forever.

I regret my actions last night. It was impulsive to act that way and I'm disgusted with myself. Knowing that I'm not ready to be with anyone, it wasn't fair to try and initiate something with him.

Maybe my father had it right. I should've taken some time off to get help instead of thrusting myself back into the spotlight. I could've dealt with my issues.

I hang up with Brody and with shaking hands, down the rest of the vodka in my water bottle.

Tomorrow.

I'll stop drinking then.

I can use the weekend to sober up and then fly out to San Francisco on Monday to wrap up the contract.

NFL STAR NOT SEEING VS MODEL

Maybe hold off on purchasing any *Bratya* wedding gifts just yet. Less than twenty-four hours after photographs surfaced of the couple, Katya Egoricheva and Brody Rodgers are crying foul.

Both Egoricheva and Rodgers spoke at the annual NCADV dinner Thursday evening. They were seen leaving the event together and even stopped for coffee on the way back to Egoricheva's downtown condo. Photographers snagged photos of the couple in a rather intimate embrace as the NFL star left early Friday morning.

A rep for the Selvaggia model claims that she and the wide receiver are "absolutely not dating" and calls allegations that they are, "absurd."

"Katya has been through so much over the past year and the last thing she's looking at is a serious relationship."

The wide receiver's agent agreed, "Brody has nothing but the utmost respect for Ms. Egoricheva, but they are nothing more than friends."

Only time will tell, but at the moment it looks like as if Bratya is never going to happen.

See Previous Article: Katya: Red Handed

EIGHTEEN

KATYA

"THERE SHE IS. We were beginning to wonder if you were going to show up." Chris taps a perfectly manicured fingernail on the linen tablecloth before flashing me a fake smile.

"Sorry I'm late." I sink into an empty chair and immediately reach for the menu in front of me. I don't know why I'm here. These women used to be like sisters to me, but lately I just feel like I don't belong. And it isn't just here—I don't feel like I fit in anywhere.

"Kat, we haven't seen you in months. What have you been doing since...I mean, are you well?" Hana places her hand on my arm, gently lowering the menu in the process.

I nod quickly and reach for my water glass, instantly wishing that it contained vodka. "I'm fine."

Chris fixes me with an intent stare. "You're fine? You do a shoot for *Selvaggia*, which went viral. Katya, you accomplished something that most people only dream of doing—you were on your way up to the top with Tyra and Heidi. Yet, you aren't in Cali signing the damn deal. That just screams 'fine' to me."

"That's not fair, Chris! She's been through a lot in the last few months." Aja speaks up, her jet black hair catching in the light above our table, giving it a metallic appearance. Out of the three, I'm probably closest to her. She's the only one I trust enough to stay in contact with.

I swallow another sip of water, feeling completely out of place here. *When did lunch with friends become a foreign concept for me?* The table is full of tension and I know I need to say something.

"I don't think I'm going to sign the contract."

Chris's eyes widen in shock. "You're not signing with them?" She lowers her voice as several other tables turn in our direction, "You've been handed everything on a fucking silver platter, all because you were abducted. And now you're saying that you're just going to throw it all away? Is this because of Brody?"

"Hey—she needs a break...it's a demanding industry we're in." Hana pointedly stares her down.

I tug on the collar of my blouse, suddenly feeling too hot. "I... I can't do this right now. I'm sorry." I shove my chair back across the carpet and quickly stand, dizziness washing over me in waves.

"Kat, don't leave. I won't bring it up again. I'm sorry you got your feelings hurt. You wanna take time off to screw football stars. I get it." Chris smirks as she talks, her lies plainly written all over her face.

Hana stands up as well and reaches for me, but I brush past her and toward the front of the restaurant. I want nothing more than to run out of here, but I know that I'm on the verge of losing control, so I take a detour toward the bathroom and lock myself in a stall.

Inhale. Exhale.

Breathe in and breathe out.

Center yourself, Kat.

My hands shake uncontrollably. I'm twenty-four hours sober and in this moment, I want a drink more than I want my next breath.

I blink away the tears, resting my head against the cool metal of the stall.

"Yves Saint Lauren, Coco Chanel, Giorgio Armani, Donatella Versace..."

Dr. Farrell said when you feel like losing control, sometimes it helps to recite something from memory. She said she's had patients recite the Pledge of Allegiance, the Serenity Prayer—even street names from their home town. I plan to spend the weekend memorizing a small passage to recite, but this is the best I can come up with off the top of my head.

The bathroom door gives a slight groan as it's pushed open. "I really don't know what her problem is. She has the entire world in her hands and she's walking away from it."

"Chris, it can't be easy on her. She was held captive for months. I don't think I'd be able to sleep at night, knowing the man responsible was still out there." Hana's voice is soft, and I hold my hand over my mouth to quiet my ragged breathing, continuing to rattle off designer names in my head.

"I read a report that said Landon raped her daily—"

"Where did you hear that?" Aja cuts Chris off.

"It was in one of those online newspapers. The article was removed after a day and the paper issued a full apology to Kat over it. Said they fired the investigative journalist for slander."

Hana gasps. "I can't imagine what she must be going through if that's true."

Chris laughs. "Oh come on, Hana. You've seen Landon Scott. I'd gladly let him put me in cuffs to have his way with me. The two of them dated for years, for Christ's sake. You really believe he raped her? Look at his picture and tell me that's a man who would ever have to force himself on a woman. Sorry, but I don't buy the rape victim story—at all."

My throat tightens and my breathing turns shallow. I shake my head from side to side, trying to force my brain to focus.

Not this memory. Not now...

"Katya? Oh Jesus, baby, what happened to you?"

I blearily opened one eye, the other was completely swollen shut. I took in my surroundings. I was still in the house. The stench of blood and urine were strong in the air.

"Landon?" I searched for him before remembering that he was the reason I was in this mess.

There was movement near me. "I'm here, baby. Who did this to you? Tell me and I'll take care of it."

I breathed a sigh of relief.

He was back from whatever drug-induced stupor he'd been in. He'd get us both some help.

I clenched my jaw as I rolled onto my back, little puffs of air escaping my lips as my nose was clogged with dried blood. Pain radiated through the upper half of my body with the movement. "Landon?" I asked again, tears forming.

He covered my body with his. "My Katya. Who did this?" He kissed along my neck even as his hands skimmed across my sore ribs, causing me to moan in pain.

Landon sat back and began unbuttoning my shirt. I knew I needed to protest, but he appeared to be normal again, and I liked him fussing over me like he was. "Your ribs are bruised, hopefully they're not broken. Katya, who did this to you?"

I brought my hand up and lightly rested it on his. "Y-you did this."

He shook his head. "No. I could never hurt you. I love you."

I squeezed his hand. "Landon, you did this to me."

He reared back as though I'd slapped him and shook his head again, the look of horror frozen on his face. "No."

I felt the need to comfort him. "I'm okay. I'm fine."

He shook his head yet again. "No you're not. Jesus, Katya. Don't make excuses. Was I drinking?"

I brought my hand up to his face, letting my fingers idly stroke the scruff he called a beard. "You weren't acting like yourself. I don't know if you took something or you were drinking."

Landon moved his hands up to my shoulders and removed my shirt completely, as though I were a small child. "Let me take care of you. Let me fix this."

I turned my head away and he teared up. "I broke you. Let me put you back together, please?"

I wanted to run from this room with its mildewed mattress, but I was frozen by his emotion. I didn't want him touching me...loving me...as though it made up for the abuse I'd just suffered at his hands.

He undid the clasp on my bra and pulled it free before removing my pants. I was completely exposed in front of the man, who only hours ago, beat me until I lost consciousness.

Landon stood up and quickly pulled his shirt over his head. His ab muscles were a testament to how hard he worked, and I felt that familiar tugging in my stomach. He gave me a shy, lopsided smile as he removed his jeans and boxers. A part of me was still on board with fighting for my life, but the other part was focused on getting him inside me.

The thoughts made me sick.

He rolled a condom on and guided me back onto the mattress with his body. His hand snaked between us and found its way between my legs. "You're already wet for me. Let go and let me take care of you."

I felt the urge to vomit at his words. I was aroused by the man who'd just battered me. I shook my head again. "No, it's not right. Not like this."

He gently rolled me onto my stomach and guided my hips back onto him. "Shhhh... let me fix this." At that, he pushed himself all the way into me, his hand twisting my long hair. "Your hair just begs to be pulled."

I focused on the mattress, watching my tears as they joined the multitude of stains. It created a pattern, each teardrop highlighting a new one.

Landon's hands moved to grip my hips and he leaned down to place a soft kiss on my shoulder blade. "You feel so good." His hand caressed my hip before moving lower; his fingers resting lightly against me.

I moaned involuntarily and he laughed softly. "I know just what you need." His fingers moved faster and his thrusting increased. I wanted to fight it, but instead found myself moving to his rhythm.

"Yes, let yourself go."

My body hurtled toward an orgasm and I came loudly. "Landon!"

He groaned my name and stilled. It was then that the weight of what had just taken place crashed down on me.

He'd just raped me...hadn't he? It wasn't like I expected. On television, it was always obvious that the act was nonconsensual, but this? This was confusing. I didn't want to, but I enjoyed it. I'd said no, but did nothing to physically stop him. What was wrong with me?

"I wanna stay inside of you forever. Just me and you."

"No!"

"You changed your mind didn't you?"

I blink at the people in front of me. One of them looks a little like me, but my long hair is gone. I stare at the reflection of the other woman holding a pair of scissors. I was just in the bathroom, listening to a woman I once considered a friend destroy my character. Now, I'm in what is obviously a hair salon, and I have no idea how I got here.

"Um, where am I?"

The stylist's eyes widen and she glances around for help. "You're at *Salon Metro*."

I shakily bring a hand up to my hair. It's cut into a short bob that barely reaches my chin. The salon floor is littered with the other eighteen inches of my hair. "I asked for this?"

She bites her lip nervously. "Yeah. You came in here and said you wanted it all gone...that it was just a reminder of him." I thought maybe you had a bad break-up. She studies me more closely. "Wait. Aren't you—"

I nod, my eyes wide with fear, pleading for her to keep quiet.

Her mouth forms a grim line. "I should've recognized you when you walked in. I'm so sorry to hear about what happened to you."

I hold up my hand to stop her. "Please. I can't. Not right now."

She nods slowly and begins sweeping up the hair.

I glance over to see my purse sitting on the counter before checking my watch. I can't account for the last two hours.

Two hours...just gone.

I stand and fumble through my purse for my wallet.

"Don't. It's on the house. Just take care of yourself. Is there someone I can call for you?"

I shake my head. "No. Thank you."

I flinch when I catch my reflection in the glass as I walk out. I don't even recognize myself—it's incredibly disorienting. I've only taken a few steps through the downtown evening crowd before my legs begin to shake and I have to lean against the bricks of a nearby building for support. I don't even know where my car is.

My phone chirps and I pull it from my purse.

New Facebook Message.

I slide the bar across, unlocking the screen and my nightmare.

Landon Scott

"Life gives you surprises. Fate gives you pitfalls. You yourself are a murderer by your own actions. Just know that the gates of Hell will open to you in the end. You know what you did. Time to prepare."

I glance around the crowded streets before dialing my father's number. He answers on the first ring.

"*Solnyshko*, is everything okay?" His worry comes through loud and clear, even with the spotty reception downtown.

"Papa, it happened again. I lost two hours—just gone. And then, just now, I got a message from his Facebook account. This is getting worse." I draw in a ragged breath, trying to keep from crying.

"Where are you? Are you hurt? I'm coming to get you."

I run my hand across my face and look around, fully taking in my surroundings for the first time. "16th Street Mall, near Glenarm. I cut off all of my hair, Papa. I came to and my hair is gone." My chest tightens and I tremble in fear. I'm about to have a panic attack on a busy sidewalk.

"Katya, I am coming to you. Stay where you are. Okay?"

I nod, before the phone is pulled gently from my hand.

"I'll stay with her until you get here. I shouldn't have let her leave in the state she's in. Just park outside of *Salon Metro* and I'll walk her out." The woman who cut my hair smiles kindly at me as she patiently answers my father's questions before ending the call.

She leads me into the salon and toward a small couch in the back. "Just wait here. I'll grab you some water."

"I'm sorry, I didn't catch your name earlier." This woman just saved me the embarrassment of a panic attack in front of a large crowd of people, the least I can do is find out her name.

She turns back toward me. "It's Piper. Is there anything else you need?"

I shake my head. "No. Thank you, Piper."

NINETEEN

KATYA

"KATYA, is there anything that stands out to you about where you were downtown? Did you see anything suspicious?"

Mike sits across from me, looking over my phone.

I blink slowly. "I thought you weren't coming until next week?"

He sighs. "We've been over this. We talked last week and I told you I'd be here this week."

I shake my head. "No, we just spoke two or three nights ago."

My father walks back into my living room carrying a mug of hot tea. "Detective, she is not sleeping well."

"Nikolay, you and I both know she's trying to avoid sleeping all together."

They continue discussing what the messages could mean as I excuse myself to the kitchen, snagging my phone from the coffee table on the way. I grab my water bottle of vodka from the fridge and take two long drinks to calm my nerves. I'm not falling off the wagon...it's just a sip.

This isn't the end of the world.

I mean, my dead ex has somehow found a way to message me from beyond the grave. Other than that though, all is well.

As if disagreeing with me, my phone chirps loudly and I cry out, nearly dropping the bottle in shock. It takes several tries to open the message; my fingers are shaking so badly.

Landon Scott

I desire the things that will destroy me in the end...

Both my father and Mike are in the kitchen within seconds. I hand them the phone and lean over the island, trying to force air back into my lungs.

They read over the message.

"Jesus Christ." Mike hands the phone over to my father and brings both hands up to his temples.

"Katya, you're sure you haven't talked to anyone? You didn't mention it to a shrink or one of your girlfriends?" His words are laced with panic.

My father cuts him off. "Detective, my daughter has already told you that she didn't talk to anyone."

"Yeah Nikolay, she also wants us to believe that it's only water in that bottle of hers too. You'll forgive me if I don't trust her judgment right now."

I slap my hands against the granite surface. "And you're nothing but a dirty cop whose judgment is more questionable than mine. Yet, here we are."

My phone starts chiming again.

Landon Scott tagged you in a post.

Landon Scott tagged you in a post.

Landon Scott tagged you in a post.

It's my missing person flyer, posted repeatedly down Landon's page. They're all captioned, *"What do you know about the disappearance of Katya Egoricheva?"*

"Mike, you said he was dead!" I shriek the words in pure terror.

He reaches out to touch my arm. “He is! I swear to you!”

I roughly push him away. “Then who the fuck is on his account?”

Sobs wrack my body and my father pulls me into his chest, holding me steady. “Detective, where is Landon Scott? I paid you to do a job. It appears that job was not done.”

I stiffen slightly. Is he implying that Landon could actually still be alive?

“Mike—I’ve been to every psychologist in the area, but nothing helps! Do you know what that’s like? I’m scared to fall asleep...I’m scared to stay awake—I used to love the city and now I’m scared to even leave my building! You’re saying there’s a chance he’s still out there?” I scream the words through my tears.

Mike yanks a cell phone from his back pocket. “Here. You want proof he’s gone? Look!”

He holds his phone up to us and my knees buckle. Landon’s corpse stares back. His skin is tinged a greyish-green, well what isn’t covered in blood is. I turn away and bury my face in my father’s jacket, disgusted by the sight of him.

Mike’s voice softens. “It’s not him. I told you I took care of it. Now, what I’m trying to do is figure out who’s behind this. I need your help, Katya.”

I refuse to look at him. “Mike, I’ve told you everything I know. I haven’t spoken to anyone about it. I can barely talk about what happened to me, much less what happened to him.”

“Nikolay, you’ve got to get her out of here. Until we can trace these messages, I don’t think it’s safe for her.”

My father guides me onto a bar stool, scratching at his chin as he mulls over Mike’s words. “Detective, believe me when I say that I know a thing or two about hiding. I will keep my daughter safe.”

He came to the United States in the late seventies, leaving Russia and the Cold War behind him. I once tried to get him to open up about growing up there, only to find myself disappointed.

“My Katya, life was different for me back then. This is my home now. We cannot dwell in the past.”

I suspect that he was involved in espionage—he would never confirm it, even if he was—but why else would the United States government ensure that he never wanted for anything financially? His accent is the only reminder of the life he left behind. He came to the United States and fell in love with an all-American girl—Patricia, or Patsy as she was known to all who loved her. Mama was only nineteen when she met Papa, who was thirty-four at the time. He called her his child bride, never imagining that she would leave this earth before him. I'd love to say that I didn't become jaded until Landon broke me, but cancer shattered my optimistic nature when it stole my Mama from me. She's been gone for five years and I still don't like mentioning her in front of him. I can't stand to watch his eyes go dark with pain.

"Katya, will you agree to it? Where are your thoughts?"

His voice jars me back to reality and I massage my forehead, warding off the stirrings of a headache. "I'm sorry. I'm just trying to process all of this."

My father moves closer to me, speaking with regret. "I failed you. I let that monster keep you captive. I should've done more—then maybe you could live your life in peace."

I place my hand on his arm, resting my head on his shoulder. "Papa, you did everything you could to find me. We can't think about that now." I want to hide beneath my comforter until the memories fade. I don't want to confront the very real possibility that there's a copycat out there, just lying in wait to finish what Landon started.

He kisses me soundly on the forehead. "*Moye Solnyshko*, listen to me. You have done too much. Let me help you—if the city is overwhelming you, then maybe it's time you left."

"I say we get her out of Denver tonight. I've got my guys working on tracing everything. Without knowing who or what we're dealing with, it's for the best." I lift my head and give him an incredulous look, as he fires off several messages from his phone—not the same phone containing pictures of Landon. I don't even want to dwell on how far down his corruption goes at this point.

I slide off my barstool. "I'll do it. If you think it'll keep me safe, I'll leave. I don't know what to tell my agent—they're expecting me to fly out to California on Monday."

"I have that cabin up in Cedar Ridge—we used to visit there when you were young, don't you remember? You loved the solitude. And you wouldn't have to work; I could take care of everything for you. Your body and mind need time to heal."

I shrug. "Papa, I'm fine. I've built a life here in the city. I just need some time away while Mike resolves this...issue. I'm not giving up my condo or anything permanent."

Mike nods his approval before stepping out of the kitchen, his phone pressed to his ear. "Get someone on this now..."

Papa's eyes fill with tears and he shakes his head at me. His voice is so quiet that I almost miss his words. "My Katya, you are not fine. You won't allow yourself to live because you're still stuck in that basement waiting for death."

MODEL ON HIATUS

Denver, CO- Just as she was expected to gain her Siren status, model Katya Egoricheva is taking a break. The troubled beauty has been embroiled in scandal since her return to the runway months ago.

Selvaggia is allegedly standing by while the model takes some time off. However, their reps were unavailable for comment at press time.

This development comes on the heels of the most recent scandal involving Ms. Egoricheva and NFL heartthrob, Brody Rodgers. The pair were photographed together just two days before the model packed her bags and left town.

"Brody is pushing Katya to move to Dallas. He's ready to settle down and start a family," said a source close to the lingerie model, "She's tired of trying to make the long distance thing work and is willing to relocate for him."

In recent weeks, the football star has been frequently seen in the Denver area, "just blocks from her condo."

When we reached out to Rodger's rep we were told that he was not "discussing my client's personal life any further." This is a change from a few days ago, when reps completely denied the possibility of a relationship between the two.

Katya's agent had this to say, "My client has been under a tremendous amount of stress since returning to work. Right now, she's taking some time off and asks that her privacy be respected."

Here's to a Bratya reunion in our future.

TWENTY

TRAVIS

May 2015

I'M SITTING on my back deck, watching the moonlight reflect off of Lake Cedar when Charlie gives a low growl.

I lean back in my chair, completely concealed in shadows. Two figures come within feet of me on their way to the cabin next door.

"I'm sure it's a little dusty, but we can get someone to clean it up for you." The man has a thick Russian accent. I vaguely remember someone once saying that the owner of the property next door was foreign. Not like I've seen any signs of life from that place in the almost two years I've been here though.

"And you're certain that leaving me without my Jeep is the best solution?" That voice is definitely female and one that sounds vaguely familiar. I strain to hear it again, wracking my brain to place her.

"*Dushka*, we went over this. It's better this way. No—" His voice cuts off as he unlocks the door and goes inside.

Charlie settles down, placing her head near my feet again. With the fear of detection gone, I check the time on my watch—one thirty in the morning.

Seems a bit early for moving day.

Various lights kick on in the house, illuminating the backyard and shattering the darkness. I sigh deeply and Charlie's ear perk up. "I'm fine," I grumble at her.

I stand up, stretching my arms overhead. Hopefully whoever is moving in doesn't plan on getting friendly. I moved here to be left alone.

I don't need anyone interfering with that.

TWENTY-ONE

KATYA

MY FATHER LOOKS around the old cabin, pride radiating from him. This place has always been special to him.

"I'll get fresh sheets on the bed for you and tomorrow, we'll go into town and get some groceries." He talks as he moves from room to room, completely in his element here.

I wasn't fond of the idea of leaving, but it was the safest option available. I just need Mike to figure out who's sending those messages and then I can go back to my normal life.

Forget this ever happened.

I open the small dresser in the master bedroom and begin putting my folded clothes inside. I didn't bring a lot with me. Mike made it seem like this would all be resolved within a few days.

"If you don't want to go to the store with me, just give me a list of things you'd like to eat. I know your trainer has you eating certain foods. I don't mind taking care of this." His voice carries down the hall as he searches for sheets.

I smile to myself. Maybe Papa has the right idea. It's kind of nice to be taken care of like this. He comes back into the bedroom, carrying an armful of linens.

"You've had a long evening. Let's get you into bed." I take the sheets from his hands and we begin placing them on the bed.

"I'm not a little girl anymore. Perhaps we should reverse roles, me taking care of you."

He makes a noise of protest. "Bah, Katya. I will rest when I am dead."

He pauses as the words sink in. "I didn't mean—"

I continue working the fitted sheet over the mattress. "Papa, it's fine. We're both exhausted. Let's just get this done and get some sleep."

He nods grimly. "Absolutely."

MY FATHER'S words from earlier haunt me as I lay in bed.

Am I still stuck in that old farmhouse, just waiting for death?

I want to believe that I'm getting better with each passing day, but when I see my reflection in the mirror, the truth slaps me in the face. My skin has taken on a yellowish pallor and my cheeks are sunken in. I have permanent dark circles under both eyes from lack of sleep. The makeup artists have had a hell of a time trying to make me camera ready lately.

I'm falling apart, and the worst part is that I have no idea how to even begin to pick myself back up again. I've put on a brave face for everyone around me, pretending that I'm no longer a victim, but it's all a charade.

I know that I can't keep going on like I have been—I can't keep these secrets locked away forever. It's as if Dr. Farrell opened up this spring inside of me and the truth of what happened has come rushing to the surface. I'll have to cancel my appointment with her next week or find a way to do it by phone.

I'm also going to need to reach out to Aja and apologize for leaving so suddenly yesterday. Maybe she and I can spend more time together when I get home. I can be the old Katya again; I just need to try harder.

I glance over at the clock and see that it's almost five-thirty in the morning.

I've done it. I made it to morning without giving in to sleep.

I'm going to need several pots of coffee to make it through the day, but I feel that this is a small victory.

TWENTY-TWO

KATYA

Two weeks later

"OKAY, we're moving into the summer months so when you open, make sure to fill the dog bowls out front full of water. We don't want anyone's furry child getting heatstroke. On that same note, no pets are allowed inside the restaurant. I'm fine with it myself, but it's a health code violation."

I nod while quickly jotting little notes down for myself.

No dogs. Check.

I made it two weeks living with my father before I was ready to scream. He was under the impression that I was going to lie in bed all day while he took care of me. I have to give him credit though, he witnessed the alcohol withdrawals and still stuck around. The fact that it didn't seem to bother him further convinced me that there's more to his past than he's willing to share.

I finally told him that he had to go back to the city. Mike was no closer to finding the copycat, but I couldn't stay cooped up inside that cabin a moment more. My father bought me a bicycle before agreeing to leave, and I don't think the dust had even settled before I rode into town to find something to do.

Sitting made me antsy, so I needed to keep myself busy. I noticed the 'Help Wanted' sign as I rode by the *Cedar Ridge Brewery* and I looped back around almost immediately. I didn't need a job; I had enough money saved up to keep me comfortable for a while. I did want something to keep me occupied though, so I applied for the waitressing position and was hired on the spot to start the next morning.

"So, Kat, we like all new employees to start with a kitchen shift. Just to familiarize everyone with the ins and outs of the restaurant. Wayne is our executive chef. He'll teach you everything you need to know and then we'll have you shadow Summer for the lunch shift."

"Sounds great." So, I wasn't exactly truthful with my name. I told the owner, Daniel, that nobody called me by my legal name even as I handed over my driver's license. I need to be careful. If the media finds out that there's a waitress named Katya living in the mountains of Colorado, they'll go crazy.

I'm probably making a bigger deal out of it than I need to, as no one here seems to know who I am. I expected there to be more of a fuss when we went to the grocery store that first day, but no one even batted an eye.

Truth be told, it's kind of exhilarating to be anonymous again.

Daniel walks me into the kitchen. "Okay Wayne, this is Kat. She's new here and needs kitchen orientation. I'll be out in the brewery if you run into anything. She's a quick study though."

A tall, slender man walks around the metal island. I take in his Coke-bottle glasses and scraggly beard, and find myself wondering if he drives a windowless van. He probably frequents playgrounds when he isn't stuck cooking at the restaurant.

Regardless of my immediate assessment, I stick my hand out to shake his, only for him to stare at it disgustedly. "First rule of the kitchen, wash your hands."

"OKAY, when you're getting a drink order on a table, check and see if any other tables need refills as well. You should be able to pass through the dining room and know immediately what every table needs."

I nod and scribble the note down in my notebook. Summer has the patience of a saint. I've had her repeat everything at least twice throughout the day, but nothing seems to faze her.

"Let's have you try it now. The dinner rush is slowing down. I think everyone is downstairs listening to the band." The floor vibrates below us in confirmation.

The sky outside turns a cotton candy shade of pink as the sun sinks. I nod at Summer and walk through the dining room.

Table 4 needs more soda.

Table 7 needs a check.

I'm totally getting it. I turn on my heel when I get to the end, as though the room is my catwalk. The smile on my face falters a bit when I see him though.

Elevator guy.

He finds an empty booth and slides in, his yellow Labrador at his feet. I remember Daniel's words.

No pets allowed.

I look around to see if anyone else is going to handle it, but no one seems to have noticed him come in.

Great. Looks like it's up to me.

I wipe my damp palms on my apron and approach him, clearing my throat to get his attention. "Hi, um- I don't know if anyone's already told you, but you can't have pets in the restaurant."

He's been staring down at the empty table up until this point.

No menu.

Nothing.

He slowly lifts his head and I see recognition flicker in his eyes. "She's a service dog."

"I know. I mean, I remember you saying that before...when we met in the city. It's just that Daniel said no animals allowed and it's my first day so—"

"It's fine, Kat. Travis is a regular." Summer guides me away from the table and back to the beverage station.

"I'm sorry. I just wanted to follow the rules," I look over the half wall to find him staring down at the table again. "Is he okay?"

Summer follows my gaze. "Travis isn't really big on talking...or socializing...really anything involving people. He just keeps to himself mostly." She grabs a Styrofoam cup and fills it with ice and unsweet tea. "Take this to him and let him know his pizza will be out in ten."

I try to refuse. "What? You mean I have to talk to him again? I think I'm probably the last person he wants to see right now."

Summer laughs. "He doesn't like anyone. Don't take it personally." She reaches into a small cabinet under the counter and pulls out a container of dog biscuits. "Give Charlie one of these and you'll be back in his good graces again. That dog can't resist treats."

I reluctantly take the tea and dog biscuit and walk back toward his table. He doesn't even look up as I approach. I slide the tea and a straw over to him before kneeling down. "Hey Charlie, sorry I almost got you kicked out. I brought you a peace offering though." The dog wags her tail happily, gently taking the biscuit from my hand.

"Char." Travis's voice must be a warning of some sort because she drops the biscuit and sits down immediately.

I slowly stand back up. "I'm sorry. I didn't ask if it was okay for her to have treats. Summer just suggested it and said to tell you that your pizza will be out in ten minutes. Sorry." I apologize again before turning away.

"You cut your hair."

I turn back to find him staring at me as though I've sprouted two heads. My hand comes up to touch the shortened locks. "Yeah, I did. One of those impulsive decisions."

He nods slowly. "I liked it better long."

I open my mouth and then close it again.

Did he just insult me?

I stand rooted to the spot as he watches me curiously. "You just gonna stand there until my food's ready?"

"No—I just—never mind."

My eyes sting with unshed tears as I walk back to the kitchen. This has been a trying day. I've never worked in a restaurant before and there's so much I don't know. I was prepping tomatoes this morning with Wayne when I cut my finger. Just seeing the blood made me feel woozy.

Wayne was not amused. "What's the matter? You've never had a cut before? Suck it up, buttercup. We've got bandages in the first aid box behind you."

I'd shakily applied the bandage as he continued his tirade.

"That's the problem with young people these days. Mommy and Daddy do everything for them. They've never experienced suffering or struggle. And what happens? They turn into entitled little snots, expecting the world to bend over backward. I bet you expected the entire kitchen to stop just now and fix your boo-boo. Girls like you are part of the problem—never had to work for anything. I bet everything's just been handed to you."

I'd shaken my head and diced the remaining tomatoes, wanting nothing more than to get the hell away from him.

From there, I'd dropped a tray of drinks on the floor and shortchanged some customers—who wasted no time in complaining to Summer. Needless to say, I was really looking forward to the end of my shift.

"You okay, Kat? Don't be upset. Nobody has it figured out their first day. You should've seen me—I managed to dump an entire beer on some guy's lap. I went home and cried myself to sleep. You'll catch on."

Summer smiles brightly at me, her teeth blindingly white. She cleans her black-rimmed glasses on her shirt before putting them back on. Her face is makeup free, dark hair pulled up into a messy bun, yet she looks completely at peace.

I have a feeling we're not on the runway anymore, Toto.

"I'm sorry, Summer. This has just been a long day."

She nods understandingly. "You've been here since nine this morning. Why don't you call it a night? I'll take care of Travis. We can start fresh tomorrow, okay?"

"Okay." I quickly untie my apron, all but running to the back to grab my purse. She doesn't have to tell me twice. I even manage to avoid looking at Travis when I walk out.

I bend down to unchain my bike when my purse begins vibrating. I pull my phone free and answer.

"Hey, Mike. You calling to tell me I can come home and give up my dreams of becoming a mountain-woman?"

"Where are you, Katya? I've been trying to reach you for hours." His clipped tone tells me that this isn't going to be a positive conversation.

"I got a job. I needed to get out of the house." I place the lock and chain inside the basket on the front of the bike.

"I'm at the cabin. We need to talk." He ends the call and I look across the street to the neon lights of the liquor store.

I could just go in and look.

Maybe hold a bottle in my hand.

Cedar Ridge Liquors.

The lights flicker and hum.

Like a siren, they call to me.

TWENTY-THREE

TRAVIS

"WERE you an asshole to my new server?" Summer drops the pizza box with a thud onto the table before placing her hands on her hips.

I shrug. "She tried to kick Charlie out."

"Damn it, Travis. I need the help. Don't run her off please."

I pull some cash from my wallet and throw it down on the table in front of her. "If you would take the time to inform your staff about Charlie, we could avoid these unpleasant little conversations every few months."

She sighs. "She won't bother you again. Look, I really like this one. So cut me some slack, please?"

I grab the pizza box, balancing my drink on top of it as I hold onto Charlie's leash. "You got it, Summer. Let's go, Char." We walk down the steps side by side.

Summer's probably right, I shouldn't have been an asshole to her. I just didn't expect to ever see her again after that morning in the elevator. I thought I was safe seeing a therapist in the city. I never imagined Ms. *"You can't bring a dog inside"* would show up in Cedar Ridge. Of all the places in the world, she had to pick here?

Shit.

She'd cut her hair and it framed her face in such a way that I wanted to reach up and run my hands through it.

That shit just won't fly.

I do feel a little guilty thinking of the way her brown eyes filled with tears when I told her that I'd preferred it long. I shouldn't have said that to her. It was a dick move. I just don't want her thinking we're friends, or worse—announcing to everyone in the brewery that she saw me on my way to therapy.

No one needs to know anything about my life.

I fire up my truck once Charlie and the pizza are squared away inside. No matter how much I try to avoid it; thoughts of her invade my mind.

Kat.

With her facial features, I'd expected something more exotic, I guess. I've just gotten back on the road when it hits me that she must be the one who moved in next door. That's why her voice sounded familiar the other night. Other than tonight though, I haven't seen or heard anyone. The house being lit up like a runway at night is my only indicator that someone's still there.

Maybe I should walk over and apologize for my behavior. On second thought, maybe she should apologize for hers first.

My headlights illuminate someone walking in the middle of the road, so I hit the brakes. It's her, pushing a fucking bicycle.

I put the truck in park and step out. "You always make a habit of walking in the middle of the road? It's a good way to get yourself killed."

She turns back toward me and I see the bottle in her hand. It's obvious that she's been crying. "Oh, it's you again." She unsteadily moves the bike over to the shoulder and continues walking.

I stand with my arm on the hood of the truck, wondering why in the hell I stopped in the first place. "Are you barefoot?"

Kat sways on her feet as she glances down. "Yep."

I take a couple of steps in her direction. "At least let me give you a ride home."

She tilts her head back and takes a swig from the bottle before answering. "I'm fine."

I fight the urge to rip the bottle from her hand and take a drink myself. Instead, I move back toward the truck to find Charlie staring at me disapprovingly. "What? She said she didn't want a ride. I'm not gonna force her." Her head drops back down onto the seat disappointedly.

I shift back into drive and follow slowly behind her. If she won't let me give her a ride, the least I can do is follow her home. Make sure she arrives in one piece.

She weaves back and forth, pushing that damned bike. It dawns on me as I follow her that she left the restaurant only twenty minutes before I did.

So, how is she already wasted?

TWENTY-FOUR

KATYA

MIKE'S SITTING on the front porch swing when I walk up, the lights from Travis's truck casting my shadow onto the cabin. Mike stands up and comes toward me worriedly.

"Who's this?"

I shrug before dropping my bike near the path on the side of the house. "Some guy I pissed off."

I've just kneeled down to retrieve the vodka and my purse from the basket when I hear his voice.

"Is she okay? I just wanted to make sure she made it home safely."

Mike's boots crunch over the gravel as he moves away from me. "She said she upset you. Did you hurt her?"

I laugh at the absurdity of it all before falling backward onto my ass. Almost immediately, I begin crying again.

If Travis hadn't been so cold...

If Mike hadn't stressed me out with his call...

"I wouldn't have ended up in a liquor store buying Stoli. But no, I'm reduced to paying twenty-six dollars for 'premium' vodka." I huff out a breath as I gather my heels, vodka, and purse in my arms and try to stand back up.

"What in the hell are you rambling about over here?" Mike grabs hold of my arm and helps me to my feet.

Charlie jumps down out of the truck, whining, and Travis leads her into the house next door.

He's my neighbor?

"Hey, I'm not finished talking to you." Mike calls after him.

I place my hand on his chest. "Don't—he's fine. It's me."

Mike steadies me as we walk up the steps to the front door. "Couldn't just wait and see what I had to say, could you? You had to go and get blitzed beforehand."

I take another swig of the vodka before dropping my heels and purse on the living room floor. In hindsight, heels were not a practical choice for waitressing. I was going to need to find some tennis shoes if I wanted my feet to survive. "What do you need, detective?"

He sinks down onto the couch. "Katya, I thought you stopped drinking. Your dad said you were sober when we last spoke."

I shrug. "So, I started again tonight. It's just a minor setback."

He presses a hand to his head. "You can't keep doing this to yourself. Eventually, you're going to have to work through what he did to you."

I close my eyes and take another drink. "I'm doing the best I can. Is that why you drove all this way? To make sure I wasn't drinking again? Because that seems like a wasted trip. You could've texted, 'Katya, are you still drinking your life away?' and I would've said, 'Yep. Fucking everything up like normal.' And you wouldn't have had to drive up here. Mission accomplished."

The room spins slightly, and Mike shifts in and out of focus. I like being at this point. It isn't too far gone yet. My body's flooded with warmth and my mind is quiet, but I don't feel sick or out of control yet. And for the first time all day—my feet aren't hurting.

Serene.

Tranquil.

"Look Katya, I don't have good news. We've looked into those Facebook messages and posts. The messages are coming from multiple IP addresses. The guy's pinging all over the place. He's probably hiding behind a proxy server to mask his location." He gets up and retrieves something from his jacket. It's the catalog, the one from my condo. I hadn't imagined it. I touch the cover, tracing the words across my body. "This was on your bed. Do you know anything about it?"

I nod. It's the same catalog I found under my comforter that first night home. I'd torn the condo apart looking for it. Then, I'd called the police, confident that they would find someone. Instead I'd been treated as if I were a crazy person. I finally quit calling them. Where before I'd been certain that someone had been inside my apartment, I began to doubt myself. I thought that maybe all that time with Landon had ruined my intuition.

"I'm not giving up—but you can't go home until we find him." Mike pulls the bottle from my hand before taking a long drink himself.

"Do you think it's the same guy that was leaving things on my door? Has anything else been left?" My hands tremble as I reach for the bottle again.

Mike looks down. "Yeah. There's been one other note left. I had people watching your front door, but I guess he spotted them. The note was found on your Jeep down in the parking garage. Security cameras came up blank though. How he got into your condo is beyond me."

My heart starts beating faster. "And...what did it say?"

"It just said, "*You deserve the moon and the stars laid at your feet. Give me one more chance.*" He wants you to think it's Landon, obviously."

At that, I drink until nothing remains in the bottle, but any feelings of serenity are long gone. I drop the bottle onto the hand-carved coffee table my Papa made for my Mama after they were married, and it lands with a loud thud.

Then I push myself up off of the couch and onto my feet, pacing the wooden floor of the cabin. "I can't stay here forever, Mike. You promised me you'd end this. And you still don't know who this guy is?"

He stands and comes over to me. "I said I'd fix it, just—"

"This is your fault! You could've arrested Landon. People would've seen him for the monster he was, but you took justice into your own hands. You swore to uphold the law and you broke your vow then. Why should now be any different?" I turn to walk away, but he roughly grabs hold of my arm, pulling me back toward him.

"I'm getting real fucking sick of trying to explain why I did what I did. You wanna accuse me of being corrupt? Fine. Just remember who saved your ass that night."

I slap him hard across the face, his eyes widening in surprise. "I never once asked you to do that!"

His jaw clenches shut and he pushes me back against the wall. "Don't hit me. You hear that? Can you process what I'm saying with all the alcohol in your system?"

I growl and strike again, hitting him in the head and chest. He grabs both of my arms and pins them above my head. We're both trying to catch our breaths when it happens.

One minute we're ready to claw each other's eyes out. The next, he leans closer to me, breathing me in, and that's all it takes. I move my head until his mouth meets mine. He releases my hands with a low groan and I move them down to cup his face.

This is a real conflict of interest here. My brain could be flashing warning signs, but in my drunken state, I take it as encouragement to continue.

Mike lifts me up and my legs move eagerly around his waist.

"That way." I murmur the words against his mouth, while pointing, and he carries me unsteadily down the hallway. I couldn't make it work with Brody, he's too close to me, but Mike? Mike is different.

I just need to get it over with—prove that I'm not broken.

Mike gently lays me back on the bed, before unbuttoning and pulling my black slacks down like a man possessed. His hands move up to strip off my *Cedar Ridge Brewery* t-shirt, and all that's left on is my underwear. I sit up and unhook my bra, tossing it at him as I lay back down.

I expect him to strip down, but he surprises me by moving over my body, licking and sucking…I clench my eyes shut.

Pleasure…find the pleasure, Katya.

"Katya, you naughty girl. I'm starting to think you like being mine." Landon's mouth moved over my body and I moaned involuntarily. My ribs were bruised, or more than likely cracked, and his mouth seemed to know just how to cause me more pain. He inserted another finger into me, my body stinging in response.

It hurt. It hurt so badly.

"You like this? Is it okay?" Mike's voice pulls me back to the present, as his fingers slip beneath my panties and I stiffen in response.

Just get it over with.

I can do this.

I just have to focus on breathing through the pain.

His hand moves away from my body, his ragged breathing the only sound in the room.

I hesitantly open one eye. "Why'd you stop?"

He laughs humorlessly. "Really? You're lying there as if I'm about to hurt—Jesus, Katya. Have you been with anyone since it happened?"

I sit up and reach for him. "No, but you could fix that."

He shakes his head and backs away from me. "Absolutely not. We're not doing this."

"What? Why not?"

Mike moves closer to me again, fighting a battle with himself. "I can't. It wouldn't be right."

I pull the t-shirt back over my head, while muttering, "Since when did you start caring about what's right?"

He holds his hand up. "Stop. Enough with the blaming. There's another woman—"

I cover my face with my hands. "You're married? Oh my g—"

He cuts me off. "I'm not married. Just fucking listen, for once in your life. I was involved with someone when this shit went down. I lost her because of it. I have to live with those regrets for the rest of my life. So, quit sitting over there acting like you're the only one with problems because of it."

I lower my hands. "So, you're not married? That doesn't explain why we can't—"

"Stop, Katya. You think I don't want to? Jesus, your body is perfect. And honestly, most guys in my situation wouldn't hesitate to fuck a supermodel, but I'm not the type of guy who's gonna stick around for breakfast though."

I walk over to the wall he's leaning up against, wearing nothing more than my t-shirt and underwear. "I don't expect you to stick around. Hell, you can leave right after we're done."

He pulls me back into his arms and leads me toward the bed. "I can't. Katya, I saw you that night. I saw what he did to you—I've read the medical report a thousand times, for Christ's sake. I look at you and I see the photos that were taken in the hospital. Every cut, every bruise, every abrasion documented in writing and full color photos. I know he raped you, but I can't put you back together. I can't have a one night stand with you—not with knowing all that I do."

He roughly wipes at his eyes and I realized he's crying. "I don't need your pity, detective."

"You think I pity you? No, I honestly can't even begin to fathom how you survived four months with him. I get it— you drink until you don't see his face when you close your eyes. I drink because every time I close my eyes, I see this image of you from that night." Mike pinches the bridge of his nose, his eyes focused on the floor.

I wrap my arm around him and he pulls me into his side. "I'm sorry, Mike. I'm so sorry. It's like I'm just beyond saving, irreparably damaged."

He shakes his head. "You're not. You've been to Hell, but I truly believe that you can find your way back. You might have to fight to get there, but I think that if anyone can do it, it's you. Come here." He shifts me over on the bed and moves onto the floor, grabbing a pillow to place under his head.

My eyes grow heavy, but I fight the urge to sleep.

"Sleep, Katya. I'm here. I'll wake you up if it gets bad."

"Would you have killed him without the money?" I ask the question mostly to keep myself awake a few moments longer.

He's so quiet that I begin to think he's fallen asleep. "I didn't think the baby—Kaden, was going to make it. Hell, if I'm being honest, I didn't think any of you were going to make it. David is my best friend, and I thought that if he was going to lose everything, he had a right to look his family's killer in the eye and do whatever he wanted to him. Your father offered me money, a lot of it, and I didn't hesitate to take it.

"Forty grand is a lot of money. I thought I could set it aside—buy Lauren a ring. You know, happily ever after shit. I didn't ever consider that my actions with Landon would ensure that I wouldn't have a future with her. So, to answer your question, I would've done it without the money—even knowing what it would cost me."

My eyes drift closed again. "I wouldn't have let you. I would've let him kill me first." I mumble sleepily before sinking into unconsciousness.

TWENTY-FIVE

TRAVIS

I SIT on the deck watching the sky lighten with Charlie. The steam rises from my coffee cup as I bring it to my lips, taking a small sip. The cup features a kitten hanging from a metal bar by its claws.

Hang in there, it's almost Friday.

I almost threw it away, but this idea that everyone struggled to get through the work week—it just seemed so normal. And I like feeling like I belong, even if it is just by possessing a coffee cup with a damn cat on it.

The screen door squeaks from next door and I jump at the sound. I'm still not used to having neighbors—sure, the other cabins fill up during the summer months, but that's still a few weeks away.

The man from last night sits down on the back steps and puts his boots on.

"Trouble in paradise?" I don't know why I bother saying anything. A normal person would've pretended that he didn't hear them yelling at each other last night.

The man finishes lacing up his boot before coming over to my deck. "We're not together. She's just been through a lot recently."

I take another sip of coffee as a duck floats by on the lake. "She always drink like that?"

Without an invitation, he walks up onto the deck, taking the empty chair across from me. Charlie raises her head up off of my foot to inspect him before losing interest.

He holds out his hand. "Michael Sullivan."

I reluctantly reach out to shake it. "Travis Logan. You don't sound like you're from around here."

He shakes his head. "I'm not. Just visiting from Texas. As for her drinking, no. Like I said, she's been under a lot of stress lately."

I should offer him a cup of coffee. Instead, I play the asshole card again. It's my default when I'm uncomfortable. "Well, Michael. Everybody's been through shit."

He nods and leans over to pet Charlie. I stand up angrily. "Don't touch her. She's a service dog."

Charlie's ears perk up and she moves in closer to me.

Michael stands as well. "I'm really sorry. I need to get back on the road anyway. Just—could you dial it back a bit with her?"

Charlie whimpers a warning as I take a step toward him. "Dial it back? Don't worry, I won't say another word to your girl. Message received."

"That's not what I meant, man."

Before Charlie gets too worked up, I turn and walk back into the cabin with her, letting the screen door slam shut behind us.

She's been through a lot...

No shit. She's such a fragile looking little thing, I bet having a bad hair day is a trauma for her.

TWENTY-SIX

KATYA

"KNOCK, KNOCK!" The cheerful voice calls out from the other side of the front door.

I force myself into another sit up before getting up to answer the door. Mike left only a few hours ago, so I'm not exactly expecting company. A shorter woman with a brunette bob similar to mine grins widely at me. "Katya, you're all grown up! I can't believe it!" She adjusts her glasses while looking around me, as if she's expecting someone else to appear.

I extend my hand toward her, but she pulls me into a warm hug. "Is Niko around? He's the one who asked me to stop by. It's been forever since I've seen him." She releases me and adjusts her blouse.

I shake my head. "I'm sorry, but you are?"

The woman laughs suddenly. "Of course you wouldn't remember me—you were so young. My name's Jeanne—Jeanne Mueller. I have a cabin across the lake. My husband and I spent a lot of time with your parents when they would come up during the summer months.

"I heard about your mother passing—I am so sorry, Katya. Patsy was a wonderful woman. My Clark passed on not long after she did. You get used to someone being there, and then one day they're not."

She clears her throat. "Goodness, listen to me rambling on about the past, while you're probably wondering why I'm here. Niko asked me if I still ran my little cleaning business, said you'd need some help around here."

"Oh, Jeanne. That's really not necessary. I have plenty of time to clean up after myself." I'm not surprised my father did this. If he has his way, I'll never be allowed to lift a finger again.

Her smile fades a bit. "I just thought...well, never mind. I brought you a casserole to welcome you anyhow. I'll just get it out of the car." I watch her walk back to her car, like a baby giraffe trying out its legs for the first time.

She must not wear heels very often.

She did put a lot of effort into her outfit and seems really disappointed that my father isn't here.

She's got a crush on him.

It's kind of adorable actually.

Jeanne comes back over carrying a foil-covered dish. "I've got the heating instructions written on the foil. It should last you a while."

I take it from her. "Thank you, Jeanne. You know, I was thinking that it might be nice to have someone come clean every few weeks or so."

Her face lights up. "You're sure?"

"Absolutely." It shouldn't be too hard to convince my father to come back up for a weekend visit.

Just because my life is in shambles doesn't mean I can't bring a little positive to his.

I SIT in one of the Adirondack chairs on the back deck, curled up in a blanket, watching the stars. I lived for four months in darkness. Now, I can't stand to be inside when it's dark. I'm only relaxed when every light is burning bright. Oddly enough, being outside is a different story. I feel safer under a sky full of stars—as if I'm hidden away from trouble.

This is what I was missing in Denver. My life's always felt frantic —between my schedule and then finding the notes, I've never had a moment's peace to just breathe. Everyone is so afraid of what I might do if left alone.

My cell phone vibrates on the table next to me and I sigh. Unfortunately, moments like this never last long.

"Hello?"

"Katya—finally. I got your message earlier—I was beginning to think you were ignoring me."

"Alexa, I didn't have any updates for you until this morning. The detective said they have no leads. He feels it's safer for me to remain here until they get this under control. There were more notes left."

"Okay, I'll get with Cindy and we'll work out something. Maybe we say you've entered into an undisclosed treatment facility for exhaustion. We could continue to play up the 'Bratya' romance, but we'll need Brody's help for that." I can hear the papers rustling in the background.

"I support whatever you need to do, Alexa. And I got the contract you sent. I'd like to have my lawyer look everything over before signing. Once things settle down, I'll take care of this."

She exhales loudly into the phone. Clearly, she was hoping it was already done. Nine months ago, I would've signed immediately. Chris was right to wonder if I'd lost my mind. This is what I've been wanting for years. The exclusivity is alluring and the pay would be steady. I just don't know if I'm capable of committing to the brand exclusively when my personal life is in chaos.

It'd be like them hiring Britney Spears, circa 2007. I'd already chopped eighteen inches of hair off. Realistically, I'm probably only one crises away from shaving my head and bashing in a paparazzo's car with an umbrella.

"Katya, I get it. If you sign the contract, you're bound to them. There'll be no modeling for other houses in the meantime. You'd still get the NFL campaign, along with the runway shows though. Just keep that in mind while you're deciding. There's not going to be a better offer for you."

We hang up and I close my eyes. I probably could've protested Mike's advice. My father would've hired a security detail to follow me around, and my life would've gone on as normal. I'd have felt as though I were suffocating, but I would've put on a brave face and powered through it.

No, the truth is, I don't want to go back. Not yet. Last night with Mike made it painfully clear that I'm not healing like I thought I would. And I'm afraid of what I might do if I go back now. A shaved head would be nothing in comparison to waking up next to someone I couldn't even remember taking to bed in the first place.

The thought causes me to shiver and I pull the blanket tighter around my shoulders. I just wish there was a way to sort all of this out without feeling like I'm letting anyone down in the process.

I pull my notebook off the small table and grab my flashlight. Dr. Farrell recommended that I get a journal to keep track of how I'm feeling. It's less of a journal and more just disjointed ramblings.

I'm letting everyone down right now.

I wish there was a way to keep everyone happy without losing my sanity in the process...

Why does someone want to hurt me?

What's the meaning of the song lyrics?

I continue to wrack my brain again for any clues into the identity of the copycat, when movement near the edge of the lake catches my attention. I switch off the flashlight and instinctively shrink down into the chair, trying to make myself as inconspicuous as possible.

It's so dark beyond the yard, that it's a struggle to see what's out there. The figure moves a little closer and I realize it's someone running with their dog. I glance at my watch and see that it's a little after eleven—a little late for an evening jog.

The person appears to be running directly toward me and I hold my breath in fear until I realize it's Travis and Charlie. He slows to a jog as he reaches his back deck and Charlie disappears from view. I can't really see anything but the reflective patches on Travis's shirt.

"Travis?"

He jumps in surprise, his breathing heavy from the run. "Jesus, Kat. You walk in the middle of the road and hang out in the dark, surprising strangers. You really do have a death wish, don't you?"

He has no idea.

"I didn't know anyone else would be out here. I'm sorry if I scared you."

Charlie's collar jingles as she pads across the deck to the door. Travis follows behind and his footsteps seem amplified on the deck slats. "I'm fine. Have a good night."

"You too." I shift to stretch my back before shakily turning the flashlight back on and re-opening my notebook.

Why does he have to be my neighbor? He's a prick—

an incredibly handsome prick, but a prick nonetheless.

I wonder if Charlie's ever considered biting him and running off?

I'd bite him...

That doesn't look right. I should scratch that last sentence out.

The screen door slams shut again and I jump, throwing my pen in the process.

He laughs. "You're still out here?" Without waiting for an answer, he comes over to my deck and sits down in the extra chair next to mine. His hair is dripping beads of water onto his face, as if he just got out of the shower.

I quickly shut off the flashlight and close the notebook, clearing my throat awkwardly. "So...um, how was your run?"

Charlie rests her head on his lap and he scratches her behind the ears. "It was running. Not much to it."

Well, this is going about as well as I expected.

I nod and pick at the fabric on my sweatpants. I don't know why he bothered coming over here. I would ask, but—

"Were you writing in your diary?" Travis points to it, the corner of his mouth turning up in a slight smirk.

I press the journal against my chest. "That's none of your business. Why are you even here?"

"I feel like we're getting off on the wrong foot," He holds his hand out to me, "I'm Travis, and this is Charlie."

I take his hand, trying not to dwell on how it dwarfs mine. "Kat."

He doesn't let go right away and I count the seconds in my head until it feels acceptable to pull my hand back.

"You don't sleep." He stares intently into my eyes as he says it and I uncomfortably look away.

What is he? Some sort of handshake psychic?

"I sleep."

He shakes his head. "Your house is lit up like Clark Griswold's house at all hours of the night. You don't sleep, just admit it."

"I sleep. How would you even know what my house looks like during the night? Are you watching me?" I pull the blanket back up around my shoulders.

"I'm not watching you—just an observation. Chill out, Princess."

I take a deep breath. "I think it's time for you to leave."

He stands up and walks off the deck, tossing over his shoulder, "Not sure why I even bothered."

I stand up and drop the notebook into the chair. "I don't know why you did either!"

He reaches for his screen door. "Hey Princess? If you're going to sit in the dark; try not to get yourself killed." I can hear him laughing to himself as the door slams shut behind him.

Asshole.

TWENTY-SEVEN
TRAVIS

I SHOULD'VE STAYED AWAY. I don't know what I expected... that she'd welcome me with open arms after I insulted her like an insensitive dickhead?

Nope. Never gonna happen.

"C'mon, Trav, get it out of your head." I turn the truck radio up a little louder, trying to drown out thoughts of her.

Charlie sits up in the seat, eyeing me blearily. If she could talk, I'm sure she'd give me an earful about the whole thing.

"I'm done, Char. No more trying to make friends. It's just you and me." She lays back down, giving a small groan of disapproval.

You and me both.

I only left the house because I needed food. The plan is to just grab something to go. That plan goes right out the window as I pull into the near empty parking lot. There's no way I'm making it out of here without her seeing me.

I walk in and immediately see Kat working the dining room, so I pass right on through into the bar area. I'll just order a pizza and be on my merry way. The bartender, Gavin, takes my order and goes back to ignoring me.

Perfect.

I don't see the point to small talk. And I obviously suck at it, if last night is any indicator. No, you shouldn't waste time talking unless you have something to fucking say.

She walks over to grab a couple of beers sitting at the end of the bar, pretending I'm not sitting a few feet away. It irks me.

"Kat, you wanna go see a movie when your shift ends?"

Her head pops up in surprise. "Um, I actually have plans for after work, Gavin."

Gavin leans against the bar drying a pint glass, as if her answer means nothing to him. "Maybe next time then, yeah?"

She nods and scurries off with the beers. I give Gavin a death glare as he goes to grab my pizza while Charlie gives me a look that clearly says, *"Hey asshole, what was all that talk in the truck?"*

I shake my head, hissing, "I know what I said. Don't give me that look."

"Uh, here's your pizza man." Gavin drops the box and backs away as if my craziness might be contagious.

I throw some cash on the bar and walk out, running right into Kat in the process.

She steps back immediately. "Sorry, I wasn't paying attention."

I reach out a hand to steady her, questioning the decision as my hand is halfway to her. I freeze and end up holding it out awkwardly before blurting out, "Do you like board games?"

She presses her lips together, trying not to smile. "Yes...why?"

"Okay, just checking." Then like a complete fucking lunatic, I walk out of the restaurant, mentally kicking myself every step of the way.

What the hell am I doing?

Board games?

That's what I came up with?

I WAIT until her house lights kick on before taking a deep breath and walking over. I hold my hand up to the door, debating on whether or not to knock, when she opens it and jumps back with a scream.

"Sorry! It's just me...sorry."

She brings a hand to her chest. "What the hell is wrong with you?"

A lot actually...

I hold up the box in my hand. "I just came over to see if you wanted to play a board game. I can't sleep. It's stupid—I can come back another time."

"Stay. I'll make coffee."

I pick my jaw up off of the floor and follow her inside. "Are you sure? I just thought, you don't sleep...I don't sleep—"

Kat purses her lips and I can tell she's about to kick me out again. "I sleep. I happen to have a lot going on right now with my work schedule, so it's thrown things off a bit."

"You mean waitressing?"

She sighs heavily. "I—" Her phone begins ringing as if on cue and her expression becomes unreadable as she glances over at it.

"Really, I can just go if it's not a good time." I can't seem to do much more than stick my foot in my mouth anyway.

"No. Stay." She snatches the phone off the coffee table on her way into the kitchen and I shrug helplessly at Charlie. I'm still not entirely sure why I thought this would be a good idea. I just hate sitting up alone at night, letting the memories take center stage.

Maybe chasing down an alcoholic insomniac wasn't the best plan I've ever had, but it's too late to change anything now.

ANOTHER ASPIRING MODEL GOES MISSING

June 15, 2015- Yesterday marked six months to the day since Selvaggia model, Katya Egoricheva, was rescued. Now, authorities in Denver are hoping for a similar outcome in the case of another missing model.

Christine Miller, 27, from Littleton, was last seen at approximately one AM on June 14th. Her roommate and several friends reported her missing hours later, leaving police scrambling for answers. Miller was last seen at *Bleu*, a popular bar downtown, early Sunday morning when she became separated from her group of friends.

"We were having a drink, and Chris's phone rang. She stepped outside to take it and never came back," said Aja Cole, who was with Miller on the night she went missing.

According to police, surveillance footage from the area captured Miller leaving the bar around one-fifteen AM. "It's my understanding that the friends assumed Miller left with someone else when they were unable to reach her by phone. They got in touch with her roommate early the next morning, who informed them that she never arrived home that night," said Arapahoe County Sheriff's Det. Shane Strohn.

As police search for clues, it's impossible not to note the similarities between this investigation and the disappearance of Egoricheva late last year. The Selvaggia model was abducted by former boyfriend, Landon Scott, and held for over four months before being rescued by police. Scott disappeared after an altercation with police officers and has not been seen since.

If you have information related to this case, contact the Arapahoe County Sheriff's Office at (303) 795-1111.

TWENTY-EIGHT

KATYA

"YOU OKAY, PRINCESS?" Travis's voice pulls me from my thoughts. Chris has been missing for four days now and the media is having a field day comparing it to my case. After hearing what she said about me behind my back, I couldn't imagine anyone wanting to take her. That being said, I do hope that she's found safely. Even if she is a horrible person, I wouldn't wish what I went through on my worst enemy.

I look down at the table that's only half cleared. "I've just got a lot on my mind. Did Summer not put your order in?"

The main dining room's been empty for about half an hour, with everyone moving downstairs for the live music. I just need to finish cleaning these last few tables, roll some silverware, and then I can go back to the cabin to relax.

"Yeah, she took care of it. I just noticed you staring off into space." I can't tell if he's messing with me or not, so I turn to face him. He's leaning against a nearby booth, his expression unreadable.

"Why do you call me Princess?" Ever since that night I surprised him in the dark, he's referred to me as Princess. If the man smiled once in a while, I might take it as a compliment.

Travis picks at the material on the booth, suddenly avoiding eye contact. "You just seem like a princess."

Definitely not a compliment then.

"Okay. In that case—your food will be out shortly, *asshole.*" I grab the remaining dishes.

He begins laughing and I turn to stare at him in shock. He's doubled over the booth, his shoulders shaking. This is so out of character for him that I'm unsure of what to do. I'm half expecting him to stop and demand that Daniel fire me on the spot.

I start to cringe when his head pops up, but he's smiling from ear to ear.

I breathlessly whisper, "Long dimples...just like I suspected." This is not good. With the Mike situation fresh in my mind, I cannot develop feelings for anyone right now. Game night was the extent of all that I can offer someone right now.

His chuckling stops and he wipes a stray tear from his eye. "What?"

I shake my head. "I didn't say anything."

He smirks. "Have a nice night, Princess."

I turn and walk toward the kitchen with the dirty dishes, tossing over my shoulder, "Later, asshole."

I can still hear him laughing when I hand the dishes over to our dishwasher, Corey. I bump into Summer on my way out of the kitchen.

"Travis was in rare form tonight. Didn't know the man knew how to smile."

I hide my own smile and feign ignorance. "Is he? I hadn't noticed. Are we good to go here?"

She unties her apron, suddenly seeming unsure of herself. "Yeah, about that. Would you like to come over? I know you're new around here and I thought that maybe we could keep each other company."

I pause, trying to think of an excuse, but she stops me.

"You don't have anything else going on. You and I both know it. C'mon, I won't take no for an answer. I'll even give you a ride."

I agree, even though I had been secretly hoping that Travis would drop by again. It's been a few days since he showed up on my doorstep, but I've left the porch light on every night since, just in case.

He seemed to have enjoyed staying up with me, drinking coffee and losing at everything from *Uno* to checkers. I mean, I assume he enjoyed it...we didn't really talk. Like at all.

We'd played round after round of games until the sky began to lighten. Then we'd taken our coffee and sat on the deck, watching the sun rise. I found that I liked Travis a lot more when he didn't say a word.

SUMMER LIVES in an old two-story house right on the edge of town. It's been transformed into two apartments, with the upper floor being hers. "What can I get ya? I've got coffee, bottled water—I think I might even have a bottle of wine somewhere."

I fight the urge to ask for wine. "Just water. Thanks."

She leaves and goes into the kitchen.

"Nice place you've got here, Summer." *Normal people compliment people on their houses, right?*

"Thank you. It's small, but perfect for just me."

I expected to see pictures of her family or friends, but the walls are bare. There's a threadbare couch with a quilt thrown over the back and a small area rug near the television. Other than that, the place is empty.

She comes back in and hands me a water before sitting down on the couch. I sit on the opposite side, studying the empty room.

"So, did you just move in?"

She takes a drink of water before answering me. "No. I've been here for about eight years. I'm just a minimalist, I guess." She laughs as she says it, but it sounds forced.

"Does your family live here too?" I start peeling the label on the water bottle. I suck at small talk.

Summer sets her glass on the floor near the couch. "I don't have family, Kat. I was in foster care growing up, so I never stayed long enough for any place to feel like home. I just got shuffled from home to home until I turned eighteen. Then I aged out and became my own responsibility."

I peel more of the label even as my face burns with embarrassment. "Sorry, I shouldn't have mentioned it."

"It's not like I was abused or anything. Mainly, I was just ignored—which suited me just fine. So, do you miss modeling, Kat?"

I start to answer, before I realize what she's just asked. Instead of speaking coherently, I end up choking on the saliva in my mouth.

This was a bad idea.

She gently pats me on the back as I cough and splutter. "Sorry, that's probably not the best way to ask someone. I kind of sprang it on you."

"How did you know?"

She grins mischievously and grabs a stack of magazines off of the floor, shuffling through them until she finds the Selvaggia catalog with me on the cover. "I thought you looked familiar from day one. And then it clicked when I watched you carry a tray the other day. It's all in the way you carry yourself. Why are you slumming it in this little town when you could be hanging out with celebrities in California?"

I regain my composure when I realize she doesn't know about my abduction or rescue. She only knows me as a pretty face on a magazine cover. "Well, I'm not quitting. Just taking some time off to rest. This place seemed as good as any to do that. I would appreciate you maybe not mentioning it to anyone. I just want to enjoy being anonymous for a little while."

I fake a smile and Summer narrows her eyes as if she doesn't believe me, but doesn't push the issue further. We sit quietly, the tick of the clock on the wall breaking up the silence.

I peel the rest of the label off of the bottle and begin folding it in my hands when I ask the question that's been on my mind, needing to steer this conversation back into neutral territory. "So, what's the deal with Travis?"

"I don't really know much, and believe me I've tried to find out more. I've yet to find anyone in town who knows the whole story. Why? Are you interested in him?"

"No—I was just curious. He always has the dog and doesn't seem overly friendly. That's really the extent of what I know about him." The label grows smaller and smaller as I fold it in my hands. This is definitely not what I envisioned when Summer invited me over. Maybe it's just been a while, and every new friendship has this period of uncomfortable awkwardness.

"Overly friendly? No need to sugarcoat it."

I smile. "So, he's an asshole and maybe I told him as much tonight."

Summer claps her hands together. "You did not! That is too good. God, to have been a fly on the wall for that."

"He laughed when I said it, like it was the funniest thing he'd heard in a while. I thought that was an odd reaction."

She nods. "Well, he's kind of an odd guy."

I don't say anything in response and we slip back into silence, the seconds turning into minutes. I risk a glance at the clock.

"It's getting kind of late."

Summer jumps up off of the couch. "Yeah. I'll give you a ride home if you want?"

I happily agree, all too ready for the night to be over. I'd hoped that Summer and I would click instantly, but the opposite seems to be closer to the truth. I know one thing for certain though as she drives me home. She's hiding just as much, if not more, than I am.

MODEL RECEIVES THREATENING MESSAGES

As police continue their search into the disappearance of Christine Miller, a shocking video popped up online overnight. In the video, which has since been taken down, a woman who closely resembles the missing model was filmed begging for her life before the camera cut away to a masked individual.

The individual, using a voice disguiser, called on Katya Egoricheva to publicly release the details of her kidnapping and the location of Landon Scott before "any more lives have to be lost."

Detective Shane Strohn, with the Arapahoe County Sheriff's Office, released the following statement, "At this time, we are launching a full investigation into the authenticity of the video leaked on Twitter last night. We are hopeful that we will gain insight that will lead us directly to Ms. Miller."

A number of disturbing tweets were also posted around the same time as the video, from Twitter user *@katyasecret*. One of the messages was even retweeted by Egoricheva's ex, Landon Scott, who is still being sought by police in connection with the model's abduction last August.

Katya Fan Club *@katyasecret* -June 28
"*@katyaEgoricheva* What do you know about the disappearance of Christine Miller?"

Landon Scott *@lscotttx* Retweeted

Katya Fan Club *@katyasecret* -June 28
"*@katyaEgoricheva* Where's Landon?"

Katya Fan Club *@katyasecret* -12h
"*@katyaEgoricheva* Come out come out wherever you are."

Katya Fan Club *@katyasecret*- 12h
"*@katyaEgoricheva* I'm going to find wherever you're hiding, and I'm going to finish what he started."

All of the tweets have been removed as of the time of this writing, but not before fans of the model reported them to police. Police were also alerted to a Reddit thread that implied Egoricheva faked her abduction, based upon photographs of the model.

"Anytime a beautiful woman goes missing and turns up later unharmed, it raises a lot of questions. Look at her eyes in all of her modeling pictures, she's hiding something."

"She looks a little obsessed with herself. I think it's been mentioned before that she could've done this to get attention."

It should be noted that Egoricheva was heavily battered when she was rescued by police back in December. One of the officers involved in the rescue even identified Landon Scott as Egoricheva's captor. Unfortunately, this has not stopped internet detectives from calling everything about the abduction into question. Egoricheva's agent did not return our request for comment, but police say the model is fully cooperating with their investigation.

TWENTY-NINE

TRAVIS

"WHERE'S SUMMER?"

Daniel looks up from the computer on his desk. His office is the size of a broom closet, I'm not certain they didn't build the room around the desk. He spends most of his time out in the brewery, so I guess the cramped space doesn't bother him all that much. "Oh, she and Kat are working the downstairs bar tonight. Did Erin get you set up with dinner?"

The alcoholic is working the bar? I can't see how that could go wrong.

I shouldn't judge Kat based on the one time I saw her drinking. It's not as if I've seen her drinking since then, but I did notice how badly her hands shook when we played board games that night. It's only natural to assume she's hitting the liquor cabinet the minute she gets home. Leave it to a recovering alcoholic to sniff out a regular one.

I nod and hold up the small pizza box. "Thanks man. I'm gonna get home before it gets cold."

He nods. "Anytime. See you tomorrow?"

I laugh. "Probably."

I get to the front door and stop. If I go straight, I'll be in the parking lot. If I go right and down a few more stairs, I'll be in the bar. Charlie looks up at me questioningly. This is not part of our routine.

I envision the way Kat's eyes light up when she calls me an asshole and I grin to myself.

Decision made.

Most people went out of their way to avoid me because of my charming personality. Hell, Kat insisted on placing me in her section every night that I came in just so she could utter the phrase, "*What'll it be, asshole?*" In my own twisted way, I looked forward to it. Watching her green eyes turn murderous when I called her Princess was just the cherry on top of the sundae. Not that she acted much like a princess. I'd seen her bust her ass just as hard as Summer did. The two of them were like some waitressing dream team.

"I'm going to sit in the bar—I'm not gonna drink. I'll just, you know, sit and have a club soda or something."

Charlie turns her head to the side, looking puzzled.

"Don't judge me, Char. Normal people sit in bars. C'mon."

This has absolutely nothing to do with the fact that Kat is working. I've been wanting to check out the bar for a while now. I'm just looking for a place to sit, not searching for her short dark hair.

"Hey Travis! What're you doing down here?" Summer yells over the music and I stupidly point at the bar.

"Just grabbing a drink!" Charlie's hugging my side protectively and I have to maneuver around her to grab a bar stool. She obviously doesn't feel comfortable with me being down here.

The band's doing a pretty good cover of John Mayer's *Come Back to Bed*. It's funny that bars have been smoke-free for the past nine years, yet the entire downstairs area still reeks of stale cigarettes. It's like it's embedded in the walls.

I look past several couples dancing in the middle of the room and finally spot her. She's leaned over talking to a group of people at one of the larger tables near the back. She smiles and tucks her hair behind her ear, unaware that I'm watching her just a few feet away.

Seeing her like this makes me wonder why I've been staying

away. It had been nice, staying up all night with her. There'd been no expectations and no judgment.

I wasn't a damaged monster; I was just Travis.

Maybe I'll just keep an eye on her from here, make sure she stays sober for the rest of her shift. From the looks of it, almost every man in the bar has the same idea. I don't like the way that makes me feel. It's the same feeling I got when Gavin asked her out. I need to reign those feelings in—get myself under control.

"What can I get you, man?" The bartender leans over and I reluctantly turn away from watching her to answer him. My eyes scan the rows of bottles lining the back of the bar.

Whiskey...a bottle.

"Just a club soda and lime, please." I turn my chair back around to face the band. They end the song and take a break, crowding the bar area for drinks. The jukebox kicks back on and the volume in the room goes up.

I'm watching her face so I miss what happens, but I see the exact moment her entire stance changes. Her eyes widen and she stops clearing the table in front of her. I slide off the stool and grab Charlie's leash, leading her through the crowd.

The song playing is country, some old Garth Brooks stuff. Nothing out of the ordinary appears to be going on, but Kat's breathing changes. She begins hyperventilating, holding onto the table to keep herself upright.

"You okay, Princess?" I step closer and see that her eyes are unfocused. I place my hand on her shoulder and she jumps in fright. "Kat?"

She bolts up the stairs and out of the bar.

What the hell just happened?

Summer gives me a worried look from across the bar and I point toward the stairs, letting her know I'll handle it. Maybe someone touched her? She was standing close to a group of guys known for getting out of control when drinking, but they seem harmless tonight. They're deep in discussion on how to cover up name tattoos.

"Well, she's your ex now— so obviously you did curse the damn thing by getting her name tattooed on your ass."

I shake my head and lead Charlie up the stairs after Kat. No one's seen her in the upstairs dining room so I check the parking lot. I'm about ready to give up when I catch a flash of movement from the side of the building.

I notice that her breathing has become more labored as I get closer to her.

Triggered.

The word pops into my head, unannounced.

"Christian Louboutin. Valentino. Zac Posen." Each word comes out sounding strangled, as if she's choking.

"Recitation can be helpful when you feel yourself losing control during an episode. It keeps your mind focused on the task at hand."

I approach her cautiously. "Kat? It's Travis. Can you hear me?"

She briefly makes eye contact with me, trying to control her breathing in the process. "I-I'm fine. It's f-fine. You can go back inside."

She shakes from head to toe and is clearly in the middle of a full-blown panic attack. "You're obviously not fine. You can't stop shaking." She's staring off past my shoulder and I follow her gaze to the liquor store across the parking lot.

"You want a drink right now, don't you?"

She nods, "I do, but I can't. I've been sober for almost a month. A whole month. That doesn't mean much to most people, but it's a long time to me." Her voice cracks and I'm certain she's about to start crying. Charlie presses herself into my leg, as if urging me to speak up.

"Let me give you a ride home."

Kat looks up at me, her eyes brimming with unshed tears. Then, she does the last thing I expect her to do. She wraps her tiny arms around my waist in a hug, gripping tightly to the back of my t-shirt.

I stand frozen with my arms out to the side before awkwardly patting her on the back. Charlie gives a small warning growl. She hasn't seen anyone hold me like this since Annie.

"Easy, Charlie. We're good."

I'm good.

This feels nice.

She's so little and I can feel every tremble that passes through her body. Her tears wet the front of my shirt and I wrap my arms around the back of her shoulders, pulling her in closer to my body.

I should end this before either of us gets the wrong idea, but I like the way I feel with her in my arms. For once, I don't feel broken. I'm protecting someone—it's a feeling I didn't even know I missed.

She pulls away and I reluctantly release my hold on her.

Her eyes are red from crying, but she gives me a slight grin. "How about that ride, asshole?"

In spite of the shit situation she's in, I start laughing. "Whatever you say, Princess. Whatever you say."

The ride back to her place is quiet. She occasionally brushes a stray tear from her cheek while staring out the passenger window. Charlie is wedged in between us, giving excited little pants—as if she arranged this whole thing herself.

I turn on the radio just to have some sound.

"No country, please." She gives me an anxious look and I switch the stations until Led Zeppelin's *Kashmir* comes on. Kat relaxes again, softly humming to herself.

Damn.

Maybe I was wrong about her. I figured she'd be into that bubble gum pop bullshit they call music, not classic rock. I park the truck in my driveway and help her out of the truck.

She has a death grip on my arm as we get closer to her front door. "Please don't leave. I can't be alone right now. Please..."

"Okay..." I have no idea what to do right now. A part of me wants to leave her here and make a mad dash for my cabin, while the other part of me wants to lift her up in my arms and hold her until she's better.

What the fuck is wrong with me?

She clings tightly to my t-shirt and I scratch the back of my neck, debating what to do.

"I could go to your house if you'd rather do that. I just don't want to be alone when I'm feeling like this. Please."

The *please* settles the whole thing. I put my arm around her and steer her toward my place. "Fine, but just so you know, I don't keep any alcohol in my house."

THIRTY

KATYA

"THAT'S FINE." I don't tell him that I have several hidden stashes of vodka around the house—stashes I absolutely planned on raiding. I don't need to be left alone when I'm feeling vulnerable like this. He helps me to the grey couch in the living room, gently pulling my hands from his shirt, before going into the kitchen.

His house smells like him—not like cologne or body wash, but him. It's not at all unpleasant—in fact, it's actually stirring up some conflicting feelings within me. I should be trying to sort through the emotional response I just had, not working to decode his scent.

How did something so small trigger such a reaction?

I was lost in my own thoughts when I heard those familiar bars and an icy cold sense of dread coiled its way around my body. I didn't check to see if anyone in the bar was watching me, didn't even stop to process it, as I ran outside.

All I could think as I leaned against the building, trying to catch my breath, was 'he's back.'

That fucking song—it was a sign. I'd forced myself against the bricks, in an attempt to make myself smaller, but I couldn't calm down enough to think rationally. How would the copycat know what that song did to me?

I'd inhaled a ragged breath, trying to decide my next move when I saw him.

"Katya, it's been awhile. Did you miss me?" Landon sat on a bench across the street from me, grinning from ear to ear.

How?

My legs almost gave out then and there. He'd stood up and walked toward me just as a minivan turned onto the street. I knew they were going to collide, but the minivan just passed right through him and continued on as though nothing was amiss.

"You're dead!" I'd hurled the words at him as he moved closer. There was dried blood all over his face and chest.

I blinked and then he'd been right in front of me. "Of course I'm dead. Look at me!"

I closed my eyes and began rocking at that point, afraid to open them for fear that he'd pull me down into the depths of Hell where he most certainly resided. "Narciso Rodriguez. Isaac Mizrahi."

"I said look at me!" He'd roared the words right into my face, but I refused to look at him. I wanted to convince myself that he wasn't real, but everything about it felt real. The hairs on my arms had even stood up in response to his voice.

"Marc Jacobs. Alexander McQueen. Vivienne Westwood. Coco Chanel. Vera Wang. Gianni Versace."

I tried to tell myself that it wasn't happening.

His voice moved further and further away, as if he was being summoned back to the underworld.

The icy feeling in my body didn't go away though, and I fought to catch my breath. "Christian Louboutin. Valentino. Zac Posen."

C'mon, Katya. Breathe in. Breathe out. It wasn't real.

"Kat? Are you okay?" I blink slowly, taking in the unfamiliar surroundings of Travis's house.

"I'm okay. Just trying to process all of it."

Travis sits on a chair near the couch, both he and Charlie

watching me with anxious faces. He leans forward and tries to place a cool washcloth against my skin, but I move away and force myself to sit up.

"Please don't. I'm okay." I glance around the small living area, noting the fact that there's not a lot of furniture, but what he does have is organized perfectly. It's also apparent that he lives alone. That makes me happy for some reason.

He folds the cloth over and over in his hands. "You were triggered. Has it ever happened to you before?"

I exhale slowly and nod. "Yeah. This was better than the last time though." I laugh, hoping he'll get my joke, but his face doesn't change.

Why, of all the people in the world, did this have to happen in front of him?

He looks down. "Do you want to talk about it?"

I massage the back of my neck, forcing my stiff muscles to relax. "Do you?"

His head jerks up in surprise. "What would I need to talk about?"

Frustrated by his ability to dodge questions, I sigh. "You're the one with the service dog, so you tell me."

I expect him to kick me out, but he shocks me instead. "How about you tell me what triggered you tonight and I'll tell you why I have Charlie. Fair enough?"

My mouth hangs open and all I manage is a small nod.

"You do actually have to talk though, Kat, or the deal's off." His voice takes on that familiar grumpy tone and I fight back a smile before taking a deep breath.

"Okay, it was the song. Let's just say I heard that song a lot during a really low point in my life and I'd be perfectly fine with never hearing it again." It's the most honest I've been since my session with Dr. Farrell. I give him my most serious look. "Your turn."

Travis puts the washcloth down and scratches an invisible itch on his arm. "You lost your mind because of a song? Jesus, I thought someone grabbed you or said something—but you're saying you fell apart over a country song?"

My heart beats faster in anger and I resist the urge to punch him. Mainly because I'm certain that Charlie would bite my head off if I did. Yep, I definitely liked him better when his mouth was shut.

"The song just brought back some bad memories. Are you going to interrogate me further on whether or not my reaction was appropriate? Because I thought we had a deal."

He shrugs and smirks as though it doesn't matter. "I like dogs. That's why I have Charlie."

"Are you kidding me right now? You had me open up to you and that's what you give in return? You really are an asshole aren't you?"

He jumps up from his chair, towering over me, and I flinch in anticipation. I know he's going to hit me. I keep my eyes clenched shut, but nothing happens.

I open one eye just as Charlie gives a small whimper. Travis leans down and pats her on the head, watching me curiously. "It's late. Why don't I walk you home?"

"Aren't you going to tell me the real reason you have Charlie? I was honest with you." I pick at my fingernails, my hands still trembling in fear.

He gives me a tight smile. "I did tell you the real reason, but I think you'd be better off at your place right now, Princess."

Right.

Maybe he thinks I'm weak.

Maybe he's right. I latched onto him during the episode without working through it myself. Who could blame me though? The long sleeves on his Henley are pushed up, revealing a left forearm covered in tattoos. It looks like a name is woven around his forearm, but I'm not close enough to say for sure. I want to spend more time studying each of them, but my eyes move up to his muscular biceps and chiseled jaw line. He hasn't shaved in a few days, but the stubble makes him even sexier.

Sexier?

Get a hold of yourself, Egoricheva.

I want to see those dimples again. I've only seen him fully smile once, but when he does, look out world. The man really is nice to look at, well when he's not scowling at me, like he is at the moment. "Look, Travis, I'm really sorry if I said or did anything to upset you. I didn't mean it."

Charlie puts her front paws on his thigh and he looks down at the floor. "Just go, Kat. Please."

I stand up slowly, my muscles protesting the movement. He can't even look at me right now. Charlie licks his face, probably comforting him for having to put up with me for the past half hour. My purse is lying on the coffee table and I have to reach around him to get it.

"Again, I'm really sorry."

He grabs my purse and thrusts it into my hands. "Just get the fuck out!"

I run the few short steps to my front door, tears springing to my eyes as I shut and lock it behind me, while trying to figure out where I went wrong.

"I WAS WORKING downstairs with Summer. Things were going really well too. I wasn't thinking about anything—my mind was just at peace. Then, that song came on and it all came rushing back. I wasn't free anymore. Every verse carried me further and further away until I was sitting back in that basement, begging for my life."

Dr. Farrell nods at me from the laptop screen as I talk, jotting notes here and there for reference. "What happened next?"

I didn't expect to be able to reach my therapist after hours and left her a voicemail. However, she called me back right away and scheduled a video chat for us. I'm assuming this is due to the obscene amount of money my father is paying her and not my stellar status as a patient.

When I left Travis's house I was ready to scream, drink, cry—all three if it meant I could gain some peace. But it wasn't just him. It was that song too. A combination that left me completely stumped inside. I suddenly needed an instruction manual to figure out my emotions.

I'd put my purse down and headed for the bathroom. The entire night had left me feeling sick. If music and people were all potential triggers, then how could I ever expect to return to normal?

Was Travis a trigger?

I'd turned on the faucet and splashed cold water onto my ashen face. Travis stirred up some confusing feelings inside of me. When I grabbed onto him outside the restaurant, he hadn't stopped me. He seemed to be holding just as tightly to me too.

Don't forget he almost hit you...

Did he though?

It was the hardest part of an episode—trying to piece together fact from fiction. I'd been conditioned to flinch when someone got too close to me, this was nothing I hadn't been told a thousand times before in therapy. So, was I merely reacting out of habit or had he truly meant me harm? The effects of trying to determine fault had left me sick and exhausted and I knew I was going to need a professional.

I walk her through the past few hours, hesitantly including Landon's apparition showing up unexpectedly. All I want is to be normal again, but I'm pretty sure normal people don't see spirits.

"You're not losing your grip on sanity, Katya. You recognized that he was not really there. Your anxiety is what concerns me the most right now. In times of severe anxiety, it can begin to play tricks on your mind—leading you to see and hear things that aren't real. If you were 'crazy' as you mentioned, then those hallucinations would not disappear once the episode was over. You took the right step in contacting me; and together, we'll work through this."

Mike swore to me that Landon would never bother anyone ever again. It's the only thing that's tethered me to sanity. For a long time, it was the only thing that kept me here.

"The problem is that he never really left though. It sometimes feels like he lives in my subconscious, ready to strike when I least expect it. How do I combat that?"

I feel like I'm finally settling into a routine here—not like I've had much of a choice. Until the police find Chris and the person responsible for all of this, I'm stuck here. I just don't want to spend my days plagued with visions of him. The man stole so much from me when he was alive, he shouldn't have that right in death too.

"Katya, you've got to be patient. Recovery doesn't happen overnight. I think we just need to take it one day at a time. The last time we talked, you were going to take up a hobby. Have you come up with anything?"

Let's see...hobbies.

I rest the laptop on my knees and recline against the back of the couch. "Well, my agent calls me for daily updates. My nutritionist calls me to go over what I've eaten. And my trainer calls to push me into working out harder. When I'm not doing that, I'm working at the restaurant. The only free time I have is from midnight to five in the morning and I'm usually too busy trying to keep myself awake to even think about a hobby."

"Is modeling something you enjoy doing?"

It used to be.

"I guess I don't know anything else. I've done this as long as I can remember."

"Have you thought about walking away from it? Maybe trying something different?" She watches me intently, and I note that she's in full makeup—at six in the morning.

I don't want to discuss my career right now. The knowledge that I'll have to make a decision soon already weighs heavily on my mind, along with everything else.

"I'm not ready to leave it all behind, if that's what you're asking. I've worked too hard to get where I am, only to walk away because of what a broken man with sociopathic tendencies did to me!" I immediately cover my mouth, shocked at my admission, but Dr. Farrell doesn't appear to be bothered by it.

"What about relationships? Would you say that's becoming easier?"

I cringe, thinking about the night I almost kissed Brody and the way I reacted to Mike. Both times were fueled by alcohol and shame over my brokenness.

"I've thrown myself at two men over the last month. I've gone from assuming I'd sworn off men forever, to jumping on the two closest to me. Last night, with Travis, it left me feeling unsteady. It stirred up feelings that I haven't felt in a while. There must be something horribly wrong with me. I feel like a slut."

She shakes her head. "Katya, absolutely not! What you're experiencing is completely normal. Think about it—you've submerged these feelings for months. You've attempted to go on as if the event never happened, so you swing like a pendulum between hyper-sexuality and completely avoiding the opposite sex.

"You attach yourself to a man who you see as a savior to you, for example, Mike. If you kiss a man, touch him, let him touch you back — then you're not damaged. Your trauma didn't affect you. This is a completely common response among survivors. You think you're avoiding the issue altogether, but your brain is zeroed in on it. So, you engage in these compulsive behaviors, without fully knowing why. Your brain is trying to fix what it sees as broken."

Everything Dr. Farrell said is right on target. Up until this point, I haven't been sure why I've felt this need to prove to myself that I'm okay.

Because I'm not.

I honestly have no idea what healthy looks like anymore...on any level. I eat what my nutritionist recommends I eat. Before that, Landon controlled what I consumed. I train and conform my body to the specifications my trainer laid out. Before that, Landon pushed my body into a state of starvation. I used to know how it felt to be in a committed relationship. Now, I'm not sure that I'm capable of anything more than casual sex.

"Be safe, Katya. Listen to what your mind and body are telling you. You need to align the two before you find the healing you need. Don't replace Mike with Travis. Take your time."

Now, to figure out how to go about doing that. Maybe I misread the situation between us last night. Would I really know if I was ready? Would he ever want someone as broken as me?

I get up and make a pot of coffee. Maybe I'll sit and watch the sunrise, try to gain some perspective. I balance the steaming mug in my hand as I open the back door, almost tripping over a small mason jar filled with wildflowers. I step over them to put my coffee down before kneeling to retrieve them. They still look fresh, so they must've been recently picked. There's a small handwritten note attached to the jar.

"I'm sorry."

I blink to clear my vision before putting the jar up on the small patio table. I sit down in my chair and sip my coffee, thinking back to our first meeting in the elevator that day. I almost drop the mug when I recall his words.

"That's funny, because the seventh floor is nothing but psych offices."

He got off on the seventh floor that day too. He drove an hour and a half into the city to see a therapist because he has no one to talk to here. The thought fills me with incredible sadness.

I look back at the flowers and the answer is as clear as day to me. I may not be able to save myself, but I know without a doubt that I'm going to do everything in my power to save him.

I just have to convince myself not to fall in love with him in the process.

THIRTY-ONE

TRAVIS

I REGRETTED my actions the minute the door slammed shut behind her. Charlie immediately jumped into my lap, licking and pawing at me to keep me grounded. Once she knew I was going to be okay, she'd given me a dirty look before settling down at my feet—as if I personally offended her by throwing Kat out.

I was a jerk. I tried to take care of her. Who could've predicted that helping her would hurt me though? I've kept my shit under control and then she comes to town and it feels like I'm losing control. The monster inside of me pushes to take over again. I've fought to keep it buried for nine years—I'm not about to lose that battle because some girl with beautiful eyes has demons she can't seem to defeat on her own.

I am curious to know what really happened to Kat. A part of me even wonders if I might've misjudged her. Or maybe I'm full of shit, and she's nothing more than a spoiled brat who doesn't know how to handle being an adult.

Either way, I can't stay here to find out. I lay out my backpack on the bed, checking twice to be sure I have everything I'll need. The plan is to head straight to the airport, but once I lock the door, I make the mistake of looking over at her house.

Grumbling under my breath, I go back inside and grab a mason jar from the cabinet before heading down to the waterline to pick a few wildflowers. If Charlie could talk, I'm certain she would ask me what the hell I think I'm doing. This is not me at all. "Just trying to be the bigger person, Char. Make amends and all that shit."

She yawns loudly, clearly not buying my story.

Before I can change my mind, I scrawl an apology on a piece of scrap paper in my pocket, placing the jar on top of it near her back porch. I can hear her talking to someone and I press my forehead against the side of the cabin, my hand ready to knock.

What am I doing?

I lower my hand and back away slowly. As I drive away, I try not to watch her cabin grow smaller in my rearview mirror.

THIRTY-TWO

KATYA

July 4, 2015

I KNOCK on the door again, on the off-chance that maybe he just didn't hear me the other five times. The clouds build in the sky, threatening to drop rain at a moment's notice. I've been standing here for ten minutes, but it's obvious that Travis is still gone.

Five days.

I went to thank him the morning he left me flowers, but his house was dark and the door locked. I'd hung around outside for most of the day, expecting to see him or Charlie, when I finally gave up and went into work.

No one seems to know anything about why he left, well, no one but me. I have no idea where he might be, but I take full responsibility for him leaving at all.

"Katya?" I jump at the sound of my name

"Papa? What are you doing here?"

He walks over to Travis's deck, looking concerned. "I came up to bring you your Jeep. The detective informed me that they are still as inept as they were when you were gone. I did not like the idea of you getting around on nothing but a bicycle indefinitely. Why are you over here?"

I look down at the deck, chewing my lip. "I was just checking to see if Travis was home. I thought he might like some company for the fireworks show they're doing later—well, if it doesn't rain first."

I walk back over to my cabin and he takes my arm. "Perhaps you'll let an old man be your date for the show?"

I smile and kiss his cheek. "Papa, you know I'd love nothing more. I've missed you."

"My Katya, I would have visited more often, but I didn't want to risk being followed. I'm going to have some friends look into—"

A car door slams from the front of the house and he looks over at me as if to ask if I'm expecting company, but I shake my head. He holds a finger to his lips and motions for me to stay in the back before walking around the side of the house.

"Papa—" I whisper.

He doesn't respond and it's completely quiet. After a few minutes, I leave my assigned spot and walk around to the front. He's got his arms wrapped around Jeanne.

His voice is low. "Zhanna, it's been so long."

Zhanna? Only my father would "Russianize" someone's name.

"Uh, hi. What's going on here?"

They pull apart and Jeanne grabs a bag from the front step. "Food. I brought you food for the fourth. Thought you might need some company, but Niko's here so you should be good. I'm just gonna—"

"Zhanna, stay," He clears his throat and looks at me, "I mean, if it's alright with you, Katya."

I push aside any feelings of discomfort and smile brightly. "Sure. The more the merrier, right?"

"AND THEN NIKO thought he could just pick the turkey up off the floor and put it back on the table." Jeanne stifles another giggle, trying to finish the story.

"Did it work?" I take a small sip of wine, cringing a bit at the taste. She'd offered me a glass and I'd accepted, even as my father narrowed his eyes at me. He didn't need to worry; there was no way I was getting drunk on this stuff.

My father shakes his head, pinching the bridge of his nose. "Absolutely not. Patka was onto me immediately. We had a cat at the time —this little demon of a thing. Just as I got the bird settled onto the platter, your mother walked in. I thought I'd done it until she pointed to it disgustedly. There was cat hair all along the side of it."

Patka...I haven't heard him say it in so long. To everyone else, she was Patsy, but to Papa she was his *Patka*—the Slovak equivalent. My chest tightens at the memory.

"I don't think anyone could've ever pulled the wool over Patsy's eyes. That woman saw everything. She seemed to always know what was going on, regardless of where everyone was. Remember when Katya disappeared on that hiking trail, Niko?"

My father stands up and walks over to the edge of the deck, overlooking the multitude of boats sitting silent on the lake. The rain is holding off for now; they might even be able to make it through the entire fireworks display.

"You okay, Papa?"

He nods, but doesn't turn back around.

"I shouldn't have brought it up. Niko, I'm sorry." Jeanne gathers up the empty plates and gives us a moment alone.

"Papa?"

His shoulders shake silently and I realize he's crying. My chair scrapes across the deck as I push away from the table and go to him.

He pulls me into a rough hug, his tears wetting my hair and face. "Katya, I'm so sorry. Everything you went through. Patka always had this intuition when it came to us—she would've found you in a heartbeat. I feel like I failed her and you."

Guilt.

The same plague that had weighted me down for months afflicted him as well. He stayed away because of it; afraid that he no longer deserved my love.

"Papa, I drove to meet him. I put myself in that situation. I believed everything he told me—why would you be any different?"

I let him hold me until there are no more tears from either of us. The fireworks begin and we move our chairs together. The sounds echo off the sides of the mountain, shaking everything.

Papa reaches for my hand. "I need you to know this. I've contacted some friends to look into these messages you're receiving. I will find this person; I will not wait for a detective to take care of it this time. Do you understand, Katya?"

I squeeze his hand and watch the sky light up with color.

THIRTY-THREE

TRAVIS

July 4, 2015

"I KNOW I say it every year, but your dad and I were thinking of driving into town to watch the fireworks—"

"No, Mom, I'll be fine here."

She continues rocking in the chair next to mine. I know she wants to say something else; her entire body vibrates with the tension of keeping it bottled up. It's the same argument we have every year. She wants me to be the guy I was before Iraq—the man who'd take over the ranch when it came time. Hell, I think she'd settle for a son who could enjoy Independence Day without losing his shit.

I flew from Colorado to Oklahoma, just like I'd done every year since Annie left. My parents have a ranch with eleven hundred acres. You know what you don't have to worry about when you have that much land? People. It's quiet, even more so when my parents drive into town. I usually sit in a rocking chair on the front porch with Charlie and contemplate what I'm doing with my life.

It's where I was when I thought of opening up a gym. Coincidentally, it's also where I was when I talked myself out of it.

"Are you going to Arlington this trip too?" Her quiet voice pulls me from my thoughts.

I nod. "Yeah. I need to see the guys."

We slip back into silence, with her searching for a way to relate to me, and me trying to figure out how to be the son she lost nine years ago.

"Your dad is looking to bring some help on—he's getting older, you know."

I continue rocking, watching the sun sink lower onto the horizon. I miss seeing these sunsets, but I can't imagine living here permanently.

"I think he should bring some more help on—it'd be good for him to slow down a bit."

She sighs heavily, the rocking chair squeaking as she moves faster. It's not the answer she wants, but it's the only one I can give. She reaches over and grabs my hand. "Trav—I just want you to be happy. You know that right? Wherever you decide to be, I just want you to live your life to the fullest. You're going to be thirty-eight in a few months. Don't let life pass you by."

I squeeze her hand and we watch the last bits of daylight fade away.

I don't have the heart to tell her that I don't think there's anywhere in the world where I'll fit in—no magic place where I'll find happiness.

THIRTY-FOUR

KATYA

July 26, 2015

TWENTY-SEVEN DAYS.

He's gone for good.

I just know it.

I've slipped into a lonely routine—I go into work and keep to myself, counting down the hours until I can leave again. Then I drive home and sit on Travis's back porch with a bottle of vodka, pouring my heart out to his back door. Then, I promise myself that I'll stop drinking and acting like a crazy person.

I don't know why I keep going over there. I told myself it was insane after the first time, yet here I sit, night after night. A few nights ago, I stood up and pressed my cheek against the rough wood of the door, tears streaming down my face. I don't know how long I stood like that, but I imagined for a moment that he was just on the other side of the door, his face pressed up against the wood too. I imagined that he heard every word I said and for once I didn't feel alone.

Aja has called almost every day to check in and keep me posted on Chris. Hearing her voice has only emphasized my feelings of loneliness. I want this whole thing finished—I want them to find Chris and the person responsible for all of it.

I want life to go back to normal...or at least back to comfortable. I don't understand in this day and age how someone can post things online and remain anonymous.

Maybe the copycat was hoping to push me to insanity by leaving me those messages—unaware that I was already there.

I survived Landon Scott...nothing else comes close to that level of fear. And as long as I stay hidden away in the mountains, I'll be fine.

THIRTY-FIVE

KATYA

August 14, 2015

IT'S BEEN sixty-one days since Chris Miller was last seen. Police suspect the video that was released is real, but according to Mike, they still have no leads.

There hasn't been any recent activity from Landon's social media accounts and with increased security at my condo, the notes stopped altogether as well. I'm starting to wonder if the copycat just lost interest.

Travis has been gone for forty-six days. I could've sworn I heard Charlie bark the other morning though. It was just past four and still dark out. I'd gone to the window and looked, but there were no lights on at his cabin. I actually think I might've imagined it—the lack of sleep sometimes caused hallucinations.

"Kat, table four's ready for their check—you okay?" Summer touches me lightly on the arm. I've been staring at a bottle of honey for who knows how long while lost in thought.

I blink to clear my head. "Yeah, just daydreaming I guess." I print out the bill I need and try to focus on the present. The one-year anniversary of my kidnapping was a few days ago. I celebrated by calling in sick and drinking myself into a stupor.

Yeah, drinking.

Dr. Farrell wanted me to find a hobby...turns out, drinking is my hobby. Well, that and watching classic movies to keep myself awake at night.

I've made little deals with myself. My first one was if Travis came back within a week, then I would stop. Then I decided if they found Chris and whoever was responsible, I would quit. Cold turkey.

As long as I have these goals, I feel that I'm still in charge.

I hand the table their check and refill another's glasses, while keeping my eyes on the door. I don't know why I've got it in my head that today will be the day he comes back.

Maybe it's because the Broncos are playing their first pre-season game against the Seahawks and the restaurant is packed with people. There's no band playing tonight—instead Daniel has set up the projection screen so people can watch downstairs. It's brilliant on his part. We've been slammed since lunch, as if the *Cedar Ridge Brewery* has become the unofficial tailgating spot for everyone in town.

Wayne's even gone as far as making a game day menu, while Summer adorned every available surface of the restaurant in orange and blue decorations. I never really got into football before I met Brody, so I only know the basics of the game.

Erin, another server and back-up bartender, is handing out plastic necklaces with the Broncos logo on them. You'd think this was the Superbowl, not a pre-season game. Daniel keeps saying that this is their year as he runs around the restaurant like a madman.

"Mark my words, Kat. Osweiler may be playing tonight, but this is Manning's year. He's not gonna retire until he gets another ring."

I nod and smile, as if I know exactly what he's talking about.

Brody and the Cowboys had played the Chargers last night, and while he carried the team most of the game, they couldn't pull off a win. I made sure to watch the highlights once I got home from work, so that I'd have something to reference when he called to check in on me. Usually, I just took notes from the sportscasters. Brody, to his credit, has never accused me of plagiarism though.

I've just finished clearing a table when he walks in. The noise in the restaurant dims slightly and I turn around, expecting to be let down just like I've been every other time over the past few weeks. He's standing near the hostess stand, with Charlie excitedly wagging her tail, when his eyes meet mine.

I hold up my hand in a wave, feeling as though time might've actually stopped. I know that it's a stupid thing that people say, but the noise around me ceases and it feels as though we're the only two people in the room.

I try to hold tight to my plan of being his friend and not letting my emotions control me, but the corner of his mouth turns up ever so slightly and I know that I'm a goner. It could barely be considered a smile by most people, but this is Travis.

I gesture to the cleared booth in front of me, but he shakes his head and points to the small upstairs bar.

"Game's on." He mouths at me as his tongue runs over his lower lip. And I nod stupidly, as if I haven't been preparing for the damn thing all day.

He sits down at the bar with Charlie at his feet. It's the closest I've ever seen to him interacting with others.

What kind of service animal is she?

Maybe he has a seizure disorder. I know that in severe cases, service dogs are trained to recognize the signs and get their human to a safe place.

I'm unaware that I'm still staring until he looks over at me. I expect him to look away once he realizes it's only me, but he doesn't. He holds my gaze and my body feels hot and cold simultaneously. His beard is fuller than it was the last time I saw him. He looks unkempt and wild, and like a moth to a flame, I'm drawn to him.

"Bozhe, pomogi mne."

God help me.

I whisper the words and then nearly jump out of my skin when Summer touches me.

"What did you just say? Was that even English?" She cocks her head to the side before following my gaze over to where Travis is sitting. He's back to staring at the television above the bar.

"I just—why does he have a service dog?"

She glances at him before leading us downstairs. With the place being so busy, servers are working both upstairs and downstairs to keep things running smoothly. "I don't really know. I've never asked."

Denver scores and the downstairs crowd erupts into cheers, ending anymore Travis talk. Summer goes into manager mode and sets me up in the computer by the bar before leaving me with Brett, the downstairs bartender. It's only eight, but everything is in full swing.

Servers move effortlessly between the bar and crowd, with kitchen staff bringing food down in between. I stare longingly at the row of brightly colored bottles sitting on the back of the bar, finally forcing myself to turn away.

I could do this.

No one needs to know that sometimes I sneak a shot in the middle of my shift, just to keep my hands steady while carrying trays.

Just a few more hours and I'll be home.

THIRTY-SIX

TRAVIS

I WAS GONE for two weeks and I thought about her every damn day. I never liked being on the lake on the fourth of July—I didn't know how I'd react. So, every year, I convinced myself that putting up with a week of my mom nagging me to move back to Oklahoma was somehow better than being triggered by fireworks. Usually, by the end of the week, I was wishing that I'd taken my chances on the fireworks.

After the first week was up, I'd made my yearly trek to Virginia to visit Carlson and Moore. There was something about being at Arlington that just put everything in perspective for me. Standing in the field of white gravestones, surrounded by those that made the ultimate sacrifice, I could reset. I remembered what I set out to do the day I got sober.

When I made it back home, I'd stood on the back deck watching her cabin for signs of life. I made deals with myself—if her lights came on, I'd go over there and apologize to her face. I'd tell her the real reason I had Charlie, but her house remained dark that evening. So, I stayed away. When I woke up the next morning, I told myself that I'd do it if she was on her deck. She wasn't and I was off the hook yet again.

I avoided the restaurant, living off of the MREs I had stockpiled in my pantry. She came by almost every night when she got off. I doubt I would've known, had Charlie not bristled up and stared at the back door. I kept all of the lights off, so she never realized I was home. If the moon was bright enough, I could make out her silhouette as she leaned against my door. Sometimes, she talked as though I was there. Other times, she cried.

Those times were the hardest. I'd pad quietly over to the door and press my face up against the wood, feeling connected to her somehow. I knew she was still drinking; I could hear the liquid sloshing around in the bottle most nights. The more she drank, the more emotional she became. It had taken everything in me to not throw open the door and pull her into my arms.

The Broncos score and everyone erupts into cheers and clinking of glasses. I smile and raise my club soda. When I woke up this morning, I knew I couldn't hide forever. Charlie was getting fed up with me not walking her until late at night. She'd been trained to keep me in the light, so I was constantly turning lights off only for her to turn them right back on, as if she wanted Kat to catch us.

The game goes to a commercial and I start to look away when a battered woman appears on the screen. The bar goes quiet, everyone staring at the various cuts and bruises marring the woman's skin.

"Turn it up, Erin." Pete demands. The man has to be pushing eighty by now, yet he's in here almost as much as I am, barking orders like he owns the place. Like the scene of a car accident, all of our eyes are glued to the image in front of us.

"It's hard to believe this picture was taken four months ago. When I was planning my future, I envisioned something else entirely."

My pulse speeds up. I know that voice. The battered woman on the screen disappears and a gorgeous woman clad only in lingerie stalks down a catwalk.

Kat.

Someone else speaks up. "Isn't that—?"

"I'm Katya Egoricheva, Selvaggia model, and these photographs were taken before and after my abduction. Twenty-four people are physically abused by an intimate partner every minute in the United States and one out of every five women will be victim of severe physical violence by an intimate partner."

Oh my God. Her hair was longer and she was curvier, but I know without a doubt that Kat and Katya are one and the same.

"I'm Brody Rodgers, wide receiver for the Dallas Cowboys. One out of every five women will be raped in their lifetime, half of them by someone they know and trust. When 12.7 million people are being physically abused, raped, or stalked within a one-year period, we cannot turn it into a blind spot."

Statistics on domestic violence engulf the screen and I feel sick to my stomach. I've been nothing but an asshole to a woman who was savagely beaten by someone she trusted. I've told myself she's a princess, some spoiled brat who has no idea how to function as an adult. She appears on the screen with that guy who plays for the Cowboys and I can't look away. She looks so frail next to him; a shadow of the woman she'd been on the runway. Not so different from how she looks now.

Katya. I smile to myself, belatedly realizing that she does have an exotic name to match her features.

"I am one out of five."

What happened to you?

The Cowboys' player looks at the screen. *"And that's one too many in my playbook."* I hope he never plans to find a career in acting. He's better on the field.

The bar's completely silent, everyone gathered around the screen. Wayne has even left his beloved kitchen to see it. He stands, wringing his hands together. "Oh no...no, no, no—said she was entitled—what was wrong with this country—Jesus."

I give him a puzzled look before taking in everyone else's reactions. Erin has her hand pressed against her mouth, tears running freely down her cheeks.

I'd wanted to believe that the woman living next door to me could never understand what I'd been through. I thought she'd never know what it was like to feel like an outcast in the middle of a crowd. I see how wrong I was. No one in this room gave a damn about her until now. Now, she'll be given pitying looks every time she enters a room and gossiped about the minute she leaves.

It's why I've played my cards close to my chest. I don't need anyone's sympathy. I quit doing interviews not long after getting home from Iraq. I didn't want to spout off bullshit as truth and I damn sure didn't want anyone judging me for my choices. I look back up at the screen and see what no one else can.

It's all an act.

Katya continues speaking, but her voice has taken on an almost robotic tone. "*No more turning a blind eye. No more, 'she seems fine.'*" I know what she told herself before doing that commercial. She convinced herself that she was helping others and completely dissociated herself from the victims in the process.

The football player continues. "*No more, 'she shouldn't wear that,' or 'boys will be boys.' If you see something, say something. Join the NFL and Selvaggia in our campaign to end domestic violence.*"

"*Please visit the website to learn more about how you can help out.*" Katya and Brody look lovingly at each other and it infuriates me more than it should.

She leans into his arm as he concludes, "*No more statistics. No more excuses. It ends with us.*"

"Did you know she wasn't just beaten? She was held for months." A man I don't recognize holds up his phone from the other end of the bar.

"It says here she was raped." Another person calls out.

Charlie begins whining, picking up on my anxiety. I want them to stop, to let it go, but the voices grow louder.

Rape?

What the hell did they think they were doing to her right now? They were raping her all over again, poring over details and facts that should've never been made public.

"STOP!" I shout the words and the bar goes silent again. "It's nobody's goddamn business what happened to her!"

Can't they see? Just because they saw her on television, it doesn't mean they can relate to anything she's been through. They don't know her. They have no idea what she felt.

Oh Jesus.

She's working downstairs. If I saw it up here, then that means...

I slide off my bar stool, an upset Charlie following closely behind me. I can't leave her here. Not when I've been so wrong about everything. I'd been so cruel to her the night she was triggered. I'd even gone as far as mocking her for being upset over a song.

I hurry down the stairs to find the bar completely quiet. Summer's hunched over the bar top, hyperventilating. I search every face in there, but Katya's gone.

"Summer?"

She sucks in a breath and turns to me, her face a deathly shade of white. "Did you know, Travis? Did you know who she was?"

"No. I never took the time to find out. Jesus, Summer, are you okay? Did you know who she was?"

She continues panting, using the bar to hold herself up. "Um, I'm fine. Just a little in shock. I knew she was a model, but I never imagined—" Her voice cuts off and she begins sobbing.

I've just taken a step toward her when I hear it.

"If I'd known she was hiding that under those t-shirts, I might've spent a little more time getting to know her." The guy is old enough to be her father and is clearly three sheets to the wind.

"What the hell did you just say?" I growl the words without quite meaning to and Charlie instinctively blocks me from taking another step, using her body as a barrier. The guy laughs and holds both palms out toward me.

"No need to flip out man. We're all having a good time here. I wonder if Daniel knew she had 'assets' like that when he hired her."

He chuckles at his own sick joke, while everyone else looks back to me to see what I'm going to do next. Not wanting to leave them disappointed, I grab the guy by the collar of his shirt, hauling him up out of his seat and onto a nearby table. Beer bottles hit the concrete floor and shatter, but I'm beyond caring.

"What the fuck, man?" He scrambles to remove my hand, his buddies not moving from their seats.

Charlie lets out a low growl and jumps into me, breaking my contact on him.

"I'm fine, Char. I'm fucking fine!"

"Jesus, Travis! What the hell?" Summer glances back and forth between me and the guy on his back.

What the fuck am I doing?

Am I about to beat this guy's ass over a woman I'd just been an asshole to only a few months ago?

"Nothing. I was just leaving."

I release him and grab Charlie's leash. The bar's still quiet, no one interested in the game anymore. They all share similar looks of horror. They've finally seen the monster inside. Summer follows me up the stairs.

"You wanna explain to me what that was back there?"

I turn back to her. "That guy's an asshole."

She cuts me off. "You're an asshole, Travis. Like all the time. Nobody's trying to kick your ass over it though. You know that group is always trouble when they're drinking."

I give a frustrated sigh. "They can't say that stuff about her—not after seeing what was done to her. I won't allow it."

I walk back upstairs and look around the restaurant, but Katya's nowhere to be found.

"You can't fight every person who makes a crass comment, especially when you consider that you yourself were a jerk to her not that long ago."

I shove my hands into the pocket of my jeans and respond sarcastically. "Don't pick fights with people. Got it, Summer. Thanks."

She checks inside the women's bathroom. "She's not in there. I think she bolted the minute she realized what was happening.

I turn away from her and walk out into the parking lot. I know her father brought her a Jeep about a month ago, but I can't see it in the crowded lot.

"Where do you think she's gone?" Summer stifles another sob, seeing her like this is so out of the ordinary. She's a tiny little thing, but her personality is huge. You can always hear her laughter across the restaurant. In all the time I've lived here, I've never seen her sad.

I sigh again. "Just stay here. I'll check her cabin and give you a call if I find her."

Summer buries her face in her hands. "I invited her over. I thought I'd tell her that I knew she modeled and she'd open up to me. It was nothing, but this morbid curiosity to know why she was here. I could tell it made her uncomfortable. I just can't fathom what she must've gone through."

We reach my truck at the same time. "Summer, she has a drinking problem. Surely you noticed that, yeah?"

Her eyes darken. "What? How do you know that?"

"So, you did know. I think it's safe to assume that she went through some pretty heavy shit. Let's leave it at that."

She looks down at Charlie. "I didn't—I mean; I didn't know for sure. I suspected it though. I know a little bit about life with an alcoholic. She displayed a lot of the same signs."

I open the door and Charlie jumps in, having settled back down now that she knows I'm not a danger to myself or anyone around me anymore.

"You promise you'll let me know the moment you find her?"

I note the worry lines on her face and the fear in her eyes. "Let me find her. Can you manage the bar on your own?"

She nods. "I'm good. The game's about to end and it'll clear out early."

"She's been through a lot tonight. She might not want to come back here. You've got to be prepared for that, Summer."

"You know I have a million questions for you now, right? I've seen you almost every day for the past two years and not once have we discussed anything about your life or how you ended up here, yet you're an expert on trauma now."

I shake my head and start to close the door. "Not now, Summer."

"No, not now, but someday. Someday we'll put all of our demons to rest." She says the last part more to herself, stepping back onto the sidewalk outside the front door, her arms crossed over her chest for warmth.

THIRTY-SEVEN

KATYA

I SHOULDN'T HAVE EVER AGREED to do the PSA, I know that for certain now. I'd gotten comfortable up here and I forgot. I forgot that the campaign has the power to undo my anonymity. All it would take is one person mentioning my name to the media and it'll all be over.

I can't stay here and wait for that. I run through the cabin, throwing my things into suitcases. The copycat will know where I am as soon as the media does.

My phone continues to ring in the background.

Five missed calls from Summer.

Three missed calls from my father.

One missed call from Brody.

I can't talk to any of them.

"Marc Jacobs. Alexander McQueen. Vivienne Westwood. Coco Chanel. Vera Wang. Gianni Versace." I recite the list, trying to keep the anxiety at bay a little longer.

What had I been thinking?

There would never be an escape. There's nowhere I can go that people won't know who I am. I inhale and exhale, tears spilling onto my cheeks.

A knock at the door startles me.

"Katya? It's Travis."

I shake my head from side to side, covering my ears. He's only here because he saw *it*. He probably needs to get a few more digs in at my expense.

No, I can't face him right now.

He pushes the door open and silently takes in the fact that I'm curled up into a ball, rocking back and forth on my living room floor, before he cautiously takes a step toward me.

"Katya, let me help you."

I shake my head again. "I'm fine, Trav. Can't you tell?" A maniacal laugh works its way free. I'm going mad.

Using Charlie as a crutch, he kneels down next to me. "Katya, take a deep breath in. Inhale and exhale, nice and slowly. I want to talk and I want you to listen. Is that okay?"

I glare at him. "When you're done, can I tell you to fuck off and then disappear for a month?"

He grins, a real grin, his dimples and blindingly white teeth on full display. "If you want to, then yes."

I reluctantly nod my agreement and he begins. "I felt horrible for telling you to leave that night. I ran away—it's something I'm good at doing. I was only gone a couple of weeks before I had to come back. I thought running would fix things, but I thought of you every damn second I was away. I wanted to know how you were...wanted to know more about you. So, I came back."

I hold up my hand and he stops talking. "You mean you've been here this whole time? Why haven't I seen you?"

He focuses on the wall behind my head, not quite meeting my eyes. "I was laying low, giving you your space. I had enough MREs to keep me fed for a while." I open my mouth to argue, but he keeps talking. "I know you came by every day. I heard you and I wanted to let you in, but I still had shit of my own to work through."

I'm furious. He's been behind that door for weeks, hiding from me. I'd poured my heart out some nights sitting on that porch. I never imagined he'd hear me. I'd wanted to be friends with him, but he's nothing more than a coward.

"Get out."

He blinks in surprise. "Are you serious?"

I brush away more tears and nod. "Yep. How did you so eloquently put it? Oh yeah. Get the fuck out, Travis."

"I didn't finish though."

I roll my eyes. "Let me guess. Once you knew I was a Selvaggia model, you had a change of heart. Thought you'd see if my real life body looks like it does in the catalogs?"

His eyes widen in shock and he slowly shakes his head. "No. I came to find you before I even saw the commercial. I owed you an explanation for why I disappeared. That's it."

I push myself up and walk over to open the back door. "Great. You explained. Now go."

Using the wall as a brace, he slowly stands back up. "I'm sorry for what I said that night. I was ignorant to assume I knew anything about your life."

I purse my lips and gesture for him to go. Once he walks out onto the patio, I slam the door shut behind him, the glass rattling from the force of it.

I swallow the lump in my throat. I did the right thing. He's only trying to make up for his behavior because he found out who I was.

Am.

Who I am.

The door opens again and before I can get a word out, Travis has crossed the room over to me. He takes my shaking hands in his, his eyes glistening.

Is he about to cry?

I don't think I can manage if he does.

"Katya, you asked me before why I have Charlie." I watch his Adam's apple bob up and down as he swallows, and I hold my breath.

"I have PTSD. She knows when I'm going to have an attack, sometimes long before I do. That night, when I tried to help you, I got low. I thought I could battle your demons without confronting my own, but I was wrong. I didn't want you to see me like that, so I kicked you out. I'm not good at opening up, but I need you to see me as I am. I'm just as fucking broken as you are."

I pull my hands free from his, finally exhaling, before making my decision. I take another step closer, wrapping my arms around his waist and pulling his body into mine. He breathes a small sigh of relief and brings his arms around me, while Charlie's cold snout presses up against my leg.

I could stay like this forever. My mind is quiet and I don't have to ask. I know that Travis wants to save me just as much as I want to save him. I'm just not sure if either of us will survive the attempt.

"CHESS?"

The coffee pot grumbles to life as I call back. "What?"

Travis's laugh carries into the kitchen. "Never mind. I don't think I even know how to play. What else do you have in here?"

I can hear him digging through the built-in cabinet next to the fireplace. I haven't even looked through it to see what's been left behind.

"What about checkers? We both know that one." Travis digs through the cabinet before holding up a dust-covered box.

I carry two cups of black coffee in from the kitchen, placing them on the side table near the couch. "What's with the games?"

He shrugs easily. "We played games before. You don't sleep, right?"

I bite my lower lip, trying to decide how to answer, when he stops me. "No, not in here, Katya. Out there, we'll put on a mask and act as though everything's fucking peachy, but in here let's be honest. Tell me the truth."

I shake my head. "No. I try not to sleep. I don't want to relive it."

He nods, satisfied with my answer. "So, we won't sleep together." His cheeks turn red once he realizes what he's implied. "I didn't mean that. We can sleep together. Fuck. No. That's not right—I'm out."

I begin wheezing with laughter. I've gone from gut-wrenching sobs to hysterical laughter in a span of a few hours. Travis watches me with a bemused expression.

"You think that's funny?"

I snort in response, which in turn makes me laugh even harder, and I'm pleased to see that there's a huge grin on his face as well. I take a deep breath. "Sorry, I'm fine now." I immediately begin again, my shoulders shaking with silent laughter.

He looks down at the games spread out on the floor and then back up at me. "What do you do to stay awake normally? I always see the lights on."

I wipe my streaming eyes. "I watch a lot of classic movies...and um—well, I drink."

He nods, his index finger tracing along his jawline. "I used to drink. It's nice to be numb for a little while, yeah? To not feel as though your nerve endings are going to electrocute you."

I sit down on the couch near him, with my legs tucked under my body, the mug of coffee warming my hands. "How'd you end up with PTSD?"

He begins stacking the games up on top of each other. "I was in the Marines. Spent some time in Iraq."

His lips form a tight line, so I don't push him further. "I bet I can kick your ass at checkers again."

His eyes light up. "You're on, Princess."

I want to know where he went for those two weeks. I want to know what happened to him in Iraq. Most of all though, I want to do anything and everything in my power to keep him smiling.

NO DEAL FOR BOMBSHELL EGORICHEV

In perhaps one of the strangest turn of events, Katya Egoricheva announced her retirement from the fashion world today. The model was expected to sign a Siren contract with lingerie powerhouse Selvaggia when news broke that she would not be returning to the runway.

Multiple sources claim that negotiations between the two broke down earlier in the week and ended with Katya calling it quits. Brody Rodgers, the wide receiver for Dallas, has been spending a lot of time with Katya in recent months, leading many to speculate that he's behind her decision. According to one insider, "I think Brody has a lot to do with her decision to quit. He wants her all to himself, and she doesn't know how to say no."

Rodger's rep did not respond to requests for comment, while Katya's rep dismissed the rumors almost immediately. "My client has chosen not to pursue a working relationship with Selvaggia at this time. She asks that the media respect her privacy."

This announcement comes just as the investigation into the disappearance of Christine Miller approaches its second month. With no leads, hopes of finding the model alive grow bleaker every day. "Katya was very close to Chris, so it's not surprising that she would put her own career on hold until she's found safe," said a close friend of Egoricheva's who asked to remain anonymous.

The question on everyone's lips is: where is Katya? Her absence from the vigil held for Christine Miller in downtown Denver last night was conspicuous. In fact, the model has not been seen since early June, around the same time Christine Miller went missing. Initially, it was assumed she was in Dallas with her new partner, Brody Rodgers, until he was spotted having dinner last week with an unidentified woman.

Trouble in paradise? Neither of their reps would confirm anything at press time, leaving us to speculate on Bratya's fate.

THIRTY-EIGHT

TRAVIS

"IS SHE OKAY?" Summer leans over the table and into my face.

I move away from her penetrating stare. "She didn't come in today?"

Her jaw clenches and I can tell she's ready to hit me. "Obviously not, if I'm asking you. You said you'd find her and call me. She didn't show up for her lunch shift and I couldn't reach her by phone. I guess I just assumed you were taking care of it."

"Give me a break, Summer. I'm sure she's fine."

"Oh, yeah. Because when someone skips out on a work shift and isn't answering their phone, it's usually because they're fine. I should've found her myself."

I shake my head. "Can I just order a damn pizza without the questions? If it'll make you feel better, Charlie and I will check on her on the way home. Will that work?"

Summer mutters something about men being assholes before marching over to the computer and punching my order in with enough force to shatter the damn screen.

She comes back a bit later, dropping the pizza box and bill onto the table—managing to knock the salt shaker off in the process. "Here. Now go."

I place a twenty on the table and stand up. "Summer, I'll call up here and let you know how she is. Okay?"

She fidgets with her glasses while hiding a triumphant smile. "Fine. I'll be waiting."

As I drive up the steep, winding road that leads to my house, I actually feel a little nervous. What if last night was some fluke thing and she doesn't want to see me again?

"This is stupid." Charlie lifts her head up from the seat, no doubt deciding whether or not her intervention is needed.

"I should just go home, Char. She might not even want company." I park the truck on the driveway and get out. Her house is dark—I could just assume that she's asleep and call it a night. Even as the thought enters my mind, my feet move toward her back door.

Staying up all night with her hadn't felt like a chore. It had been fun, playing board games with her—even if she had cheated on most of them. Being with her felt comfortable.

I knock softly against the door. "Katya?"

I step back when I hear her coming, but nothing can prepare me for the shape she's in.

"Hellloooooooooo..." She holds on to the door frame to keep herself steady. "Come back to lose at more games?"

"How much have you had?"

She holds her index finger and thumb about an inch apart. "A little bit. Didn't you know? I'm unemployed now. I'm drinking to celebrate."

Katya attempts to twirl when she says the word 'celebrate,' and instead ends up falling right into my arms.

THIRTY-NINE

KATYA

I TRY to push myself upright, but Travis's arms come around my body, drawing me in even closer.

I hiccup loudly and he begins making small circles across my back with his hands. "Shhhh...I've got you. Let's get you inside."

My chest tightens at his words and my eyes fill with tears. I try to cover it with a careless giggle. "I'm fine. Just relieved, you know? It'll be fine. Everything's fine."

His hands move to my shoulders and he gently pushes me away until we're staring into each other's eyes. I bite down on my lower lip, hoping he doesn't see it quivering.

Travis's lip turns up ever so slightly on the right side. "Say fine one more time and I might believe you."

I shrug and go back inside. "Why're you here?"

I can't fathom why he's come back.

I'm a wreck.

A hot mess.

I glance down at myself to see that I'm still wearing an oversized t-shirt that's covered in paint stains along with a pair of holey sweat pants. I found the shirt in one of the dresser drawers, obviously left behind by my father for when he did repairs. I haven't showered and actually scared myself when I passed by the mirror earlier and saw my hair poking out in all directions like an angry porcupine.

Travis left my house around five and I spent the morning debating the pros and cons of staying in modeling. It was a once in a lifetime opportunity, but I knew that if I continued, I'd always be seen as a victim.

My agent told me that it'd made me more marketable, but I didn't want to capitalize on my trauma. Doing that PSA so soon after had been a mistake. I never imagined that something I did to help other victims would actually become a trigger for me. Signing a contract and committing myself to more exposure would've been even worse.

I clumsily sit down on the couch, somehow managing to fall over in the process. Travis carries a pizza box over and sets it down on the coffee table in front of me.

"It's hard living this way. You think every day moves you further away from the memories, but grief isn't linear. I had to figure that out the hard way. You'll have good days and you'll have bad days, but those memories never fade."

I rub my eyes, trying to stop the flow of tears, but it's as futile as trying to catch a waterfall in a thimble. "I thought that quitting would make me feel better. I expected to feel as though a weight had been lifted off of my chest—how is it that I feel worse?"

Charlie casually moves her snout closer to the pizza, all while keeping an eye on Travis. He doesn't have to say a word. He just gives her a look and she slowly moves back down to the floor with a sigh. Then he turns his attention back to me. "Did you quit because you wanted to, or because of the video?"

I think about it. "At first, it was because I knew everyone would see that video and view me as this battered victim. The more I thought about it though, I knew that if I stayed, I was allowing someone else to make my decisions for me. What I was going to eat, what I was going to wear—hell, even what I was going to say—all of it would be determined by someone else. That's not living, Trav."

He nods in agreement, silently urging me to keep talking. I settle my head against his shoulder and continue.

"Before it happened, I never considered doing anything else but modeling. It was always my goal. When I came back, it was if that goal was thrust into my hands undeservedly. And it pissed me off. I didn't want anything handed to me. Suddenly, I couldn't go the grocery store without it making the cover of *US Weekly— 'Katya: She's just like us. She eats!'* I'd broken free from Landon's captivity, only to fall prey to the media. And now, here I am, unemployed, with absolutely no future plans for myself."

He softly chuckles into my hair. "It might seem like the end of the world right now, but it's not. Today was just a bad day. I remember the day my military career ended. Honorably discharged without a fucking clue as to what to do with myself. All the plans I'd made before, just didn't work anymore.

"Then, I thought I wanted to open a gym, for other vets. Guys who needed a place where they felt like they fit in. Maybe I'd hire on some physical therapists and make it a training facility—kind of like what they've got down in the Springs for Olympians."

I turn my head to the side and look up at him. "Did you?"

He scratches softly at his beard. "Yeah, I bought that building over on Main, and then did nothing with it. It's just sitting there, empty."

"Do you think people ever go back to normal? Like how they were before?"

He leans forward until his forearms rest against his legs. "I don't think you ever go back to who you were before. I think you have to create a new normal and hope that it's enough."

"What you said about grief—it doesn't get better?"

He focuses on Charlie as he answers. "I think it's different for everyone. You might have a year with no problems, only to hear a song and fall apart all over again. That's the hard part, trying to act as though everything's fine because everyone else expects it."

I slide my hand closer to his body, debating whether or not to touch him. Staring at his profile, from his green-blue eyes down to his full lips, I'm considering my next move when he stands up abruptly—moving away from me.

He clears his throat. "I got a pizza. Thought you might be hungry."

Okay. May have misread that situation completely.

I had to stop throwing myself at men just because they opened up and showed concern for me. Well, first I had to stop drinking as it was completely screwing up my judgment. Step two was definitely going to include not trying to kiss random men.

Travis goes into the kitchen. "Plates?"

"The cabinet to the left of the sink." I lean forward and open the pizza box. Half is vegetarian while the other side is covered in a variety of meats. The smell makes my mouth water. I haven't had pizza in years—I spent all that time perfecting my body for various modeling jobs, never once allowing myself a cheat day. Well, minus the alcohol.

"I didn't know if you ate meat or not. I don't think I've ever seen you eat anything." I jump at the sound of his voice as he carries the plates back in.

"I'll eat whatever."

He grabs a slice of each and passes it to me before sitting down again. I know it's better this way, but I still feel a sense of loss when he sits across from me. The coffee table suddenly feels like an ocean between us.

SUMMER HAS BEEN SO patient with me since I ran out after the commercial aired a few nights ago. Even after I missed my shift the next morning, she re-worked the schedule, giving me an extra couple of days to recover.

She hasn't really said much since I've been back, which suits me just fine. Between my father, my therapist, and Travis—I've grown tired of talking about my feelings.

Travis walks in and I feel a small sense of panic. He seemed fine when he left after bringing me pizza that night, but I haven't seen him since. I'd told myself that we could be friends, but when I didn't see him for two days, I accepted the fact that he might not even want that.

"So, you want to take it or should I?" Summer grins wickedly at me as she combines half-used ketchup bottles—or 'marries' them as she informed me on my first day.

I look over the partition at him, trying to decide if he looks happy or upset. His shoulders are hunched over and he stares down at the table, giving nothing away.

"Relax, I'll deal with him." She pushes the ketchup bottles to the side and takes an iced tea over to him.

I drop a check off with one of my tables, while simultaneously checking on the others.

Does he even have friends? I've never seen him with anyone. Maybe he's as clueless as I am on how to make this work. I manage to walk back to the back without glancing at him again.

"Hey Summer, does Travis- um- does he ever come in with anyone?"

She stops squeezing a bottle, but doesn't look up at me. "You developing a crush on the Big Bad Wolf now? What would Brody say about that?"

I choke out, "Brody? No. There's nothing going on between us. He's just been a friend to me. You can't believe everything you read in magazines."

Yet another reason I wouldn't miss modeling. People assume they know me because they read stories about me.

Summer's shoulders sag and she sighs. "I'm sorry. That was tacky —I'm still just trying to wrap my mind around the fact that you're not only a supermodel, but a supermodel with equally famous friends. Look at me—now I sound bitter about it."

She drops the glass bottle onto the counter with a thud and walks away, leaving me incredibly confused. She knew I was a model before anyone else. I'm still not sure why seeing me on television has changed things between us.

Wayne comes out of the kitchen and hands me a boxed pizza. "Here you go, dear. This goes to Travis, I'm assuming."

"Oh, I'm sorry. I was about to come check on that for Summer. You didn't have to bring it out yourself."

He waves his hand in the air. "I'm quite capable of leaving the kitchen every now and then. Are you okay today? Feeling better? Do you want me to make you some soup?"

I shake my head, trying to keep a straight face. "I'm fine. Thank you though." So, it's completely apparent that he's seen the ad. I've gone from entitled brat to defenseless kitten in a matter of days.

Summer comes back up, and takes the pizza—saving me from having to actually talk to Travis. It looks like she's been crying, but she just claimed she wasn't feeling well before leaving me alone in the beverage station again.

I watch her and Travis and wonder again if he has friends. He'd said he was in the military and usually those men are extremely close. I feel like he told me so much, yet there's still so much I don't know about him.

Summer walks back in and refills a drink, refusing to look at me.

"Summer, I'm really sorry if I said something that offended you."

She puts the drink down and faces me. "Kat, Katya—I don't know what to call you now—"

"Either is fine." I encourage her to continue.

"Travis is a man who likes his privacy. I've been here forever it seems and never once have I had a full conversation with the man. Do your friends know you're here in Cedar Ridge?"

"No, only my agent and my father know where I am." Well, and Mike, but she doesn't need to know about him.

She purses her lips, obviously uncomfortable with what she's about to say. "Look, you're really sweet and you've been through such an ordeal. I just worry what would happen to this place if all of your 'friends' decided to come visit. People live here because it's secluded —nobody wants to wake up to camera crews camped out on the streets looking for you. This isn't Aspen—celebrity sightings are actually quite rare around here and we'd like to keep it that way."

I swallow the lump in my throat as she pushes past me to take care of her tables. She just implied that Travis is keeping his distance because of who I am and that stings more than anything else.

I take off my apron and toss it onto the counter. I've tried so hard to run away from my problems, but they just followed me here. People in Denver wanted to be my friend because of who I was, while people in Cedar Ridge want nothing to do with me for the very same reason.

I know what I have to do. I walk into Daniel's office and tell him I'm going back to Denver, while apologizing for not giving him more notice. He doesn't seem surprised, relieved is more like it.

Is everyone ready for me to leave?

I can't hide here anymore. I'll go back to Denver and I'll lure the monster out of hiding. And once he's out, I won't shrink back, I'll gladly let him devour me whole.

FORTY

TRAVIS

"IS KATYA NOT WORKING TODAY?" I try to keep my tone casual, but once Summer narrows her eyes at me I know I'm busted.

"Katya quit. Daniel said she was moving back to Denver. It's better this way. That girl was a media circus just waiting to happen."

I clench my fists and Charlie moves her head onto my knee, watching me warily. "Are you responsible for this? You defend her a few months ago, but the minute you find out she's got a past you turn on her? That's pretty low, don't you think?"

Summer sighs. "Do you want your damn pizza or not?"

"Just tell me why she left."

She drops her notepad onto the table and slides into the booth across from me. "Fine. Yes, I'm partly responsible for her leaving. She was asking me if you had friends, wanted to know more about you. I may have brought up the fact that she's dating a football player and how she'd never fit in here. Do you really want our town to turn into some celebrity hot spot because of her?"

My fist connects with the table and Charlie's head shoots up, ready to act. "Goddamn it, Summer! You really believe that? You really think that someone who survived what she did should be treated like shit because of her career?"

"Travis, please let me explain."

I stand up angrily. "I guess you're not who I thought you were. Maybe no one in this town is."

I can't believe this. How much longer until they throw me out of town because I carry my own bag of demons around?

Daniel walks in from the brewery just as I walk out. "Travis, what's wrong?"

Summer runs up behind us. "I'm sorry. If you'd just let me explain—"

She tries to grab me by the shoulder, causing Charlie to emit a low growl and bare her teeth.

"Don't. Either of you. You had someone who was trying to turn her life around—trying to be better in spite of what happened to her and you pushed her away—made her feel as if she didn't fucking belong. I hope you can sleep at night, knowing you basically gave her a death sentence."

Summer's hands drop to her sides. "Oh my god, Travis. You're in love with her."

I sneer, "Grow the fuck up, Summer," before turning to Daniel. "I want her number, since none of you assholes can be bothered to make sure she's okay."

Daniel brings a fist up to his temple, probably wishing he'd remained out in the brewery. "Travis, you know I can't give you her information—"

I hold up my hand. "Fine, I'll get it myself. Just know that if anything happens to her, it's on you."

Charlie gives another low growl and then prances out behind me. I'm glad to see that at least the two of us are on the same page. I drive back to my place, needing proof that she's really gone.

A small car is parked in her driveway and I have a small flicker of hope that she's decided to stay, until an older woman I don't recognize walks out carrying cleaning products.

"Hi, is Katya around?"

The older woman bites her lip and glances back inside, and my heart plummets with fear that she might've hurt herself. What if it was all too much for her? And here I've been, avoiding her while I sort out my own feelings. I don't want to push a romantic relationship on someone who's obviously been traumatized. That, and I also don't know if I'm capable of being in a relationship without hurting the other person.

I'd done it to Annie. I got overconfident, thinking I was better, only to snap and hurt the person I was supposed to love and protect.

"Katya went back home. I'm Jeanne, I just clean for her—well, for her father mostly." She thrusts her hand out and I gently shake it.

"Any idea on how I could find her? I wanna make sure she's okay."

She cocks her head to the side and studies me. "Are you Travis?" When I nod, her eyes light up. "Oh, of course you are. I've heard so much about you from Katya. Let me just get in touch with Niko, see if he wouldn't mind me giving you her information."

I thank her before mentioning, "You know, we're just friends, right? It's not like that between us."

Jeanne winks at me. "That's what they all say, honey. I know that look when I see it. Come on inside and let's get you to your girl."

"There's really nothing going on between us, Jeanne. I swear to you."

She smiles as though my words make no difference. "You may not see it, but I do. You could be the one to save her."

I actually laugh out loud at that one. "I'm no one's savior."

FORTY-ONE

KATYA

"IS THERE anyone else who'd like to speak?" Jo gestures to the podium in front of her and I tentatively raise my hand.

"Kat, okay. Come on up here, love."

There's polite clapping and a *'go get 'em, tiger'* from Lee as I walk up toward the front.

I place my damp palms on the wooden podium. "Hello, I'm Kat, and I was the victim of domestic violence." I pause and stare down at the various pamphlets and literature on assault adorning the top of the podium, trying to catch my breath. There's a lump in my throat and I feel as though I can't breathe. The back door squeaks as someone arrives late. I mentally talk myself through it. Then I look up at the bright lights above me, take a deep breath, and begin.

"I fell in love with a man and for a long time I let that love excuse a lot of bad behavior. He never got physical with me then, but he would say things—little comments here and there. Like, he cheated on me...a lot. He always had an excuse though. If I hadn't been traveling for work...if I'd shown more attention during dinner...if I would've dressed up more—I heard it all.

"I finally got strong enough to end things—I was living in Denver again and he was still in Texas. Last August I made the decision to visit him, and it got violent. I haven't heard from him since then, but I just wondered if maybe anyone else had experienced feeling like you don't belong anywhere?" My voice cracks and a few tears drop onto my cheeks.

Jo stands up and comes over to me. "That was quite a lot to share at once. Don't push yourself too hard, Kat." Her words give me small comfort as I sit back down in my chair. I had to tell it, had to force the words out of me or live with demons for the rest of my life.

Lee leans over and pats the chair in between us. "You did good up there. And no, you're not the only one who feels like you don't belong. I sometimes feel as though I'm on the wrong planet—I can't relate to people like I did before."

Marissa, who'd shared her story my first visit, turns around. "You should grab coffee with us after this—join our little band of misfits."

I smile at her. "I'd like that. It'd be nice to just feel normal again, even if it is temporary."

So, maybe I don't socialize with the people who knew me before. Maybe I don't seek out new friendships, like I'd attempted in Cedar Ridge. Maybe I don't think about greenish-blue eyes and the secrets and pain they seemed to be hiding.

As Jo begins talking about building a support group of other survivors—a group that can be reached anytime, day or night, I feel a sense of repulsion. I don't want to only associate myself with people who've experienced trauma. I don't want to be responsible for talking someone else off the ledge in times of stress.

Lee and Marissa begin rattling off the names of several nearby coffee houses when Jo ends the meeting, but I find my thoughts drifting.

"Kat?"

I blink and look back at them. "I'm sorry—what did you say?"

Lee smiles and I notice that one tooth is slightly turned inward from the rest. It doesn't detract from his looks; if anything, it gives his smile character. "I said I think we're going to head over to *Roasted*, maybe catch a movie after. You in?"

"Let me think about it." I stand up and follow the others to the door, almost as if on auto-pilot. My eyes remain on the concrete floor in front of me as I'm herded out of the building.

"You belong when you're with me. You know that, right?"

My head jerks up at the voice and there he is, standing near the front doors.

Travis.

I stop moving and several people slam into my back before muttering their apologies and stepping around me. A few others stop when they see Charlie.

"Kat, should we just meet you at *Roasted*?" Lee asks.

I turn to him. "Lee, can I take a raincheck on that?"

He smiles. "Absolutely. See you next week."

Then he's gone and it's just us. "You came all this way for me?"

He nods, keeping a tight hold on Charlie's leash. "You didn't even say goodbye. You were just gone."

I run my foot along a crack in the sidewalk. "It just seemed better that way, you know?"

"Not for me, it wasn't. You said in there that you felt like you didn't belong. I know what that's like, Katya, but you will always have a place with me."

I don't have to think anything over. I put one foot in front of the other until I'm in his arms. "I missed you, asshole," I murmur into his chest.

His laugh vibrates against me. "I missed you too, Princess."

"SO, how exactly did you find me?" I ask as I unlock the door to my condo. Travis and Charlie follow me, his eyes taking it all in.

"I talked to Niko. He and I met for coffee earlier today and he gave me your address. I waited around for a while and when you didn't show, I called him back. He said you sometimes attended a support group downtown. So I went there."

I set my purse down on the dining table and turn around to him. "My father met you? How was that?"

He shrugs nonchalantly, but the corner of his mouth turns up in a small smile. "It was great. He told me how much you meant to him and I shared with him the fact that you curse like a sailor."

I swat him on the arm, earning myself a warning growl from Charlie. "No, you did not! My reputation's gonna be ruined now!" I fail to hide the grin on my face.

What if he doesn't want to be more than friends though?

My hand's still resting on his muscular bicep when it hits me. I'm sober—have been since I left Cedar Ridge—and I still want him.

Badly.

"Nice place you've got here." He helplessly looks around the condo, searching for a change of subject. I would've laughed had I not been so afraid of his rejection.

"You never told me why you gave me the cold shoulder, Trav. You left my house that night and then dropped off the face of the earth."

He bends down and lets Charlie off of her leash, allowing her to roam for the moment. "I just don't want to lead you on. I can be your friend, but that's it."

I should be worried about the copycat...about what I'm going to do for work...about a million other things, but I can only focus on him.

I run my hand lightly across his arm and his eyes widen. Then I move until our bodies are touching, my hand moving up to cup his cheek. Travis shakes his head slightly, while I nod earnestly back at him.

He abruptly steps away. "It's late. I should get home."

The tears threaten to spill over as my hand drops down to my side. "Why? Why won't you let me in? Am I that broken?"

His fist comes up to his mouth and he shakes his head. "No. It's me, Katya. I told you."

"Stop it! Stop lying to me. You came all this way to get me to come back with you, yet you're already pushing me away again. Tell me why. You at least owe me that."

He turns away from me and grabs Charlie's leash and I double over, clutching my chest in pain. I physically hurt, knowing that he's about to walk out that door.

His hand reaches for the doorknob when he suddenly changes his mind. Charlie cocks her head to the side, studying him intently. He turns back to me. "You want the real me?"

I brace my hands on my thighs and nod. "Please."

He drops the leash and his hands move to the belt on his jeans. I stumble back, hitting the kitchen island with my elbow. "Wait..."

Oh Jesus, I might not be ready for this after all.

"Trust me?"

I nod uncertainly, still unsure of what exactly he's about to do. He unbuckles the belt and button before lowering the zipper on his jeans. Here I stand, transfixed in shock.

"Katya, breathe."

I inhale and exhale forcefully as he pulls his jeans down over his hips. His dark grey boxer-briefs fit his body like a glove, leaving nothing to my imagination. Then he lets the jeans fall to the floor and my lip begins to tremble.

It's what no one else has seen.

It's why he only runs at night.

It's how he knew I wasn't okay when no one else did.

Travis's left leg ends just above the knee.

The titanium prosthesis peeking out from under layers of black spandex is the only clue that he's lived through a hell not too dissimilar from mine.

FORTY-TWO

TRAVIS

I HOLD my breath and wait for her reaction. When she sinks down onto the designer tile floor meant to look like hardwood and begins to sob, I know it was a mistake. I should've left her with assumptions, instead of burdening her with the truth.

I've never been so afraid to show someone. I've been with countless women since it happened and there's always been this defiance in regards to my leg.

Take it or get the fuck out.

With Katya, it's different. I wanted her to see us as the same. I needed her to know that she wasn't the only one who was broken. Damaged goods come in all forms.

I pull my pants back up and fasten them, just as she speaks.

"So, you're not repulsed by me?"

I stand still for a second, unsure if I've heard her correctly or not. "Repulsed by you? Were you just here for this? I'm missing half of my fucking leg, Katya."

She wipes at her eyes and sniffles. "I'm relieved. I know you must think I'm crying because it bothers me, but it's tears of relief."

I know two things then.

She's absolutely gorgeous—inside and out.

She's also clearly insane.

"How would seeing that relieve you?" What I want to do next hinges on her response.

She smiles and sniffs again. "Isn't it obvious? I've got feelings for you and I think—"

I lift her up off the floor and press my lips against hers. Her hands come up and cup my face, stroking me, encouraging me to continue. Her lips taste like cherries and my tongue darts out to lick along the bottom one.

She lets out a small sigh, allowing my tongue to slip in. I'm sure most guys were drawn to her because she'd made a career out of walking around in lingerie. That hadn't done it for me though. It was her flaws...her weaknesses. All the things she'd kept hidden that I'd seen clear as day.

The fact that she got up every day and tried again, even if she'd drowned her sorrows in a bottle of vodka the night before. The fact that she'd shown back up to the restaurant, knowing that everyone had seen the commercial. All of those things made her irresistible to me.

"You okay?" I whisper against her lips. I don't want to push her too far.

She brings my mouth back to hers, while muttering. "Just kiss me, asshole."

I lightly bite down on her lower lip and she giggles. The sound just makes me harder as my mouth latches back onto hers, my tongue pushing past her lips again. I use my mouth and tongue to articulate everything I can't say aloud. My hands move up to the nape of her neck, dark strands of her hair tangling in my fingers.

I pull back and try to clear my thoughts, my forehead resting against hers. "Katya, I don't know if I'm capable of more."

The words are a confession. I can fuck her with my mouth, my tongue, but can it ever be more than that? Could I trust myself to be in a relationship without hurting her in the end, just as I'd done with Annie?

She blinks slowly, as if she's trying to wake up. "Me either."

Both of us stand awkwardly, our arms still around each other until Katya clears her throat. "So, will you stay the night with me now?"

I take in the walls of windows overlooking the mountains and Denver skyline. This condo has to be worth half a million dollars easily. It had been easy to forget that her former career paid her well when she was living in the small cabin next door. Here, not so much.

"Do you like living here?"

She shrugs and moves away from me to grab a bottled water from the fridge. "I bought it because of the view. I stayed because it never gets fully dark. It doesn't matter how late it is, there's always some form of light coming in. I um...I don't really like the dark. Want me to grab you one?" She holds up an extra bottle and I nod.

"I saw you outside a lot though. It gets pretty dark back home."

She passes me the water and we walk toward her bedroom. "Yeah, I don't know why being outside made me feel safer, but it did. Plus, I knew you were just feet away most of the time. Speaking of—how do you sleep?"

I laugh uncomfortably and take a drink, missing the taste of her already. "I don't."

She nods at my answer. "So, you gonna agree to the insomnia party or is it just gonna be me and Charlie?" Charlie rolls over onto her back, giving us an upside down smile.

"I'll stay, but my leg—"

She places her hand against my mouth. "I didn't expect you to keep that on all night. I imagine it would get uncomfortable."

"Maybe we could just lie in your bed and watch a movie?"

She pulls some clothes from the dresser before passing me the remote. "I'll be right back. Pick whatever you want."

Charlie jumps up onto the foot of the bed as I pull my shirt off, walking in circles before finding the perfect spot. I can hear water running and Katya humming from the bathroom as I sit down to take off my leg. I release the white valve, allowing the air to break the suction, before removing the protective sock and letting my leg breathe.

The bathroom door opens up just as I recline back against the pillows. "Oh, I'm sorry." Katya turns back toward the bathroom.

"It's fine. You can come in."

She walks over and sits down near Charlie on the bed. "Does it hurt?"

I massage my thigh. "I don't know how to describe it—it hurts, but more of an 'I'm used to this' kind of hurt."

She begins to reach toward me before stopping herself. 'Sorry, is it okay—I mean—"

I chuckle. "You can touch it, Katya. You won't break me."

She bites down on the corner of her lower lip in concentration and tentatively places her hand on me. She begins making small circles around my thigh, her fingers tracing along the shrapnel scars. "I never would've known. I mean, you run. You don't walk with a limp."

I bring my hand down to rest on top of hers, trying to slow her movements. I'm getting hard again, but I need to take things slow with her. My voice comes out sounding strangled. "I've...uh...I've had it for almost nine years. You learn to adjust. Come up here. Lay with me."

She crawls up the bed toward me and I think that Selvaggia might've missed their mark. Katya's sexier than ever wearing a pair of baggy sweats and a faded Pearl Jam t-shirt. She settles against my body as I flip channels, deciding on *Mr. Smith Goes to Washington.*

Her hands move over the tattoos covering my arms and chest. "What do they mean?"

I glance down to see what she's referring to. Her hands trace over the Eagle, Globe, and Anchor tattoo across my bicep. "That's the symbol for the Marine Corp," I point to words woven together underneath, "This is 'Semper Fidelis,' it means 'always faithful.' The motto of the Marine Corp." I don't want to talk about the names taking up most of my forearm—it's too personal. Thankfully, she doesn't push.

"Where did you go when you left?" Her voice sounds drowsy while her fingers make slow, lazy circles across my stomach.

I shift against the pillows, pulling her body closer to mine. "I went home to my parent's ranch in Oklahoma for a week and then I went to Virginia to um—to see some old friends."

She yawns. "I'm glad that you have friends. I worried about that with you living alone. The one thing I can't picture though is you on a ranch. I can't even imagine you in a cowboy hat and boots—do you have to wear spurs when you're there?"

I laugh softly. "I think you watch too many movies. I usually just wear a t-shirt and jeans."

Her voice gets softer. "Hey, Travis. Remember earlier when I said I didn't think I was capable of more either?"

"Yeah?"

She moves her hand up to rest on my chest. "Well, I didn't say it, but I'd be willing to try to be with you."

I softly kiss the top of her head, my heart racing with excitement. "Me too." I'm not quite ready to tell her everything just yet...but soon.

I wait until her breathing is deep and even before admitting, "I stayed for you that day we met in the elevator. I don't even know how long I sat in the lobby, just waiting for you to come out. You never did though. I didn't even know what I was going to say—I just knew that I wanted to see you again."

FORTY-THREE
KATYA

I FORCE MY EYES OPEN, trying to process what I just heard. The television's still on, some infomercial for an egg skillet. I hear the sound again and look over to my left. Travis is fast asleep, snoring next to me. His mouth hangs slightly open, his lips twitching every few seconds.

Charlie raises her head up off of her paws and eyes me warily, as if she's urging me to ignore him and go back to sleep.

Sleep.

I was sleeping, but I can't recall any nightmares. I roll over to check the clock.

Five AM.

I just slept for five hours straight. Travis inhales again, his nose whistling loudly, and I smile to myself before curling up against him. He's better than any dreamcatcher. I lay my head against his chest, hearing the steady beating of his heart. It's enough to lull me back into unconsciousness.

TRAVIS JERKS IN HIS SLEEP, waking both of us in the process. He sits up abruptly, rolling me off of him. I brush the hair out of my eyes and grin up at him.

"Good morning, sleepy head."

He looks over at me, his hair and beard poking out in every direction. "Are you okay? Did I hurt you?"

I shake my head, grin still in place. "No, but you snore louder than anyone I've ever met."

He runs a hand through his hair, his lips turning up in a smile. A real smile. "No, that can't be right. Are you sure it wasn't Charlie?"

I smile wickedly and glance at the clock again.

Nine AM.

He and I just managed to sleep a full nine hours, nightmare free. I don't know what that means, but I do know that it's a first for me.

I stretch my arms above my head. "I can't remember the last time I slept like that."

"I don't know that I ever have." Travis grabs the silicone sleeve from the nightstand. "Do you have some rubbing alcohol?"

I get up and grab it from the bathroom. Travis coats the sleeve with the alcohol and rolls it on as I watch intently. Then he grips the black compression sock and puts it on, before pulling a hard plastic sleeve over everything. The final step is pulling the prosthetic leg over to the side of the bed and using his body weight to lower his left leg into it. There are so many steps involved, but he performs the task almost mindlessly.

"How does it stay on?"

He glances over his shoulder at me. "I gotta tell ya, Princess. I don't think I've ever had anyone show this much interest in my leg before. Other parts of me? Maybe. But usually not this."

He winks as he says it and I blush when I realize what he's implying. "Oh..." I try to keep my eyes on his leg, but after his comment I can't help myself. My eyes are glued to those boxer briefs.

"It's a vacuum. See?" He threads a small metal pin through the hole in the leg, locking it onto the prosthetic. "As I put weight on it, it forces the air out of this valve, creating suction. Would you mind grabbing my backpack for me?"

I go out into the living room to grab his backpack off of the couch. I'd thought it was an overnight bag before, but as he opens it on the bed, I realize it's more of a survival kit. It looks like he even has ready-made meals down in there.

He grabs a tool that looks like pliers and connects it to his leg. "This is a vacuum pump—" He squeezes the handle several times. "It just ensures all the air's gone. See? Now, it's secure."

It's right then that I know, with him standing before me in nothing but his underwear and his hair an unruly mess, that I'm falling in love with him.

And I'm completely terrified.

This broken man who opened up and shared his secrets with me makes me want nothing more than to tell him all of mine.

LETTER

Katya,

I waited in the parking garage for you tonight. I wanted to talk about what went wrong between us.

But he was there. Him and that beast he calls a dog. I don't like dogs. Did you see it sniff the air? He knew I was just feet away from you. It didn't like that and bristled up. Good thing it was on a leash. I remained undetected. I watched you touch his arm and laugh like I was nothing.

Why? Why are you doing this to me?

After everything I've done for you. I made you famous! If I hadn't taken you...no one would even know who you are.

You owe me an explanation. My life has been nothing but misery since you left. I thought taking your friend would get through to you, but you haven't taken me seriously at all. Christine was a mean girl to you...I'll make her pay for that.

I'm going to make you take me seriously.

You think my love is temporary.

I'll show you how deep these feelings run.
I'll make you love me again. Just you wait...

FORTY-FOUR

KATYA

I HURRIEDLY CRUMPLE the note in my pocket before Travis can see it. He slams his truck door shut and turns back to me. "You got everything?"

I nod, while checking the backseat of the Jeep. I packed enough clothing to get me through the winter. I'm going back to Cedar Ridge. It's safer for me there. The note left on the windshield of my Jeep only reinforces that fact.

"I'll just follow you home."

Home.

It's funny that less than twenty-four hours ago, I'd felt like I didn't fit in anywhere. He's right though. I'll always belong with him. With him, things make sense.

His brokenness calls to my brokenness.

I'm expecting him to get into his truck, but he comes over to me, tucking my hair behind my ear. "See you in a bit."

His lips brush against mine, sending my lustful thoughts into overdrive. I feel guilty about it—as if I'm somehow less of a victim because I have these feelings.

Because it isn't just a kiss—to most people it would be considered a peck at best, not to me though. When his lips meet mine, it's as if he's throwing a lifeline down into the depths of my soul, pulling the old Katya back a little at a time.

I wait until he puts his truck in reverse before calling.

"Detective Sullivan speaking."

I sigh. "Mike, it's Katya. I got a letter."

His pen clicks in the background. "In Cedar Ridge?"

"No, I came back to Denver. I-uh- I needed a little break. It was on my car this—"

"What did I tell you about leaving? Jesus, Katya! What if he'd followed you inside? You could've been hurt or...or worse."

I follow Travis's truck out of the city, drumming my fingers against the steering wheel anxiously. "Mike, I wasn't alone. Travis was with me."

"Who the hell is Travis?"

I debate on what to tell him. *Who is Travis to me?* My boyfriend? My neighbor? The asshole who's stolen my heart? "He lived next door to me in Cedar Ridge. He came down to make sure I was okay."

Mike laughs humorlessly. "The guy with the dog? I think you might be better off with the guy leaving you notes. He seemed a little off when I met him."

Wait. Mike has met Travis?

"When did you meet him?"

"I met him the morning after...well, whatever it was between us. I tried to be friendly, but he seemed hell-bent on being a jerk. I just didn't get a good feeling from the guy—be careful, Katya."

I clench the phone tighter in my hand. "Mike, Travis is a good man. He's been through a lot, just like me. I really just contacted you to tell you about the note. I don't need advice on how to live my life."

He'd pushed me away. He doesn't get the right to give me his opinion now.

The pen clicking stops abruptly. "Fine. Get me a copy of it. I'll have someone check it out. Just—I just want to make sure you're not rushing into anything. You've been through a lot."

I end the call and fight the urge to scream. I'm not rushing into anything. I've kissed Travis and haven't thought of Landon once during it. I did that while sober—not to prove that I'm not broken, but because I'm attracted to him. I'm still listening to my body and my mind. While they aren't quite on the same page yet, they're at least in the same book.

Travis inspires me. He instills hope that I can awaken from this nightmare and walk in the light again.

It's progress, and I'm not about to let anyone take it away from me. I'll send him a picture of the damn letter and make sure I keep our conversations strictly professional from here on out.

"DOG GROOMER?" I hold up the newspaper and point. Travis sits on the other end of the couch, holding my feet in his lap. Every so often he'll run his index finger along the bottom of my foot, from heel to toe, checking my 'reflexes.'

He does it again and I jerk my foot back, eliciting yet another laugh from him. "What do you know about dog grooming?"

Shrugging, I bring the paper back down and turn to the next page. "Isn't there anything I can do?"

"I thought you weren't going to rush into anything. You've only been back a few weeks—God, your feet are like ice cubes." Travis gets up and goes over to stoke the fire, grabbing a grey woolen blanket from the arm of the chair on his way back to me.

We've settled into a comfortable routine since coming back. I still worry that maybe things are moving too fast too soon, but being with him feels so right. I don't feel as though I'm forcing myself either. Each kiss, each touch, leaves me craving more. I haven't opened up about what happened to me, but it's if he knows everything already, and he hasn't pushed me for more.

I don't know how much he read about it online. I know that I'm going to have to tell him sooner or later. It's only fair.

"Trav, do you ever think about following your dream and opening that gym?" I move the paper out of the way, as he drapes the blanket over me. I'm not sure that I'm going to last through the winter if it gets colder than this. I got spoiled living in Denver. I always knew I had until Halloween before it got really cold. Travis said that once it starts snowing, it'll stay cold until spring. While I love the snow, I have a feeling that I'm going to need to hibernate inside until it's gone.

He finishes covering me up before sinking down onto the end of the couch, my feet tucked under him. "I don't know. I guess I hadn't really thought about it much. You're really hell bent on finding something to do, aren't you, Princess?"

He leans over and squeezes my thigh playfully and I fight back a giggle, pushing his hand away. "Stop tickling me, babe—" I stop talking mid-sentence. *Did I just call him babe?*

Travis gives me a strange look. "What happened to *asshole*? That was really starting to grow on me."

I pull my knees up to my chest. "That's what I meant."

He grins and moves closer. "Is that right? Just a slip of the tongue, yeah?"

I groan. It isn't and he knows it. I tug on his shirt, pulling him closer. "I don't know what this is, and I don't want to get too comfortable just yet."

He brings his face down to mine. "Katya, I'm there too. We put up walls because we're afraid to trust—if we let our guard down, we could get hurt." He pulls back and stares into the fire.

"When I was in Iraq, I felt like I was constantly on alert. We got a call about a disabled vehicle—I was part of the QRF," Seeing my confused face, he amends, "Quick Response Force, sent to retrieve it. I was the Convoy Commander, so the vehicle I was in was at the front of the line. They train you, if you see anything suspicious you call it in. My buddy, Carlson, was cracking jokes to break the tension. We were supposed to go home right before the holidays, so he thought it'd be funny to pretend to be Santa, asked everyone what they were going to ask for when he 'came down their chimney.'

"I never told anyone, but I saw it. Piles of dirt or garbage were often used to disguise roadside bombs. Maybe two seconds before we hit it, I saw a small mound of garbage up on the left side of the road. I didn't react immediately—which wasn't the norm for me. When I came to, I was about ten yards from the Humvee. My left leg was shredded—I wasn't quite honest with you a few weeks ago—about where I went in Virginia." He pushes the sleeves up on his shirt and points to the names woven around his left forearm.

Luke Carlson and Chad Moore.

There's a date connecting the two names—November 4, 2006.

The day they died.

"I told you I was in Virginia, and that's the truth. I was there visiting friends—those two friends just happen to reside at Arlington now. My two best friends are dead. They died because of me."

He closes his eyes, no doubt reliving every second over and over again in his mind. I stroke his cheek with the palm of my hand. "You can't know that it would've changed the outcome, Travis. There wasn't enough time."

He moves away from my touch. "It could've saved everyone. I just kept my fucking mouth shut and let my brothers die. Do you know why I haven't been able to sleep, Katya? Because every fucking time I've closed my eyes, I've been transported back there. I'm trying to save them over and over again. It's a different situation each time, but the outcome is always the same.

"I wouldn't allow myself to get close to anyone and then I met Annie. She stuck with me through a lot of shit. I still couldn't sleep though. The nightmares were so real and I worried that Charlie wouldn't react in time. It took a toll on our relationship, little cracks that seemed to widen as time went on. I had another nightmare, thought my bunker was surrounded, and I hurt Annie thinking I was saving Carlson."

I swallow past the lump in my throat. "I'm sorry."

He shrugs it off. "I'd given up and then you came along. I thought you were nothing more than a spoiled rich girl. When I saw you—what had been done to you, I wondered if you might be the answer. I thought we could fix each other—these two broken people that the world had given up on. That night at your place in Denver, when you didn't turn me away, I slept. I slept without any nightmares and felt like I'd found the fucking holy grail in your arms."

I feel the same way. I haven't needed copious amounts of vodka... just him. I know just as well as he does what a rare thing that is. "Are you as scared as I am that it might go away?"

He roughly pulls me into his arms. "Yes. Every second I'm with you, I feel like I'm holding my breath, waiting for the other shoe to drop. I know I've dumped a lot on you right now, but you have a right to know. And I don't want you feeling like you have to share anything with me. Just wait until you're ready."

I was raped.

I was beaten.

I don't even know if my body still works like it should.

The words stick in my throat. I want to tell him. I want to be as honest with him as he's just been with me, but I'm not brave enough.

Not yet.

My phone rings, saving me from my pending confession.

"Hello? Papa?"

"*Mishonok*, have the police given you any more information on the letter?" He's becoming increasingly worried. He's kept his distance since July fourth; fearful that someone would follow him to get to me. *"I cannot put you in danger again."* Mike had been in contact with both of us—I was thankful that he hadn't told my father about what had happened between us a few months ago or I'm certain Papa would've moved back in with me permanently.

"Papa, *ne volnovat'sya," Do not worry.* "I haven't heard from Mike, but I know he's working on it."

He sighs. "I don't like the thought of you all alone, not with a psychopath on the loose. They still haven't found that girl, *dushka*. Are you staying in at night? What about Travis?"

As if sensing his name has been mentioned, Travis strokes my leg through the blanket and I almost jump out of my skin. He's so quiet-I'd almost forgotten that he's sitting right next to me. He gives me a puzzled look and I hold up my hand, signaling that I'll be off the phone soon.

"Papa, I'm being very careful. I swear to you. Travis has been staying with me, okay? I'll call you as soon as I hear something."

His voice cracks slightly. "I love you, my Katya."

I close my eyes. "I love you too, Papa."

My head's hurting. I love my father, but he wants me to live as a caged animal until it's safe. There's always this pressure to live my life constantly looking over my shoulder—I'd done that in Denver. I didn't want to go back to that here. He worried enough for both of us, I don't know why he insists that I join him.

"You speak Russian like your father." It's a statement. A log crackles in the fireplace, sending sparks upward, and Charlie raises her head off of the rug to watch it.

I nod, massaging my temples to ward off the ache. "I do. Only when I talk to him though."

Travis gently pries my hands away from my head and replaces them with his own. "So, if I wanted to call you Princess in Russian, what would I say?"

I press my lips together, trying to hide my smile. "You picked an easy one there—*printsesa*. It sounds pretty much the same."

His hands drop to the base of my skull and his mouth moves closer to mine. "My *Printsesa*, Katya. I'll keep you safe. You have my word on that."

FORTY-FIVE

TRAVIS

I'M in over my head. Hell, Annie and I had been so reserved in our affection with each other, while I feel like Katya and I are on warp speed. I'd told her that I'd pick up dinner for us, but I really just needed to clear my head.

She'd brought up the gym and doing something with it and it scared me. I'd grown content to let the damn thing sit empty. It had been a crazy naïve dream to turn it into something, but when she mentioned it tonight, I'd considered what it'd be like to actually throw caution to the wind and pursue it.

I imagine the people that I could help, but more than that, I can see Katya running it right alongside me. We'd open it up to survivors of all kinds, help them train their bodies and heal their minds. The thought fills me with fear and excitement. I haven't been able to see a future with anyone except Charlie before. It makes me feel normal again; making plans with her.

Real life shit. Not the half-assed existence I've been calling a life.

"Hey Travis." Summer walks up to the hostess stand and I almost turn around and walk right back out. Cedar Ridge doesn't have a lot of choices for food. It's between here and the sandwich shop down the street.

"I just need to place an order to go—without your opinions this time, please."

She bites her lip as if she's going to say something, but keeps her eyes on the computer screen in front of her. "What'll it be?"

I order my usual large pizza with two drinks and her eyebrows raise slightly. "So, it's true. You went and got her?"

Charlie nudges my leg with her nose and I sigh. "Yeah, is that a problem?"

She immediately shakes her head. "No. I'd like to apologize to her. I was out of line. Do you think she'd be open to hearing me out?"

I'm pretty sure that I'm making the same expression that Charlie does when she isn't sure what I'm saying. "You want to apologize to her? This isn't some twisted plot to get a few more digs in?"

She pushes her glasses up on her forehead and wipes at her eyes. "No. I...I let my own past cloud my judgment of her. It wasn't fair and I've felt awful ever since. Could I stop by later?"

"I think she'd like that, Summer. She needs friends right now—not to be made to feel as if she doesn't belong."

She agrees and goes back to the kitchen to get our order. I hope she got my message loud and clear. I've read every article I could find online regarding Katya's abduction. There's very little in the way of facts; most everything I can find is celebrity speculation.

She'd gone to Texas to see her ex and then dropped off the face of the earth for four months. When they found her, she was severely malnourished and dehydrated. One report said she'd been raped repeatedly, but it looked like they later retracted that. Another claimed she'd done it all as a publicity stunt, which made no fucking sense. What woman would allow herself to be beaten and starved, not to mention the various broken bones she sustained, all for fame?

No, the truth of what happened is somewhere in the middle of it all. I just have to keep looking. The ex-boyfriend went missing not long after she was rescued and police still had no leads. She hasn't let on that anything's wrong, but why else would her father be so concerned? He's worried that this guy's going to come after her again.

I click on another article and read through it. The name Michael Sullivan sticks out and I realize that he's the guy who was at her cabin that night. I'd thought they were lovers, but he was the detective on her case—the guy responsible for finding her. Maybe I'll reach out to him and see what he can tell me, offer him my help in the process.

I study the picture of her lying in a hospital bed that *TMZ* so helpfully released. I memorize every cut and bruise, until I can see them with my eyes closed. And I decide then and there, as I wait for our food, that I'm going to find Landon Scott. And I'm going to make him wish he'd never laid a hand on her.

WE EAT in front of the television, Katya still bundled up in blankets on the side of the couch closest to the fireplace. Her eyes are glued to the screen, and I can't help but admire her profile. She takes a small bite of pizza, catching me out of the corner of her eye.

"Why are you staring? Do I have sauce on my face?" She brings her napkin up and dabs awkwardly around her mouth.

I disagree and smile. "No, I just like watching you."

Her cheeks brighten and she looks away. "Oh..."

"Is that okay, *printsesa*?"

"*Ty lutshe fsyeh na svyetye*" Her eyes sparkle with amusement as she says it and I have no idea what any of it means.

"Did you just call me an asshole in Russian?"

She giggles and takes another bite of pizza, refusing to answer me until she's done chewing. "Maybe."

I lunge to grab her and she scurries off of the couch, laughing wildly. "Don't you dare!"

Just as I catch her and lean down for a kiss, there's a knock on the door. I groan in frustration. This had better be good.

Summer stands awkwardly on the front porch and Katya shoots me a questioning look. "Did you know she was coming?"

"Yeah, she wants to talk to you. I'm just gonna run home and feed Charlie—give you two a chance to catch up." I hurried out before she had a chance to speak.

We make it inside my cabin and I lean against the door as I close it. "Jesus, Charlie. Did you see the look on her face? I thought she was going to kick my ass for that. I probably should've mentioned that Summer was going to be stopping by."

Charlie yawns and pads over to her food dish expectantly.

"Alright, alright. Let's get you fed."

I get Charlie squared away and then check to see if Summer's truck is still parked out front. It is, and I suddenly don't know what to do with myself.

If I go back over there, I run the risk of getting pulled into whatever it is they're having. So, I sit down in my recliner and turn on the television, flipping aimlessly through the channels.

I should call that detective.

I pull out my phone and look for his number at the bottom of the article.

"Detective Sullivan speaking."

I take a deep breath. "Detective, it's Travis Logan. I'm calling about Katya."

FORTY-SIX

KATYA

"I CAME by because I owe you an apology for the way I treated you."

I stare daggers at Travis as he all but runs back to his cabin. "Come in. You'll freeze out here."

She rubs her hands together near the fireplace. "Do you remember that night that you came over to my place? I wasn't exactly truthful with you about my past. I think both of us were keeping our secrets close, but in light of everything that's happened, you deserve to know.

"I was...God, you'd think after this many years, it'd be easier to talk about it. When I turned eighteen, I was released from the foster care system. I met a man when I was nineteen and um, we got married. I was starving for affection and desperate to belong to someone, so I ignored a lot of the warning signs."

I reach out and take her hand in mine. "Did he hurt you?"

She takes off her glasses and wipes tears away with her free hand. "No, never physically. He just was so damn convinced that he had his drinking under control and in the eyes of his family and friends, he was a saint. It got harder and harder to make excuses for his behavior. I loved him, but hated who he turned into when he was drunk.

"We were in a car accident and he ended up in the hospital. His family was very wealthy and I was so afraid they'd try to pin it on me to make him look better, so I took off. I pulled enough cash from the bank to keep me comfortable for a while and I left in the middle of the night."

She pauses and works through the emotions while I squeeze tightly to her hand. "Take your time."

She nods. "I ended up here. When I saw that commercial with you in it, I started to worry. What if the paparazzi showed up here? What if a picture of me made it back to him? I've just been so afraid that he'd find me and I'd have to run again. I took it out on you, but it's not your fault. It was a shitty thing to do and I'm so sorry."

I gently pull my hand away from hers and wrap her up in a hug. "It's okay, Summer."

She's sobbing in my arms when Travis and Charlie walk back in. He freezes and starts to back up. I would laugh at his reaction, but she's pretty upset. "Stop. You can come in."

He looks like a toddler who's been caught in the cookie jar.

Summer pulls away and wipes her streaming eyes. "I'm fine."

He grabs another slice of pizza before coming into the living room. "How come every time someone says they're fine, it's obvious that they're not?"

I shrug. "I don't know, maybe it's a reflex?"

"You guys friends again?"

I nod and drape an arm over her shoulder. "We're good. Thanks for telling her to come by...even if you forgot to mention it to me.

Summer smiles up at him with tear-stained cheeks. "Thanks, Travis. Listen, would it be alright if I borrowed Katya for the day on Monday?"

He looks to me and I agree. "What'd you have in mind?"

"Well, there's this new spa over in Snowcliff. One of my customers today was raving about it. It's only a half-hour away, so I thought we could go together, maybe grab lunch after?"

A spa day?

"I'd like that a lot."

She smiles again and stands up. "Well, I'd better get home and let you two lovebirds enjoy your evening."

I walk her out and come back in to find that Travis is missing.

"Trav?"

"In the bedroom." He shouts from down the hall.

I lock up and follow the sound of his voice. "What are you doing?"

He looks up from one of my dresser drawers. "Do you have oil...or lotion?"

I point toward the bathroom, confused by his actions. "There's some lotion in there. What do you need it for?"

He retrieves it and strolls back in with a mischievous smile. "Summer gave me an idea. I want to give you a massage."

My eyes widen. Out of all the things he could've said, I was not expecting that. Kissing is one thing, rubbing my body is quite another. I can't believe I agreed to go to the spa without considering exactly what that means. Maybe if I request a female, it'll be better. I hope.

"Hey now, don't flip out. We can go slow—I just thought it'd be something new to try." He steps closer and reaches for my hand.

I nod dumbly. "I...I think...okay."

He runs his hand through my hair. "We'll leave the lights on. Do you trust me?"

"Um, yes?" My voice squeaks and he begins laughing.

"You sure about that, *printsesa*?"

I let out a nervous giggle. "Can I keep my underwear on?"

His eyes move down my body and I watch his Adam's apple bob as he swallows. "Uh, absolutely. I'll just step—"

He stops talking mid-sentence as I strip off my sweater. I'm not self-conscious about this part. I've done enough modeling that it's the equivalent of putting on work clothes for me. My jeans come off next and I fold them over the small chair in the corner.

"Do I just lie on my stomach?"

He nods and slowly pushes the sleeves on his Henley up, as if he's in a trance.

I inhale and exhale slowly. I'm safe. Travis's hands gently touch my skin and my body immediately goes taut with fear.

"Dirty girl..."

No.

Coco Chanel. Calvin Klein. Christian Dior. Ralph—

"Deep breath. I'm not going to do anything you don't want me to do." He speaks the words softly, yet somehow loud enough to drown out the ghosts.

I focus on each breath, my body relaxing beneath him, as his hands glide across my back. He takes deep breaths right along with me and I find that just hearing him calms me. Each touch is like striking a match within me, building an inferno of desire. His hand slips under the band of my bra and I moan into the comforter.

He freezes. "Are you okay? Is it too much?"

I shake my head, keeping my face hidden. I'm sure that my cheeks are crimson with embarrassment. "You can unhook my bra if you need to."

I hold my breath in anticipation, releasing it softly when he shakily unclasps the hooks. His fingers gently knead the muscles in my back, and I ache to feel him on the rest of my body.

Travis's breathing sounds a little strained and I know that he's just as affected as I am. Before I can change my mind, I roll onto my back, looking up at him. "Come here."

He bites back a groan and pulls his shirt off, before moving over me. "I didn't plan on this, I swear. If you want to stop—"

"Shhhh...just kiss me, *krasavchik*."

Travis chuckles low against my mouth. "Now, I know you're calling me an asshole."

He moves until his lips capture mine and I don't stop him. I don't interrupt to tell him that I just called him *handsome*, not *asshole* like he assumed. I don't tell him that what I said earlier was that he's better than anyone else in the world. Those are my little secrets for now.

I arch upward, locking my arms around his neck and pulling him down closer. "Is your leg—"

"Fuck, I'm not even thinking about my leg right now." His mouth presses lightly against the corner of my mouth and then down my jawline, while his hand skims up my ribcage, leaving goosebumps along my skin.

He moves his mouth lower, his tongue making a trail down my neck and then my collarbone. I grip him tighter, silently begging him not to stop.

"Is this okay?" He murmurs and I nod breathlessly.

Please.

His tongue traces a circle around one of my nipples and I moan loudly. He takes it as an invitation to continue and licks at both of them until they harden into stiff peaks. When he takes one into his mouth, my body goes haywire, and I grind myself against him.

"You taste so good..."

My heart plummets and I try to recover, but it's too late.

Landon bit into my shoulder, drawing blood. "You taste so good I want to mark your entire body with my teeth."

I release my hold on Travis, tears welling up in my eyes.

I can't do it.

He pushes himself up, whispering to me. "Hey, baby. Don't cry. Don't cry."

His words only make the tears flow faster and he sits back, pulling me into him.

"I-I'm broken. I tried, but I can't. I'm sorry, Trav. I'm so sorry."

He shakes his head, disagreeing with me. "Don't apologize. It was just too much at once. It's okay. Look at me," I brought my eyes up to his. "You are not broken. Do you hear me? I'm not going anywhere."

"I am. I'm broken—and instead of cutting yourself open, trying to sweep up the shards and piece them back together, you should run. Get out while you can." I bury my face in the crook of his arm and weep. He doesn't say another word, just holds me until there are no more tears left to cry. Charlie sits patiently on the side of the bed, her eyes darting between me and Travis as if she's asking him why I'm upset. I give her a small smile before my eyelids grow heavy.

Travis pulls the comforter back and settles me under it before stripping off his jeans. Next, he removes his leg, before climbing under the covers and pulling me close. With his arm draped around me, I fall into a deep and dreamless sleep.

"I NEVER THOUGHT I'd say this, but a couple's massage was a genius idea, Summer." I'd told her how nervous I was on the drive over, without mentioning the incident with Travis from Friday. She'd drummed her hands on the steering wheel as she thought of a solution.

Luckily, the spa was on board with her idea and we had our massage in the same room, just feet from each other. I was so relaxed that I ended up dozing off in the middle of it.

She leans back in the upholstered chair, stretching her arms over her head. "Hey, every now and then I have some good ideas. You still feeling okay?"

I take a sip of lemon-cucumber water and nod contently. After the massage ended, they brought us to a dimly lit room to rehydrate and relax.

"You ready to grab some lunch?"

My stomach rumbles in response. "I think that's a yes."

Jeanne had shown up to clean this morning and I could've knocked her over with a feather when I told her that Summer and I had plans.

"Go, go. I'll be cleaning all day so you might as well make the most of it. Do the spa, have lunch, see a movie."

She'd shoved me out the door with a huge smile on her face. I think she was probably just thrilled to not have me following her room to room and asking her a million questions.

I reluctantly part with the thick waffle robe and put my winter gear back on, just as my phone begins vibrating inside the small locker. I grin when I see that it's Travis calling.

"Hey stranger, missing me already?"

"Katya, you need to come home." His voice is strange, and my body instantly prickles with fear.

"Trav, what's wrong?"

Summer finishes adjusting her coat and comes over. "Is everything okay?" She whispers.

"There's...there's been an accident with Jeanne. She's in the hospital. Just...just get here, please."

My hand comes up to my mouth and I stand frozen in shock. "Summer, we need to go back. Jeanne...she's hurt. We have to go to the hospital."

I begin shutting down, trying to process what could've happened to the woman who's become a sort-of surrogate mother to me over the past five months. Summer doesn't even flinch at the news. She just calmly gathers our things and puts everything on her credit card before ushering me outside and into her car.

She somehow makes the thirty-minute drive in fifteen, with me sitting and praying in the passenger seat. She parks at the entrance and orders me to get out. "Go inside. I'll park the car. Just tell the front desk who you're looking for, okay?"

I walk past the sliding doors, the smell of antiseptic hitting my nostrils immediately. Memories from that night come to life and I walk closer to the desk in a fog.

Lights flashed overhead as I was wheeled down the hall. They'd asked me for my name repeatedly, but it hurt too much to speak.

"We're going to get you checked out. Is there anything you can tell us about what's happened to you? Anything that's hurting you right now? Ma'am?"

"Miss, are you okay?" An older man sits behind the desk, wearing forest green scrubs. "Miss?"

"She's with me, Ralph." I turn toward the voice. Travis's lip just barely lifts and I know that it's bad. Charlie stands nearby, looking relatively sedate given the circumstances.

"I got you, babe. One foot in front of the other, okay?"

I look up at him, everything feeling incredibly surreal. "Trav? Is she—" I bite my lip as my eyes well up with tears.

He shakes his head. "She's unconscious, that's all I know at this point."

Summer jogs up behind us. "Is there anyone I need to call for you, Katya?"

I struggle to remember. Jeanne and Clark didn't have any children and I don't know that she has any other living relatives.

Papa.

"I need to call my father. They were...they *are* friends." I hand Summer my cell phone and sink down onto a hard plastic chair. "What happened to her?"

Travis looks down at the ground. "I went on a run this morning—I never do that, but it was nice out. When I got back, I noticed your back door was slightly open. I thought it might've blown open when Jeanne was taking out the trash. So, I went inside and she was in the living room—" He pauses and presses his lips into a solemn line. "She must've tripped and hit her head on the coffee table. I called 911..." His voice trails off and he stares off into space, both of us fighting a losing battle with the past. I lace my fingers with his and place my head on his shoulder.

"Where is she? Let me past!" I lift my head, searching for the voice.

My father bursts around the corner, two men in scrubs right on his heels. Summer appears a few seconds later, holding my phone in one hand while the other points confusedly at him.

"I called him and then he came through those doors almost instantly. I thought you said he was in Denver?"

I cross the room to him. "Papa, what are you doing here?"

He hunches over the nurse's station and cries out. "Jeanne, please. Can someone tell me if she's okay?"

Travis comes over just as a nurse asks him if he's family. "She's my girlfriend. I need to know she's going to be okay. Can you take me to her?"

I give Travis a puzzled look and then turn back to my father. "Did you say she's your girlfriend? Have you been here this whole—"

The nurse behind the desk interrupts. "They're running some tests right now. She took a pretty nasty hit to the head. If you'll have a seat right over there, I'll come grab you as soon as I know something."

My father's like a lost child. Once Travis realizes that he's not going to move, he puts an arm around his shoulders and leads him over to a chair. He begins weeping into his hands and I kneel down in front of him.

"Papa, please talk to me. It'll help you."

He mutters in Russian before meeting my gaze. "My Katya. I've been living here since July. I came for the fourth and saw her— I didn't want you to feel as though I was crowding you, so I asked *Zhanna* if I could stay with her. I just wanted to be nearby in case you needed me. She and I—we connected and our friendship gradually became something more."

I'd worried that they didn't seem to hit it off that night we watched fireworks together, all for nothing. He'd taken care of it himself. I would've been overjoyed that they found love again, but Jeanne is fighting for her life. Travis squeezes my shoulders and I lean into him.

She has to be okay. My Papa has already lost too much. When my knees begin to ache, I move off of the floor and into the chair next to him. Summer brings my father coffee and sits across from us, our eyes glued to the door. If Travis hadn't found her—No, I can't let myself think that right now.

She has to be okay.

BODY FOUND IN CHERRY CREEK BELIEVED TO BE THAT OF MISSING MODEL

Denver, CO – Quite possibly a tragic end in the case of a 27-year-old Littleton woman missing since May. Model Christine Miller was last seen by friends in the early morning hours of May 14th.

Police were called to Cherry Creek near Four Mile Park just after seven Monday morning when two joggers reported seeing something floating in the tributary. A partially clad, bloated body was later retrieved.

"They initially thought some clothing had gotten hung up on low-lying branches, but upon closer inspection, realized it was a female," said Detective Shane Strohn with the Arapahoe County Sheriff's Office. Strohn was the lead detective on Miller's case.

"At this point, we're trying to determine how long the body was in the water so we can establish a time of death." When asked if police thought that the body was Christine Miller, Strohn responded, "It's definitely a possibility, but the body is badly decomposed, so an immediate positive identification just wasn't possible. We're going to leave that up to the coroner. My job now is to find the person responsible."

According to an eyewitness who chose to remain anonymous, the body was "weighted down with various chains."

Anyone with information about this investigation is asked to contact the Arapahoe County Sheriff's Office at (303) 795-1111.

FORTY-SEVEN

KATYA

I FORCE my eyes to remain open. I've had enough caffeine to last me for days, yet it doesn't seem to be working. Jeanne's been moved into ICU, and a nurse was kind enough to take my father back to her.

As far as they can tell, she suffered a traumatic brain injury when she fell. The doctors said she had some intracerebral bleeding so they had to perform a craniotomy to relieve the pressure. The nurse initially told us that she was opening her eyes to voice commands and struggling to make sounds, but the doctors still consider her to be in a coma.

I'd fallen apart at that. If I'd been home, she might not have fallen. I could've gotten immediate help for her. Travis just rocked me in his arms as I cried. He finally convinced Summer to leave a couple of hours ago. She'd been insistent on staying by my side until we had an update. It quickly became clear that there wouldn't be any such update.

"Katya, you need rest. Let me take you home."

I blink at him and disagree. "What if she wakes up?"

He pulls me from the chair, leading me out of the hospital. "Then your father will call. You can't sit here all night."

I stare straight ahead on the drive home, Charlie's head resting on my lap. It's as if she knows I need comforting. Travis pulls onto the gravel driveway in front of my place and shuts off the truck.

"Do you want to be alone?"

"What? Why would I want to be alone?"

He glances down at the steering wheel and then back over at me. "I just feel like I might've pushed you too far the other night. I didn't know if you'd want me to stay tonight or not."

I open the passenger door. "It's up to you."

Why? Why are we having this conversation right now?

Never mind the fact that he's stayed the other three nights with no problems.

He stays in the driver's seat as I trudge angrily toward my house. Charlie jumps down after me, only to pause when she realizes that Travis isn't coming.

My hands are shaking slightly as I unlock the back door. My house smells different, unfamiliar, no doubt the product of having police and paramedics all over the place. The coffee table has been moved and Jeanne's little duster sits alone on top of it. I cover my mouth as a strangled sob escapes my chest and I sink down into the chair near the fireplace.

"Hey, I wanna talk."

I nod without turning toward him. Of course he does. He's probably had all day to consider what a flipping basket case I am.

"Why aren't you a wreck over the fact that the asshole who hurt you is still out there? Another model goes missing and the police think it's the same guy. Did you know that?"

My head begins to throb. That's what he wants to discuss? The case? "I don't wanna do this tonight, Trav. I really don't. I'm trying to move on—"

"That's bullshit!" He shouts and I jump in fright. He quickly lowers his voice. "I can't touch you without you jumping out of your skin. You are not moving on- so don't give me the same fucking story you gave the media."

I clench my fists in my lap, refusing to look at him. "So, you read the stories. You know everything now, yeah? Why bother asking me?"

He whispers, "Why won't you tell me what happened to you?"

I close my eyes against a new wave of tears. "I'm broken, Trav. I'll probably be broken forever. It doesn't matter how it happened."

He sinks into the chair next to mine, our knees almost touching. "It matters to me, Kat. It fucking matters to me. I know about being broken. That bastard should pay for what he did to you. Don't you want that, baby?"

I stand up and move away from him, pacing. "It's not that simple, Trav. Please understand."

He sits back and raises his hands up. "By all means, Princess, help me understand. What happened to you?"

I shake my head from side to side, trying to push the words back down. I can't say them—I swore to Mike that I never would. "Don't make me do this, please."

Tears cascade down my cheeks and Travis clamps his lips together in an attempt to keep himself in check.

"I can't imagine what he did to convince you to let him get away with this. I want to love you, Katya, I do, but I can't compete with him. It's like walking a fucking minefield with you—I never know what's going to set you off."

"Then leave." I spit the words at him, sobs sending tremors through my body.

He brings his hand down on the coffee table, sending the small duster flying. Charlie gives him a low warning growl, which he promptly ignores. "Don't push me away! Just talk to me...make me understand this."

The words I've buried so deep, bubble to the surface in my anger. "I was raped, Travis! Every. Fucking. Day. Is this what you want from me? He would beat the shit out of me and then use my body for his pleasure. I was raped, but there were moments I actually got pleasure from it too. So, it's confused the hell out of me. I don't even know if it was truly rape!"

He sucks in a gasp, but I can't stop. The gates have been opened. "I didn't try to escape—do you know why? Because when he raped me, I convinced myself that he still loved me. That it meant we could still work. He didn't need my body bound in chains to keep me there; he had my heart. I let him tear apart my body and my spirit. I stayed willingly. I told you, he broke me, and there is nothing you can do to fix it! That's how completely messed up I am."

Travis and Charlie both approach me, one more cautiously than the other. "Baby, you are not broken."

I suck in a ragged breath. "I'm too far gone, Trav. I can't come back from this. I was bleeding constantly. I asked the doctor about it, concerned that it wouldn't stop. Do you know what she told me? She wanted me to know that she thought I'd still be able to have children—that's what she told me as I lay there. In what world would I be considering having children? There's no way I'd make a good mother."

"I want to kill him. Katya, say the word and I will pour every resource I have into finding him. You will not go the rest of your life looking over your shoulder."

I start cackling at his words, sounding like a movie villain, and he takes a step back. Charlie quickly follows, probably afraid that I'm about to completely snap.

Maybe I am.

"That's what Mike said. That night in the hospital...I shouldn't have to go through life looking over my shoulder. So, I lied in interviews...I made it seem like my life was perfect again. And I took the secrets from that night and buried them."

I want a drink. Fuck that, I want fifty drinks. I want to drown myself in alcohol until nothing else remains.

Travis moves closer and puts his hand on my shoulder. "What are you saying?"

Another laugh escapes past my lips, this one without humor. "You wanna know why I haven't been concerned with the police finding him? He's already dead, Trav. He's been fucking dead for months."

His hand drops away from me. "How do you know? What about the other woman that was taken? He could still be out there."

I disagree. "It's a copycat. Some sick fuck who wants me to think that Landon's come back for me. He probably still lives at home with his parents—spending his time in their basement, jacking off and hiding behind proxy servers. Hell, maybe Christine's the mastermind. I have the proof that Landon's gone—so, I haven't been afraid of the copycat. I survived four months with Satan himself. What could be worse than that?"

I can see him trying to piece everything together in his mind. I place a bet with myself on how long it'll take him to run. Every thought I've had regarding the copycat just came pouring out—things I haven't told anyone. Christine had hated me after I was rescued and I truly questioned whether her disappearance was legitimate or not. My mind swirls with dark things. Things that were never meant to be brought out into the light. "I let a monster make me into one as well."

"What did you say?"

I wipe more tears away. "I said that I let a monster make me into one as well."

His hands come up again, his fingers brushing away my tears. "You and I are not different, baby. I'm broken physically and you're broken emotionally, but it's all the same isn't it?"

I grip his forearms like a lifeline. "You are not broken, Trav. You're the best person I've ever known."

He leans in closer and I see in his eyes, the exact moment that the decision is made. His lips meet mine and I fall into his depths, his mouth claiming my lips, my neck, my breasts. For the first time since it happened, I feel free. I'm finally unshackled from the prison of my past.

He knows everything and he didn't run.

I let him lift me up in his arms before remembering his leg. "Trav, put me down—your leg!"

"Baby, I'm well aware of what my leg can and cannot do."

He carries me to the bedroom and lays me gently across the comforter. I watch, mesmerized, as he strips down to his boxers—his hands deftly removing the prosthesis.

"I know you're not ready. I just want to hold you. Would that be al—"

I stand up, pulling my jacket and long-sleeved shirt off, before tossing them across the room. His eyes follow my hands as I slide my sweatpants down and kick them across the floor. "What if you didn't just hold me? What if you helped me forget for a little while?"

I unhook my bra and let it fall to the ground, my thong quickly joining it. I stand before him naked—physically and emotionally. He lays back against the pillows and hooks his thumbs into the waistband of his boxers, inching them down over his hips. I start to close my eyes out of habit when he stops me. "Keep your eyes open. I'm leaving the lights on, okay? It's just Travis and his Katya right now...no one else."

I nod slowly, my eyes moving down his abdomen, and stopping at his erection. His hand moves down to stroke himself, his eyes never leaving mine. I climb into bed next to him, placing my hand over his and allowing him to guide me. My heart beats wildly with lust and fear, but his eyes keep me grounded in the present.

He moves, easing me onto my back. "I won't say a word after this, but I need to know how you want me. Tell me what you want, please."

I grab his hand and move it down my abdomen until his fingers brush against my clit, sending a jolt of pleasure through me. "Here. Touch me here." I guide a finger inside. "And here."

He makes what sounds like a cross between a groan and a growl before obliging. His hand moves slowly against me. "Faster...please."

His movements increase and I bite down hard on my lip, until I taste blood. His eyes never leave mine and it makes my orgasm that much more intense.

I come down from my high and he stills his movements. I gently push his shoulders, guiding him onto his back. His tongue darts out to lick at his dry lips and I lean over him, tracing them with my own. Then I reach between my legs and grip him before sinking all the way down on his shaft.

He keeps his hands at his sides as I rock back and forth. I grab one of his hands and place it on my hip, while I use the headboard to speed up my movements. His eyes tell me that he's close and I move faster, his other hand coming up to rest on my other hip. I come with a loud cry and squeeze the upholstered material so tightly that I'm sure it's going to break. Travis thrusts harder into me, pushing the boundary between pleasure and pain, before coming with a groan. His hands hold my hips in place and I place my head against his chest, his heart still thumping loudly.

"*Ty spas mena*, Trav. *You save me*. Just when I think it's all too much, when I'm drowning from it all, you're right there. Ready to pull me to safety." I shut my eyes and almost immediately doze off.

I'm not sure if I'm dreaming or not when I hear him whisper, "It's the other way around. You saved me, Katya."

FORTY-EIGHT

TRAVIS

I WAKE up to Charlie staring at me from the side of the bed and Katya fast asleep on my chest. I go to shift her and my cock slips free from her body. This induces a slight moment of panic at the fact that I came inside of her without checking first. I just wanted her to feel completely in control last night.

She rolls away from me, grumbling at the disturbance. I pull my leg on quietly, knowing that I'm going to have to redo it when I get home in a few minutes. Charlie follows me as I gather up my clothes, whining softly as she moves to the back door. I let her out and grab the pen and a pad of paper on the kitchen table.

I knew the minute I moved inside of her that this was it. She's breathed new life into dreams that I thought were dead. We'd freed each other and could start brand new.

Katya,

You were sleeping so peacefully that I didn't want to wake you. I want you to know that I'll be out of reach most of the day. I'm working on a little surprise that I think you're gonna like.

I love you.

I stare at those three words for what feels like an eternity, debating on whether or not to scratch them out. I finally decide that I'm done with secrets and leave them.

I can't wait to see the look on her face when she realizes what I've been keeping from her since yesterday.

FORTY-NINE

KATYA

I STRETCH my arms above my head as memories from last night flood my mind.

Had it all been a dream?

I shift and there's a slight ache between my legs. It had happened.

I roll over to find the other side of the bed empty and my heart sinks. Grabbing my clothes from the floor, I pull them on as I walk into the living room, praying that he's still here.

Empty.

Maybe he went on a run?

I pad into the kitchen to start some coffee when I notice the letter on the table. I read over it twice and grin happily. He hadn't left after all. He's just working on a surprise. I trace *I love you* with my fingernail, trying to match the loops and swirls of his handwriting.

I need to call my father and see how Jeanne's doing. I reluctantly leave the letter on the table to retrieve my phone from my purse.

Sixty-one missed calls?

I scroll through, but Mike's name is the only one listed. I click one at random.

"Katya?"

I clear my throat. "Is everything okay?"

He makes a strange sound. "What the fuck did you do? I need you to think long and hard about the repercussions of this, because we are all going down here."

PRETTY LITTLE LIAR?

If you've turned on a television in the last few months, you've seen her battered face pleading for an end to domestic violence, but was it all an act?

According to a source close to erstwhile lingerie model, Katya Egoricheva, she wasn't exactly truthful about her abduction. This announcement comes on the heels of yesterday's tragic news, when police recovered a body from Cherry Creek believed to be that of missing model, Christine Miller.

Our source, who wished to remain anonymous for safety reasons, reached out to *TMZ* when the information came to light. Katya has long since remained mum on what went on when she was held by ex-boyfriend, Landon Scott, late last year. When we asked where the former model has been hiding, our source led us directly to Cedar Ridge, Colorado.

"She's become increasingly paranoid and delusional since Chris went missing. It's like she knew she was going to have to come clean." Among the claims that are raising some eyebrows? Katya may have fabricated rape claims to medical staff after she was rescued late last year. Our source said she alluded to the fact that it may have been consensual. When we reached out to the hospital where the model was treated, we were told that they were not authorized to release any information on past or current patients.

"She told me that she never even attempted to escape." Police have long questioned why the former Selvaggia model never sought help after being abducted even when she acknowledged that Scott left her alone on multiple occasions. The model changed her story repeatedly, but it appears that she never once attempted to leave her 'captor.'

"You wanna know why I haven't been concerned with the police finding him? He's already dead."

And perhaps the most disturbing claim Katya has made is that Landon Scott has been dead the entire time. Police have spent countless hours searching for her kidnapper. According to Detective Shane Strohn with the Arapahoe County SD, "We've reached out to the Lubbock Police Department and informed them that the search into Scott's disappearance could possibly be a homicide investigation at this point." Police said they're not considering Katya a suspect at this time, but are interested in questioning her further.

According to Psychotherapist, Alice Martin, "When someone endures abuse of any form over a period of time, it can create a shift in perception—the lines between perception and reality become blurred. It's quite possible that she has invented these claims to help herself through a traumatic time."

A representative for the former model released this statement. "My client endured horror at the hands of someone she trusted. To imply that she fabricated the events or may be responsible for Landon's Scott's disappearance is reprehensible."

Katya Egoricheva has dealt with many issues over the past year and it may be premature to pass judgment until more information comes to light. If these claims are true, then Katya needs to be held accountable for her actions. If not, then she obviously needs to be hospitalized. This story will be updated as it develops.

FIFTY

KATYA

COLD HORROR COURSES through my veins as I read and reread the article. It doesn't matter that they cast doubt on the validity of the claims—the clickbait title and bold quote are enough to ensure that I'll be blacklisted from ever working anywhere again.

There's a picture of me and Summer leaving the spa after finding out about Jeanne—worry evident on my face. In another, I'm leaving Viktor's shop in Denver, several vodka bottles tucked under my arm.

My phone starts ringing. To be honest, it hasn't ever really stopped.

"Mike? I don't know who did this."

I can hear him walking, the wind whipping into the phone, punctuating his silence. "Who did you talk to? You do know, and don't give me any excuses. It's like trying to contain a fucking wildfire right now."

I stare at the words on my laptop screen, my tears falling on the keyboard. There's only one person I talked to—Travis.

He wouldn't have done this to me.

Right?

"I- I told Travis…last night. Mike, you don't think he did this do you?"

I hear his truck fire up before he answers. "He called me the other day…wanting information on your case. Said he just wanted to help. I need you to try and remember if you ever saw him in Denver—maybe at some of the same spots you frequented."

It couldn't be him, but then how else could I explain…

"Mike I saw him when I went to therapy once. We shared an elevator. It doesn't make sense though. The last note left on my car mentioned him in it."

"Katya, he might've mentioned himself in the letter to throw us off. Has anything suspicious happened recently involving him?"

Images of Jeanne flash through my mind. I'd wanted to believe she'd just fallen, but had Travis lied about that too? "My housekeeper was injured yesterday. Travis found her and called for help."

It wasn't Travis. It couldn't be Travis.

"Stay away from him. I'm trying to get a flight to you now. Don't try to confront him on your own, okay?"

I agree and hang up, feeling lower than I've been in a while.

My tears become full-on sobs. I feel so stupid. I'd fallen in love with someone who wanted to destroy me. It's just like the situation with Landon. *And Christine?* Had Travis been responsible for her disappearance too? He disappeared for months over the summer, but convinced me that it'd only been a week.

My phone chimes with a Facebook notification. It's from Landon's account.

"I have honored your request for silence and you've washed your hands clean of this."

Isn't that an Alanis Morrisette song?

I fold myself up into a ball on the couch, shaking uncontrollably. I know it will never end, and for the first time in a long time, I wish that Landon would've killed me that night.

FIFTY-ONE

KATYA

4PM

I TAKE another swig of vodka. My body's completely on edge—the caffeine, alcohol, and adrenaline acting as a triple threat. I'd given up on sobriety sometime after my father called to tell me that Jeanne was awake, but not speaking.

It had been my fault all along. As I sat there, listening to my father cry through the phone line, something inside of me snapped. Travis had said he'd be out of reach most of the day—he was probably busy feeding every news outlet in the country information on me.

I force myself out of the chair and stumble into the bathroom to vomit...again. I thought that having someone rape my body was the worst thing I'd ever experienced, but this somehow tops that. He'd raped my soul—and exposed my every secret to the world while doing it.

I finish purging and take another swig of vodka to rinse my mouth out. Thoughts of us together fill my mind and I lean forward to retch again into the toilet. I want to scrub my skin until it falls off. I feel dirty...tainted by him.

"Katya?" Travis's voice calls out from the back door and I freeze. His voice gets closer as he moves through the house and I fold myself into the corner, shaking so violently that my teeth hit together.

The bathroom door opens and he looks over at me. "Jesus, baby, are you sick?" He begins opening various cabinets and drawers until he finds a washcloth. I upend the bottle and drink until my eyes are streaming and my body is screaming for oxygen. The washcloth falls from his hands.

"What happened? Baby, why are you drinking?" He kneels down in front of me and I swear that the concern in his eyes is real.

I hiccup and immediately lean over the bowl again, just in case the vodka is about to make a reappearance. Once I'm sure that everything's going to remain inside, I answer him. "I got your surprise."

His mouth opens in shock. "You already know? How?"

"It's all over the fucking news, Trav. So, why are you here now? Did you come to finish it? Just do it. Pull the fucking trigger and put me out of my misery."

He moves off of the floor and sits down on the edge of the tub. "What are you talking about?"

I laugh bitterly. "You told the media everything I shared with you last night! This entire time, it was you. Did you hurt Jeanne too?"

He rears back as if I've slapped him. "How the fuck could you accuse me of that? I haven't talked to anyone! What happened last night was between me and you. Where is this coming from?"

I toss my phone over to him and he reads the article, shaking his head as if he disagrees. "I swear to God; this didn't come from me! You have to believe that."

"I thought it was perfect—what we had between us. I thought I might actually get a chance at normal again. I'm such an idiot though—thinking that you could fix things. Look everyone! Travis and his magical dick are here to put Katya back together—"

He slides down in front of me again, his hands digging painfully into my shoulders. "I didn't do this to you. Look at me! Damn it, Katya. Fucking look at me!" He shakes me and my head cracks against the tile wall. Waves of dizziness and nausea wash over me and I have to blink several times to clear my vision.

"Oh, Jesus. Katya, I'm sorry. I didn't mean—I'm sorry."

My voice comes out sounding raspy after being sick all afternoon. "Is it because I accused you of living in your parent's basement like some pathetic loser? Is that what pushed you over the edge? Just get it over with. You're good at hurting people—it's what you did to Chris, isn't it? Jeanne...I should be a piece of cake. I won't fight you...just make it quick, please."

Travis releases his hold on my shirt and stands up unsteadily, backing toward the bathroom door. "You think I'm responsible for this? You think that I'm going to kill you? I just made love to you less than twenty-four hours ago—how could you think that I'd want to hurt you?"

"You fucked me to get information. Don't make it something it wasn't."

Travis's fist connects with the doorframe, sending fragments of wood onto the floor. He stares at it in disbelief, as if even he's surprised by his actions. "Fuck, if that's what you think, then maybe it's best if I leave. I'm apparently nothing but a monster, hell-bent on destroying your life."

He doesn't wait for a response from me before storming out and slamming the door behind him. I heave a sigh of relief, immediatcly followed by more tears.

It doesn't feel right. How could he be the one responsible for all of it? It doesn't make sense. I try to recall everything I've read online. It all points to him being the *anonymous source*, but that picture of me and Summer. He couldn't have taken it. He was still in Cedar Ridge and had been at the hospital. The paramedics and police confirmed that.

That picture is just one of many things that isn't adding up for me.

Oh god...Summer.

Her picture's being posted everywhere online. I have to warn her.

I drag myself to my feet, swaying into the bathroom counter in the process. I just need to drink a cup of coffee and I'll go to her. Tell her everything and then figure out a way to get her the hell out town until it blows over.

Maybe Papa can help me.

Jeanne.

I mash my lips together as more tears fall. Everything's falling apart and I don't even know where to begin in order to fix it.

I WALK INTO THE RESTAURANT, still feeling slightly off-kilter. I had no business getting behind the wheel of my Jeep, but Summer deserved the truth.

Using the wall for support, I walk toward the server station. The restaurant's packed with the dinner crowd, but Summer is nowhere to be found. I run into Daniel as I turn around. "Summer?" I question him.

He points downstairs. "Lead singer of *Bohemian Experience* got sick halfway through the set—Summer offered to fill in." He runs off to check on a table, clearly running things while Summer's gone.

I walk downstairs and there she is, looking like she belongs behind a microphone. She croons into it, "*It's you, it's you, it's all for you. Everything I do...*" sounding just like Lana del Rey.

I wait until the song ends before approaching her. "Summer," I croak. The tears and vomiting have destroyed what remains of my voice.

Her head shoots up and her eyes widen in shock. "Katya? What happened? Come here."

I walk onto the stage and she immediately pulls me into a hug.

"Summer, I fucked up. Someone released pictures of me to the press. There's one of us leaving the spa yesterday. We have to get you out of here—just until this gets resolved."

She releases me, her elbow hitting the microphone stand, sending it crashing to the floor. "When were they released? Like hours ago? Yesterday? When?" Her voice gets higher and higher with fright.

"The story broke at three this morning."

She begins shaking her head. "No. No. No. That was fourteen hours ago. I have to leave. I have to leave right now. We have to go." She steps off the stage just as a band member walks over. "Summer, you can't leave right now. Please just finish one more song."

She hesitantly agrees as he picks the stand up off of the floor. "Just this and then I need to leave.

He nods and picks up the guitar. Then she takes a ragged breath and closes her eyes. It's like night and day; her entire body relaxes almost immediately. "*Hello…it's me…I was wondering—*"

I sink down into a chair near the stage, mesmerized. She sounds amazing. She belongs on a stage, singing every night.

The song ends and the room erupts into applause. Summer blushes and steps off stage. "Let's go," she whispers to me.

Maybe my father could think of somewhere she could stay. The clapping dies down, save for one person who won't quit.

"Bravo, Genna."

Summer freezes and tightens her grip on my arm. I turn to the familiar voice.

"Brody? What are you doing here?"

He doesn't answer me, his eyes locked on Summer. "Genevieve, if I would've known that a Selvaggia model would lead me right to you, I would've contacted Tom Brady years ago."

Genevieve?

"Brody, this is my friend, Summer. She and I were just leaving."

He laughs bitterly. "Summer? You changed up your maiden name? That's what you've been going by this entire time? Did you share with them how you nearly ended my football career and then skipped town?"

"We were in a car accident and he ended up in the hospital. His family was very wealthy and I was so afraid they'd try to pin it on me to make him look better, so I took off."

Brody's a recovering alcoholic—I only know because he confided in me when he found out that I drank to cope with the memories. It was why Summer had pushed me away after she saw the PSA. She was afraid I'd lead him here. And I had.

"Summer? Brody's your ex-husband?"

Brody corrects me. "*Estranged* husband—kinda hard to serve divorce papers to someone who disappears."

She takes her glasses off and sobs into her hands. "Why are you here, Brody?"

"Looks like you still refuse to learn how to play an instrument; instead relying on a band to cover for you." He's being incredibly cruel to her right now. I don't like this side of him.

"Brody, stop."

He shakes his head at me. "This doesn't concern you, darlin'. Give us a minute, yeah?"

Daniel runs downstairs. "What's going on here?" He looks at me and mouths, "Is that Brody Rodgers?" I nod, pulling him away from the two of them and back upstairs.

"Let's give them a minute to catch up." I don't know if it's right to leave her alone with him, but it feels like we're intruding on a very private moment just standing there gawking.

Daniel sits down on a bench near the entrance, working to catch his breath. I bet this is the first time he's sat down all day. "You doing okay? I saw all the work Travis has been doing downtown the past few days. He's had construction crews there working day and night to get the old building fixed up. It's going to look so good. You must be proud of him."

My heart bottoms out in my chest. *His surprise.* He's building the gym. That's where he's been—not revealing my secrets. That means that whoever's responsible is still out there.

"Daniel, I- I have to go. Just keep an eye on Summ—Genevieve for me, please."

I run out of the restaurant as he calls after me. "Katya? Who the hell is Genevieve?"

My cell phone vibrates as Mike calls, but I hit ignore and jump into my Jeep. I have to find Travis and make this right. Someone's trying to set both of us up.

I drive past the building on Main and while there are various crews working, I don't see Travis's truck. I turn around and head up toward the cabin, praying he's there.

His truck is parked in the driveway and I hurriedly run across the gravel to his front porch.

"Travis?" I bang my fist against the wood until it throbs. His house remains quiet though. I sink down with my back against it. I plan on sitting until he comes out, but the sky grows dark and small snowflakes begin to drift down around me.

So, I stumble across the dirt path and into my house, the alcohol in my system still making me feel unsteady. My phone vibrates from my pocket and I see that it's Mike again. I slide my finger across the bar.

"Katya? Where are you?"

I grab a glass and fill it from kitchen faucet. "I'm at home—why?"

"I need to you to get into your car and drive back into town. It's not safe for you—found evidence—Facebook released records—right all along—stay—" His phone's breaking up so badly that I can't understand anything he's saying.

"Mike?"

The line goes dead and the hair on the back of my neck stands up as I catch movement outside the kitchen window.

It's probably just a deer...or a raccoon.

I need to keep calm.

I crouch down and slide a drawer open, reaching for anything I can use as a weapon. My hands connect with a steak knife and I tuck it into the waistband of my jeans. My phone vibrates with an incoming text message and I quickly pull it off the counter and into my hand.

Restricted:

"Do you ever miss me? I think of you all the time."

My heart jumps into my throat as I see the three dots appear on the bottom of the phone screen. He's typing. This isn't happening. He's found me...maybe he knew where I was all along.

Restricted:

"Baby, I see you. Let me in."

I shove the phone down into my back pocket with shaking hands. I have to get out of here and get to my Jeep. The front door rattles loudly, as though someone has thrown their body up against it, and I cover my mouth, stifling the scream that's trying to force its way out of my throat.

I pull the knife free from my jeans, gripping the handle until my knuckles are white. I try reaching Mike, but his phone goes straight to voicemail.

The cops. I need to call the cops. I press the number nine, but freeze when I hear the sound of footsteps from inside the house. The stereo kicks on suddenly and Frank Sinatra's *Strangers in the Night* fills the house.

He's inside.

I tried to ensure that he'd never find me, but it wasn't enough. Now he's back to finish what Landon started.

My heart pounds violently inside my chest and I hold my breath as the steps get closer. I think of my father and Travis. And I realize that I'm not ready to die.

Not like this.

I need to run. I'm going to have to do now what I hadn't been brave enough to do then.

I block everything else out, but the sound of the steps, focusing on where they are in the house. There's a small crash from down the hall and I know it's going to be only my only chance to escape. I hold tightly to the knife and run for the back door. The music becomes much louder, making it hard to stay focused.

I yank the door open just as a body slams into me from behind, forcing it closed again. I suck a breath in to scream and a large hand clamps over my mouth, silencing me. I have to fight back, but I dropped the knife in the scuffle and I don't know where it landed.

Fight, Katya!

I kick wildly as the hand squeezes my face. My attacker laughs at my efforts and I shudder in fear. I know that laugh.

I feel the gun press against my spine. "Miss me, baby?"

FIFTY-TWO

KATYA

HE LOOSENS his hand on my mouth. "Don't scream. You scream and I will hurt you. Do you understand?"

I nod slowly, taking shallow breaths. He moves his hand away and guides me over to the couch. "Sit."

I thought he looked like Landon when I'd first met him. Now, as he walks around my living room, massaging his temple with the barrel of a gun, the resemblance is almost uncanny. Evil might take different forms, but it all looks the same in the end.

"Lee, why are you doing this? You of all people should know what violence does to someone. Think about your wife." My voice wavers, but I won't cry.

He lightly smacks the barrel against his forehead. "My wife. Jesus Christ—how could I forget about her? Oh, because she never existed. It was the only rape support group within three hundred miles. I knew if I kept going, eventually you'd show up, and your lies would begin to unravel."

"I don't understand. Why would you go to all that trouble just to meet me?" Maybe he is a stalker, someone who'd followed the tabloids and felt like he knew me. It had happened before.

He mimics my words, making me sound like a dumb blonde. "I didn't want to meet you. I wanted you to admit you lied. You see, I wrote a little article after you were rescued—it captured everything you went through. It was going to make my career.

"I posed as a doctor and gained access to your medical file, I had to screw a nurse in the process, but—I put in the work on this one. It wasn't like before...no, this time I was going to make a name for myself. I saw the photographs and the notes. You were raped. No one else knew that. I did though. I released it and your people threw a shit fit, demanding that we retract it."

He sits down next to me on the couch, slinging his arm around me as though we're close friends just catching up. Never mind that the gun is now pressed behind my ear. "I lost everything because of you. My entire career imploded because you lied. I hate liars, Katya." He hisses the words into my ear and I stiffen.

"What did you do to Chris?" I force the words through numb lips.

"Chris? You're worried about what happened to that bitch? She was in on this from the beginning. It was so easy getting her to feed me information that I could leak to the tabloids for a few bucks. She wasn't content to just remain on the sidelines though, so I recruited her.

"I quickly realized why I worked alone too. Jesus, was she a drama queen. She thought I could fake her disappearance and make her as famous as Landon made you. She tried to make it all about her though and that's not what this was ever about. It's all about you—nobody's star can ever shine as bright as yours."

My teeth begin shattering again. "You k-k-killed her?"

There's just enough moonlight streaming in for me to see him roll his eyes. "Of course I killed her. Have you seen the news lately? It's like talking to a fucking toddler here. She wanted to scare you and use your pain to climb to the top. I wanted to destroy you. Maybe *kill* is a bit too strong of a word—let's just say we had a difference of opinion in our business relationship and I terminated our arrangement."

The chattering becomes convulsions as I process what he's saying. "Jeanne? That was you too?"

He taps the gun against his mouth. "Jeanne...Jeanne... Oh—you mean the cleaning lady? Yeah, 'fraid so. I did not want to do that, but she surprised me." He reaches under the coffee table and holds up what appears to be a coin. "I needed a confession, so I may have planted a few of these around the house. You still somehow managed to come out of that unscathed though. It's like you're untouchable—well, up until now."

I hear a twig snap from outside and try to distract Lee from checking it out. I need to stall. "How did you access Landon's social media? What was the purpose of all of it?"

He looks out the window as if searching for something or someone. "It's not hard to hack accounts. As for the letters, they seemed like something Landon would've left. Real psychopath shit. Originally, I did it hoping to lure him back to you. Then it became increasingly obvious that he was never coming back. It makes sense now—it's why you came back like nothing ever happened. Your life was picture perfect."

I ball my hand into a fist. "Picture perfect? I was drinking just to get through the day without falling apart. You didn't have to do anything. My life was falling apart just fine on its own."

"Poor pitiful Katya. Your lies caught up with you—it's why you decided to pen a full confession before slitting your wrists in the bathtub. A fitting end to a life well-lived."

I wait until he turns and then lunge for the door. "Help me! Help me!" I scream for anyone who might be outside the cabin, hoping they'll hear me over the music. Lee catches me by the leg and I fall painfully onto the hardwood floor. I land on my wrist and it begins to swell almost instantly.

"I said not to do that. Did I not say that?" He pulls me up and inspects my arm. "I don't know how we're going to explain that. Your fucking wrist is broken."

Tears slide down my cheeks and I tell myself it's because I'm hurt, not because I'm scared.

There's a knock at the door and Lee's hand covers my mouth again.

"Katya? Can we talk? I know you're in there. Please, just humor me and open the damn door. I need to know you're okay." Travis's head rests against the glass and I cry harder. Lee spins me around and roughly wipes at my eyes.

"Answer the door, but if you tell him I'm here, I'll kill him. Are we clear? Let him know you're okay and send him away. This is between us. I will have a gun on him the entire time. So, don't get any bright ideas."

I nod and try to get my breathing under control. He's allowing me to say goodbye. Travis knocks on the door again, as Lee slips into the hallway. I open the door to snow falling down around him, sticking in his hair and leaving a light dusting across his beard. I try to commit every detail to memory. I want to remember him just like he is in this moment.

"Hey. Sorry, I was sleeping." I move my wrist behind the door, hoping that he'll accept my words and leave before Lee changes his mind.

He looks behind me into the cabin. "It's completely dark in there —you're scared of the dark."

I give a slight nod. "I fell asleep when it was still light out. I'll turn some on in a minute. You better get inside; it's really starting to come down."

It's ironic. I was rescued right before a blizzard. Now I'm going to die right during one.

"What's with the music?" He reaches out to stroke my cheek and I can't stop the flood of tears. I'd been prepared to die for Elizabeth that night—a woman I didn't even know. Dying in Travis's place was a no brainer. "You okay?"

I'll gladly give my life if it keeps him and Charlie safe. Love is sacrifice, I know that now. I had a good man's love—however fleeting our time may have been together. I'll go to my death knowing that his love pieced me back together.

"I'm fine." His eyes narrow at the words and I know he's going to say something stupid. He's going to get himself killed. I step out onto the porch and pull his mouth down over mine, and I feel his body relax. I sigh against his lips. "I love you, Travis."

I break away and turn to go back inside when he grabs my wrist, causing me to cry out in pain. He looks down at it, but I pull away. "Go." I whisper the words before shutting the door in his face.

Then I bring my hand up to my mouth, resisting the urge to scream in anguish.

He's safe.

Lee walks around the corner, slowly clapping his hands together, the gun still in his grasp. "Bravo. I mean, you had me in tears. You really should've looked at a career in acting."

I push past him and go back into the living room. "I wasn't acting. He's gone now, so do it."

He follows me in. "What—no begging? Just resigning yourself to your fate? That doesn't sound like the Katya that survived four months in captivity. Even Chris begged for her life in the end. No one wants to die."

I did. If it kept the man I loved safe, I would throw myself on that sword without question.

The front door clicks open again and I freeze.

No.

FIFTY-THREE

TRAVIS

"YOU KNOW, when someone says they're fine, it usually means they're not." I walk around the corner with a smile on my face. A smile that immediately fades when I see the man holding a gun on Katya. Charlie moves in front of me, the hair on her back bristled up. She lets out a low growl, ready to defend me if needed.

Katya manages to choke out, "Trav—run. Run!"

I'm not leaving her here. I've spent the last nine years searching for someone just like her—I'll be damned if he thinks he can take her from me. I can see it in her eyes. She wants me to go—she thinks she's saving me.

She inhales loudly, but it's like she's not getting enough oxygen. She whispers one word. "No."

"Well, this changes things a bit, but I'll improvise." He points the gun at me, just as I mouth for her to run.

She shakes her head vehemently. "I'm not leaving you."

"Katya, come here." She refuses to look my way as she walks over to her captor. I know that she's prepared to die for me, but I won't allow it. She made that decision when she was on the porch with me —I can see it written all over her face.

He grabs her wrist and twists it behind her back, causing her to bite down on her lip and let out a small whimper. Other than that though, she remains silent, tears running down her face. He puts the gun to her temple and she closes her eyes.

That's not how this is going down. I watch him like a hawk. He's sloppy and he's going to slip up. I fight the urge to attack, instead studying his every move.

He leans down until his mouth is next to her ear. "Now, here's how this is going to go down. You snapped after Travis found out about Landon. The man told the world your secrets...so you killed him. And then you just couldn't live with the consequences of that. See where I'm going with this? Fast forward to you slitting your wrists in the bathtub."

She shakes her head. "No, this is between me and you—not him."

He turns to look at her, his focus completely on her. That's all I need. This guy just fucked up—he turned his back on a Marine. A Marine who is about to tear him limb from motherfucking limb.

My body barrels into his, the force knocking Katya back into the fireplace. Her head hits the bricks, and she lies there stunned. I will her to get up while grappling for the gun. She sits up just as he glances a blow off the side of my head. The moment he makes contact, Charlie lunges at him, her teeth bared.

"Katya, get out of here!" I slip behind him, attempting to lock him into a chokehold.

She makes it onto her feet, standing completely dazed in the middle of chaos.

"Katya, run!" I don't have to look up—I know she hasn't moved. The man uses my momentary distraction to slip out of my hold, and I lose my temper. "Get into a fucking bedroom!"

She runs down the hall, slamming a bedroom door shut behind her. Maybe she's calling 9-1-1, God knows some back-up would be good right about now.

The gun goes off and I maneuver myself until I've got him in a blood choke. He goes limp within seconds. I release him and lean down, trying to catch my breath. The back door flies open and Detective Sullivan comes in with his gun drawn.

"Is he dead?" He asks tersely.

I shake my head, winded from the entire thing. "He had a gun... put him in a chokehold..."

He holsters his gun before picking the other up off the floor. I stand in shock as he kneels down next to the man, placing the gun back in his hand.

"Detective?"

He doesn't answer, instead bringing the man's hand up under his chin as though they're grappling for the weapon, though it's clear that the man is still unconscious.

"Travis, look away."

The gunshot rings out, startling me, and I jerk my head back. The bottom part of the man's jaw has been blown off and is lying next to him in a pool of his own blood.

Holy fuck...the detective just killed him.

I mean, I was prepared to kill him, just not while he was still unconscious.

Katya's voice carries down the hall as she talks to the police. "My boyfriend...the guy has a gun. I need to go check."

Stay there, baby. Stay in there.

The detective pulls a wallet from a Ziploc bag, placing it into the dead guy's hands and then into his pocket. I notice that he's wearing gloves—probably has been the entire time. What kind of a cop goes into a situation already prepared to kill?

I move until my back hits the wall, sinking down to a sitting position. The bedroom door pops open and Katya comes running down the hall, the phone pressed to her ear. I'm still breathing heavily and she starts patting me down. "I'm here. I'm here. Did he shoot you?"

I shake my head, staring straight at Detective Sullivan.

"He's gone—you're safe."

She follows my gaze over to the body. "Jesus Christ."

The detective goes to her and I'm too exhausted to care. He pulls the phone from her hand, muting it. "Katya, I need Landon's ring."

She doesn't even blink; she just goes and retrieves it for him. *Is she familiar with his less than legal tactics?*

He wipes the ring clean of prints before slipping it onto one of the guy's fingers. "I was never here." Before either of us can process what's going on, he slips out the back door and into the dark.

The sound of sirens grows closer and I reach for Katya. She moves toward me just as a small whine sounds from the corner of the room.

Charlie?

I push myself off the wall, crawling toward the sound. "Char?"

My sweet girl is lying on her side, panting heavily. Blood runs from her side. "Charlie, I'm here. I'm here. Katya, help me!"

She whimpers again, trying to lift her head off of the floor and get to me. Katya grabs a blanket and presses it to her side, trying to staunch the flow of blood. She murmurs softly against Charlie's fur. "Listen to me, Char. Help is coming."

Her tail slaps against the floor; even while hurt she's still trying to comfort us. Katya kneels over her and weeps, while I cradle her head in my hands. She licks at my face and I lose it, tears streaming down my face. "You saved me a million times, Charlie. It's my turn to save you now. Don't you leave me, Char. I can't do this without you."

She gives a low whine and closes her eyes as the sound of sirens grows louder.

MODEL SURVIVES HARROWING ORDEAL AT THE HANDS OF STALKER

Terrifying details coming out of Colorado tonight. Former Selvaggia model Katya Egoricheva is safe after being held at gunpoint by an alleged stalker. The model escaped with a broken wrist and a concussion and is being treated for her injuries at a local hospital. Her attacker was shot during the attack and pronounced dead on scene.

The stalker? Lee Watkins. Watkins was a journalist with the Huffington Post. According to an anonymous staff member who worked alongside him, "He published an article on Ms. Egoricheva's rescue that was heavily fabricated. The Post was forced to retract it and he lost his job as a result. It just never seemed like he let his obsession with her go though."

Ms. Egoricheva's boyfriend and dog were inside the home during the attack; no further details have been released regarding their condition.

Police have confirmed that paraphernalia found on Watkins links him to the murders of Christine Miller and Landon Scott. "I can confirm that the decedent was in possession of some jewelry belonging to Christine Miller, along with a wallet and college ring belonging to Landon Scott," said Detective Michael Sullivan who was assisting the Arapahoe County SD in their investigation. Sullivan is widely credited for rescuing Egoricheva back in December and launching a massive manhunt to find Landon Scott.

Landon Scott has been missing since last December after an altercation with police officers. Christine Miller had been missing since May. Police confirmed yesterday that the body found in Cherry Creek was hers. An official cause of death has not been made public at this time.

We were unable to reach Ms. Egoricheva's agent at press time. This story will continue to be updated as it unfolds.

FIFTY-FOUR

KATYA

I OPEN MY EYES, trying to piece together the events that culminated in me ending up in a hospital again. I glance down to see a cast on my right hand—my wrist must definitely be broken then.

"Katya, can you hear me?" Travis leans anxiously into my face.

I nod slowly as stabbing pain shoots through my skull. "Travis?"

"I'm right here, baby." He grips my good hand tightly in both of his and my eyes well up.

"Charlie?"

He swallows and looks down at the bed. "She made it through surgery. Now, we just wait and see."

I squeeze his hand. "You should be with her, Trav."

"I waited until I knew she was going to make it through surgery before coming back to you. Niko was with you the whole time though."

"Trav, I'm fine. I mean, my head feels like it's going to split in two, but I'm good." I close my eyes at the brightness in the room and he flips the light above the sink on before shutting off the overhead lights.

"Better?"

I nod and gesture toward the bed. "Will you lay with me?"

He helps me shift over in the bed before climbing in next to me. I lay my head against his chest, listening to the steady beating of his heart. "Trav, I'm sorry. I'm so sorry for what I said to you...what I accused you of doing."

He tightens his grip around my shoulders. "Shhhh...you've been through a lot. Now, that you're awake, maybe they'll discharge you."

I lift my head up to face him. "Look at me. What I did to you is inexcusable. I'd just gotten those letters and messages for months—and then when the story broke with everything I'd told you...I was devastated." A tear slips down my cheek and Travis reaches up to brush it away.

"I was so worried about hurting you that I never even considered the possibility of you hurting me. I left you and felt nothing but rage. I wanted to drink...to hurt someone...until I felt better. Instead, I ran. I ran until I couldn't see anything but your face. And I knew then that it didn't matter what you'd said—you were it for me. I was going to do whatever it would take to make you see that. When you answered the door, things just felt off. Then you kissed me, and it was like you were saying goodbye permanently. Which, in hindsight, I guess you were."

He brushes more tears off my face and my lip quivers, ready to unleash a torrent.

"I couldn't let him hurt you...I love you."

He blinks rapidly, as if trying to keep himself from joining me. "Princess, it's been you. From that first conversation in the elevator, you've managed to get under my skin and annoy the hell out me like no one else."

I pinch him and he smirks up at me.

"You didn't let me finish...I love you too, baby."

FIFTY-FIVE

TRAVIS

June 2016- 8 months later

I TAKE a deep breath and put the truck into park.

Katya stares in shock at the house. "Why are we here, Travis?"

"You trust me?" She nods slowly and I open the truck door, climbing out. She's still buckled in when I get around to her side. "Come here, baby."

She unbuckles, taking my hand in hers, before cautiously climbing out. I grab a can of gasoline from the bed of the truck and her eyes widen further.

Charlie jumps out right behind her, taking it all in. I didn't think she was going to make it that night, but she must've known how much I—we—needed her, because she held on. I lean down and scratch behind her ears, earning a lopsided smile from her.

We came back to Texas for a wedding—not ours. Not yet.

Elizabeth had survived Landon Scott alongside Katya and the two had formed a friendship of sorts. When Elizabeth sent the invitation for her and David's vow renewal ceremony, Katya didn't even hesitate.

Once the trip was planned, I reached out to Mike for information on where she'd been held. He owed it to me. I never told Katya, but the night that Lee was killed, there was this split second after he pulled the trigger where he looked at me, gun still in his hand. I knew that he was contemplating killing me to keep their secret safe.

I recognized the struggle taking place within him.

Mike was fighting the same monster that I did. A monster who thirsted for blood and pain. Katya later told me that she knew that Mike's father was into some bad shit, but never elaborated. Mike had held that gun on me for what felt like minutes before shaking his head and lowering it. He'd refused to give in and become his old man, even if it would've ensured that no one but he and Katya knew what really happened to Landon.

When I reached out to him, he told me that Elizabeth's husband, David, had bought the house and land not long after they were rescued. He gave me his blessing to do whatever I wanted to the house.

I lead Katya closer to it and her breathing intensifies. "Baby, look at me. I'm not going to take you inside. You're going to stay out here with Charlie. Okay?"

She nods again, like a bobble head doll. I walk inside, surveying the hell she called a home for four months. It's like an episode of *Hoarders*. The walls are crumbling and there is shit piled up everywhere. The basement isn't any better—there's blood mixed with the dirt in several areas and my heart twists painfully in my chest knowing that my girl was held down here. I douse gasoline on some cardboard boxes before moving back upstairs. One of the bedrooms is littered with newspapers, but otherwise empty. I move into the other one and freeze. There's a mattress lying on the floor, with bloodstains all over it. I clench my fists.

This is what the media never saw. It's proof that she survived the unthinkable. The monster begs to be let out of its cage the longer I stare. I clear my thoughts and douse the mattress in gasoline.

When I walk back out, she and Charlie are sitting on the tailgate, both of them wearing matching expressions of anxiousness.

"You ready to finish it?" I make a trail of gasoline down the porch and into the dirt.

She nods and jumps down. "Can I—"

I hand her the matchbook and she doesn't even hesitate—just strikes one up and tosses it down. The house goes up faster than I thought it would and the heat forces us back to the truck.

I lift her up onto the tailgate before kneeling down on one knee in the dirt. Her mouth drops open in surprise. "I know it's not traditional, but hell, neither are we. I promise to protect you—to keep you safe. I brought you back here to show you that. I'll destroy anything that comes against you. You are my life, Katya. You saved me from the darkness and pulled me back into the light and I want to spend every day doing the same for you...for as long as we both shall live." I pull the ring box from my pocket and take a deep breath, my hands trembling. "Katya Egoricheva, will you do me the honor—"

"Yes! Yes! Yes! A thousand times yes!" She jumps off the tailgate and into my arms, knocking us both back into the dirt.

A glass window shatters from somewhere inside the house and we both turn toward it. The roof begins smoking as the fire crackles and pops—every flame destroying her past.

In the morning, only ashes will remain. The scorched earth will remain blackened and raw for a time, but then life will take over and rebuild. Plants will sprout from the gray soot and wild flowers will blanket everything until there's beauty in this place. Ten years from now, no one will know the unspeakable horror that took place here. They'll only see the good.

It's what I want for her.

It's what I'll fight for until my last breath.

KATYA: IN LOVE AT LAST

In an exclusive, tell-all interview with *Vogue* magazine, former model Katya Egoricheva opens up about her abduction back in 2014 and how she managed to find love after heartbreak.

"People think that you just bounce back after something like that; and I was so afraid of letting everyone down," the model, 34, noted. I thrust myself into projects and campaigns, thinking that if I kept myself busy those feelings would just go away. They didn't; if anything it just made everything worse. I became self-destructive."

This isn't the first time Egoricheva has alluded to her alcoholism. In late 2015, after stalker Lee Watkins was killed in her home, she admitted that her struggles with drinking began after she was rescued. "It became a part of who I was—the numbness was my only way of coping. It's why I left modeling. I just couldn't keep up the charade any longer."

While she may never again appear on a runway, Egoricheva is perfectly content with where her life is currently. "My fiancé has the gym and I've enjoyed working with him. Who knows? Maybe I'll become a personal trainer and he'll put me on the payroll," she said with a laugh.

The fiancé is none other than Marine Captain Travis Logan, who lost his leg to a roadside bomb in 2006. The heavily tattooed man is pretty terrifying when you first meet him, but his story is incredibly heart-warming and inspiring.

"Trav lost two of his best friends the same day he lost his leg and that changed his entire life. He went through a period like I did where the survivor's guilt was almost too much to bear," the model told *Vogue*, "He saw that there was a need for services for wounded veterans, like himself, and decided to start a gym."

Survivor's Gym is more of a training mecca rather than your average run-of-the-mill gym. It boasts a full staff of physical therapists, along with a behavioral health center. "There is so much that needs to be done for our wounded warriors, not only physically, but emotionally as well. Travis is just the best person with the biggest heart," Katya gushed.

When asked what the future held for her, she became demure. "I want what a lot of people want—marry the love of my life and have his babies. I spent too much time just existing—now, I want to live."

Katya seems ready to live out her fairy tale, but what about her ex, Brody Rodgers? Is he still pining away for the former bombshell? The wide receiver has been spending a lot of time in Cedar Ridge. Rodgers has been seen frequently with the same dark-haired woman. No one seems to know anything about her, but it appears that the football star is struggling to move past his failed romance with Egoricheva and find love again.

BRODY ROGERS' MYSTERY WOMAN

5 FACTS YOU NEED TO KNOW

As Brody Rodgers spends more time in Colorado, fans are scrambling for answers on the identity of the woman he's been photographed with over the past few months.

1. **The mysterious woman is none other than Genevieve Summers—the wide receiver's estranged wife.**

After doing some serious digging, gossip site TMZ uncovered a marriage license from thirteen years ago. The two were married right before Rodgers graduated from the University of Alabama.

1. **Summers worked in a coffeehouse when they met.**

It's unclear whether or not the two first met at the coffeehouse or on campus, but it must've been love at first sight. They were married after only a few months of dating, according to a former friend of

Rodgers'. The former barista was well known for her voice back in the day and frequently headlined open mic night at the local bars.

1. **Summers grew up in foster care.**

Summers was removed from her home by the state when police discovered that she was being abused by her parents. She ended up in the foster care system, but was never formally adopted. She aged out and immediately moved across the state.

1. **Rodgers was a tabloid favorite after a woman released photographs of him after a hook-up.**

Rodgers was not known for dating anyone until a woman posted photographs of the wide receiver passed out, claiming the two had just hooked up. The woman said she met up with the football star after connecting on a dating app. He never denied the claims and has been photographed with many different women since, earning him the 'Bad Boy of the NFL' moniker.

1. **The two are still legally married.**

Perhaps the hardest news to accept? Summers and Rodgers are still married. It appears that divorce documents were never filed, even though the two haven't been together for over a decade.

EPILOGUE

KATYA

Present Day

I DIDN'T THINK it was possible. I just couldn't fathom that there was any way for two broken people to be pieced back together. Travis may not have physically pulled me from that basement, but emotionally he saved me.

I'd lived this half-life after it happened—certain that everything would implode the minute I let my guard down. In his arms, I found peace. A man who'd been so afraid of hurting others that he'd lived in near seclusion was the only one who could fight my demons.

What do you do when you find a man that rare?

You take his last name.

Or at least that's what I did. It took a broken and damaged man to show me what real love was. Broken piece by broken piece, he glued me back together, and the girl that I once was began to resurface.

The transformation in us was so profound that both his family and my father commented on it. Together, we made each other whole.

I never received another threatening letter or message and Mike's calls became less frequent until eventually, they stopped altogether. I know that he's still pouring himself into every case, but I hope that he's tracked down the woman he lost. I hope that he's found her and in the process, found the man that he used to be.

It took a little while, but Jeanne made a full recovery. Her speech was still a little slow at times, but she never let it stop her. She and my father got married a few months ago and live together in her lake house. Even though she never had children of her own, Jeanne has easily slipped into the role of being a mom for me.

I haven't seen as much of Genevieve since Brody came to town. I know that he's spent the off-season here, but she's remained tight-lipped on what exactly went on between the two of them all those years ago.

I push the gym door open, searching for Trav. Charlie is laying on a giant bean bag near the front counter and she wags her tail when I come in. "Hey Char—you keeping things running smoothly?" Her tongue flops out of her mouth as she grins.

I lean down and scratch under her chin. My sweet fur baby.

The gym has grown so far beyond what he and I could've ever imagined. An enlarged photograph of Travis, with his arms around Carlson and Moore, takes up most of the back wall—a reminder to not take a single day for granted.

"Okay, we'll try it again. Just do what you're comfortable with." I stand up and see Trav. He's working with a man who lost his leg right below the knee in a motorcycle accident.

I'm busy admiring him when he turns to look at me. "That's perfect." I think he's talking to the guy in front of him, but his eyes never leave mine.

He finishes another set before coming over to me. "Hey baby. You wanna give those pistol squats another go?"

I laugh and shake my head. "I have no desire to ever do one of those again. I think I'm done with training for a while."

His lip turns up in a smirk. "What about this morning?

My cheeks burn bright as I look around to see if anyone else has overheard him. "That doesn't count," I whisper.

He pulls me into him, kissing the top of my head. "How'd your appointment go?"

I hide a smile, my fingers brushing against the papers in my pocket. "It was interesting...and a little surprising."

His eyes narrow. "Are you okay?"

I take a deep breath and then place the black and white images in his hands. He stares at them for a moment, confusion evident on his face. "Wait, are these? Does this mean—?"

I feel like my grin must reach my ears, it's so big. "Yeah, I just—"

He scoops me up into his arms, yelling out to the entire gym, "Do you hear that? I'm going to be a daddy!"

Several people begin clapping and I giggle as he plasters kisses across my face. I think of the legend of Snegurochka. Her heart was incapable of knowing love—the very act caused her to melt. It was meant to be sad, but what if there had been more to it? The love she felt thawed her heart, causing her to melt, but maybe her story didn't end there.

After winter comes spring. Everyone knows this. Things that were once dead are restored to their full potential. Maybe Snegurochka sacrificed herself for love and became more, not less. She didn't disappear forever when she melted...she just became something else—something better.

Just like the woman who was pulled from a basement years ago.

The end.

THANK you for reading YOU SAVE ME! I hope you loved Travis and Katya's story.

Want to dig into Detective Mike Sullivan a little more? His story can be found in the SPMC series. Book 1 in that series is THE DESERTER!

I grew up in the dark.

Right and wrong?

In my world, it was kill or be killed.

I spend my time in the shadows, doing what I want when I want. I refuse to follow anyone's rules—I own this town.

They might not see me, but my club controls everything... including her. I took Daddy's little princess and defiled her to send a message. Now, I want to keep her down here in the dirt forever.

She's crazy not to run.

Around here, there's no right or wrong. I'm the judge, jury, and executioner, and god help any fool who tries to lay a hand on what's mine.

If you're looking for a hero, you're in the wrong place.

Keep reading for an excerpt from THE DESERTER!

WANT to be the first to know when these stories are coming out? Sign up for my newsletter, join my Facebook group, Shannon Myers's Fan Group, and/or Follow me on BookBub!

ALSO BY SHANNON MYERS

From This Day Forward Duet

(David & Elizabeth's Story)

From This Day Forward

Forsaking All Others

Operation Duet

(Dakota & Zane's Story)

Operation Fit-ish

(Kate and Nate's Story)

Operation Annulment

Silent Phoenix MC Series

(Main Storyline)

The Deserter (Book One)

The Protector (Book Two)

The Renegade (Book Three)

The Traitor (Book Four)

The Savior (Book Five)

Standalones within the SPMC universe

The Keeper

The Christmas Trap

Fairest Series (Can be read as standalones).

(Charm & Neve's Story)

Through The Woods

(Killian and Ari's Story)

Wait For It

<u>Fictioned Series</u>

(Hayden & Jake's Story)

Protagonized

ABOUT THE AUTHOR

Shannon is a born and raised Texan. She grew up inventing clever stories, usually to get herself out of trouble. Her mother was not amused. In junior high, she began writing fractured fairy tales from the villain's point of view and that was the moment she knew that she was going to use her powers for evil instead of good.

After an unplanned surgery in 2014 and a long pity party, she decided to pen a novel about the worst thing that could happen to a person to cheer herself up. She's twisted like that. Thus, From This Day Forward was born and the rest, as they say, is history.

She resides in the Texas desert with a posse of men (nothing like she'd imagined in her fantasies) and a plethora of fur babies.

Find her online at: http://shannonshaemyers.com
Or in her fan group: https://www.facebook.com/groups/630229377127363/

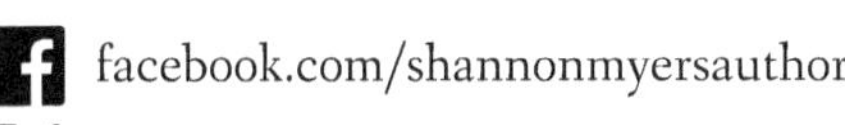

facebook.com/shannonmyersauthor
x.com/shannonsmyers
instagram.com/shannonsmyers

www.ingramcontent.com/pod-product-compliance
Lightning Source LLC
LaVergne TN
LVHW010639110826
845149LV00014B/2885

* 9 7 8 0 9 9 7 5 3 4 8 7 0 *